FEAR NO MORE

MICHAEL NELSON (known as 'Mickey') was born in 1921. He worked as a journalist before the Second World War, and during the war worked as secretary to John Lehmann, a prominent publisher and man of letters, and served as a captain in the Royal Army Service Corps. After his demobilisation, he lived with his boyfriend in Winchester and owned a bookstore there before meeting Rachel Holland, who knew Nelson was gay but married him anyway; the two remained married the rest of their lives. Nelson and his wife relocated to London, where he was well known in the drinking establishments of Soho. Nelson's first novel, *Knock or Ring* (1957), which concerned the illegal practices of the 'ring', a group of booksellers who conspired to fix auctions and share profits among themselves, drew on Nelson's own experiences as a bookseller and received good reviews. His second book, *A Room in Chelsea Square* (1958), also available from Valancourt Books, was published anonymously, and has gone on to become a gay classic. His other books are *Blanket* (1959) (published under the pseudonym 'Henry Stratton'), *When the Bed Broke* (1961), *Captain Blossom* (1973), *Captain Blossom Soldiers On* (1974), *Nobs & Snobs* (1976), *Captain Blossom in Civvy Street* (1978), and *Fear No More* (1989). Michael Nelson died in 1990.

MICHAEL NELSON

FEAR NO MORE

VALANCOURT BOOKS

Fear No More by Michael Nelson
Originally published by Quartet in 1989
First U.S. edition 2024

Published by Valancourt Books, Richmond, Virginia
http://www.valancourtbooks.com

ISBN 978-1-960241-26-9 (trade paperback)
Also available as an electronic book.

Cover by Roderick Brydon / KLRCovers.com
Set in Dante MT

For Rachel

Fear no more the heat o' the sun
Nor the furious winter's rages;
Thou thy worldly task hast done,
Home art gone and ta'en thy wages:
Golden lads and girls all must,
As chimney-sweepers, come to dust.

William Shakespeare, *Cymbeline*

PROLOGUE

They were all dead now. No one could be hurt. No one could feel betrayed. His grandfather the old general, his mother, the girl with whom he had spent one night, his old schoolmaster, the priest he loved at school and who may have caused all the trouble, but above all, the Comte de Chaumont, they were all dead.

I had returned to the château where he had spent the last days of his life to decide if I still wanted to write about him. I knew the moment I arrived that I had to tell his story, a story that had fascinated me for more than thirty years.

I picked up the bottle of champagne which the barman had wrapped in a white napkin and took a glass off the table. I went out through the open window on to the north lawn of the château. It was a June evening just after eight o'clock. Overhead, the swallows and the house martins soared and chattered. Three miles to the north beyond the vineyards the River Loire sparkled in the sun.

I walked round the west wing of the château and entered the walled garden through the gate with its rusted and creaking hinges. The scent of wisteria and roses that covered the walls was especially strong, brought out by the heat of the day and the still-warm evening.

I felt sentimental.

I stepped off the grass on to the gravel path which ran round the rectangular garden about six feet from the wall. And there it was. The marble plaque set into the stone of the wall. To its left drooped sprays of sweet-smelling wisteria; to its right clusters of the heavily scented rose, Gloire de Dijon.

I read aloud the words inscribed on the plaque.

IN MEMORY OF
LIEUTENANT ANTONY FITZJAMES RATTIGAN
1921-1942
HE DIED FOR FRANCE
REMEMBERING TOO HIS BLACK CAT WHOM HE LOVED

'To Lieutenant Antony Fitzjames Rattigan,' I said. I filled my glass and swallowed the contents in one gulp.

After refilling the glass I threw it against the plaque where it fragmented and the wine ran down the marble. It was a stupid gesture but I felt better for it.

The following day I returned to England. I brought down from the attic the black box in which I had stored all the notes, the diary and all the information I had collected on Antony Fitzjames Rattigan thirty years ago. I took the telephone off the hook and shut myself up to write his story.

I

I was discharged from the army in 1946 having been called up as a driver in 1940 in the Royal Army Service Corps. This branch of the service had been my own choice, as, after making careful enquiries, it had seemed to me that within its vast organization I would be most likely to emerge from the war unscathed and, with luck, without even hearing a shot fired in anger. I more or less achieved my object. I spent four years overseas in the Middle East and then in Italy. In the latter country I whored, drank, and thrived on the black market. There was nothing too cowardly or base to which I was not prepared to stoop. I had no sense of shame. As I have grown older I have had second thoughts about my appalling behaviour. After all, had everyone been as cowardly and slothful as me, civilization as we know it today might have been exterminated. Living under the Nazis would have been something too horrible to contemplate. So as the years have gone by I have come to respect more and more men and women whom one might simply call brave. I now realize that I owe a great debt to men and women who are commonly called heroes.

I have been an anti-hero all my life, but the knowledge has slowly come to me that I have only been able to take up that amusing and popular stance beneath the umbrella of the heroes.

Before my call-up I had been a young newspaper reporter and on my discharge, more or less from lack of anything better to do, I drifted back into Fleet Street. In spite of myself I was lucky. After several hirings and firings I found myself writing successful features, usually two a week, for Lord Beaverbrook's *Daily Express* then under the editorship of Arthur Christiansen.

The winter of 1950 had been a bad one for me. I had worked hard, but I had also played hard. Late nights and vast quantities of alcohol, that occupational hazard of Fleet Street, found me in May of 1951 feeling depressed and run down, so I put in for a month's leave which was granted. I particularly wanted to get out of England where I had been conducting a highly emotional and impossible affair with a girl on the *Daily Mirror*. We were quite unsuited to one another, and we both knew it, but one of us had to make the break, and I had decided that that one was going to be me. I had given her the chance to take the initiative as I like to think of myself as a gentleman, and there is nothing more insulting to a girl than to be left. I hate it myself.

I had decided to drive down to Nantes and follow the Loire up to Angers, Tours, Blois and Orléans, where it was my intention to turn north to Paris where I would spend a few days, if I was still rich enough, before returning to England. It was to be a slow journey, just me by myself with no attachments. In this way I hoped to rid myself of ill-health and get over my unhappy love affair.

I went into the office on Monday to say goodbye to my colleagues and to tell them to keep an eye on my desk and Remington typewriter while I was away. I have never liked leaving Fleet Street with my possessions and desk unguarded. You never know but that when you return you may find the typewriter gone and some bright young blade ensconced behind your old desk. There's an awful obsession in Fleet Street for new blood which makes it a highly nerve-wracking place in which to earn a living.

I had just locked the drawers and handed the keys to my friend the chief sub, when the telephone on my desk started to ring. I wish I had let it ring. I would have saved myself a lot of trouble.

It was Christiansen. 'The Lord wants a word with you.'

A few seconds later the voice of Lord Beaverbrook was rasping at me. 'Get yourself a plane down here right away, Nelson. Like your last two pieces on Bevin and Bevan. Very good, nice sense of humour.'

Here goes, I thought. 'Look, sir, I am just off on a month's holiday.'

There was a pause, then Beaverbrook continued. 'Can't help that. Where were you going?'

'For a drive through the Loire valley.'

'Come here first. You can go to the Loire valley later. It will still be there in forty-eight hours, won't it?'

'Yes, sir. But my car. I was taking it over to France on the ferry this afternoon.'

'Can't help that,' said his lordship.

Oh hell, I thought, I need a holiday, and I'm damned if I'm going to have it ruined, even for Lord Beaverbrook. The most he could do would be to fire me, and my stock at the moment was high and I would have no trouble in finding a job elsewhere. In fact the editor of the *Daily Mail* had been dropping hints in El Vino only a few days before that if I ever felt like moving over to Bouverie Street he would be pleased to see me there.

'Tell you what, sir. I'll fly down tonight if I can pick up a car at your end and drive back to the Loire valley.'

It meant approaching it from Orléans and following its course the other way down to Nantes, and Paris was out. Still, that might not be a bad thing. I always got into trouble in Paris and always came out of that beautiful city bloody-minded, hungover, unhappy and definitely broke.

'Do that, Nelson. See you tonight. Get the office to call through your time of arrival at Nice airport and I'll have a car meet you.'

'One thing, sir.'

'Yes?'

'I'd like to charge the rent of the car in Nice to the paper.'

There was a pause and a grunt. 'Damned cheek. But yes.'

The line went dead.

To this day I am not sure why Beaverbrook asked me to his villa. Compared to the company there I was insignificant in the extreme. But the old man had an odd habit of flying some of his less important employees down there. Maybe he thought it was some kind of reward, a way of expressing his regard for their good work. Maybe it was his one nod in the direction of democracy. But it is not my intention to write at length about my stay at his villa. I only mention it because if I had not gone there but had stuck to my original itinerary I should not have stayed at the château in the village of Les Saules a few miles east of Orléans and Lieutenant Antony Fitzjames Rattigan would not have come into my life. I would not have started to think about dangerous abstract subjects like bravery, cowardice and loyalty.

The most memorable person staying at his lordship's villa that May was Winston Churchill. I had talked with him three times before but always in the company of other journalists. That first night I was there he held the floor, and I just listened. I remember he said what I believe is now common knowledge, namely that Stalin was the toughest, nastiest, most unscrupulous leader that he had ever met. There were a great number of questions that I would like to have put to him. I noticed that the whole time he was talking, and he did more than his fair share of it, there was always a glass of whisky at his elbow. With my common streak for writing what the man in the street wants to read I would like to have asked him whether it was true that he was often drunk in the days when he led the British people through the war years. But I never got round to it. The opportunity did not arise.

Somerset Maugham was also there, but I found him a bore. The following day when I was in the garden he cornered me and started to moan about his age. He was not all that old, and it seemed to me that a man as successful as he was had a great deal going for him compared with all the millions who throughout the world had been killed, starved to death and ruined by the years of warfare which we had recently endured. I may have said as much, or certainly I must have hinted at it, for he changed his tack and started to tell me that all his success, all his books were nothing to him; that after he was dead no one would read him;

that he would be considered a failure. I cannot feel much sympathy for this line of thought. I would not have minded a quarter of Somerset Maugham's income, and I never thought much of his writing anyway.

That is all there is to say about my stay with Beaverbrook. I was no wiser when forty hours later I picked up my bag and left the villa for Nice.

In Nice I collected the car which had been reserved for me by the London office, a Citroën Light 15. This was famous for its appearance on films and television and was the car always used by the French police. It was a very tough car with front-wheel drive and Citroën kept it in production for a great number of years. At one time it became quite popular in England, but today it is hardly ever seen. I always a make a point of hiring cars produced in the country I am visiting on the principle that if it breaks down spares will be readily available. I am naturally pessimistic about cars. I always believe that they are going to let me down.

I drove westwards, through Aix-en-Provence and Arles, until I reached Nîmes where I stopped for lunch before turning north to Le Puy where I spent the night at the Hotel Regina and ate a memorable dinner at the Petit Vatel – morels, a kind of fungi cooked in cream, followed by a *ballotine* of guinea-fowl with truffles served on a bed of green lentils. It deserved its one star in the *Michelin Guide*. It is over twenty-five years since I ate that meal at the Petit Vatel but I can visualize and taste it even now as I write about it. I am a very greedy person.

I was on the road early the following day and as I drove across the Massif Central, that wild and little-explored area of France renowned for its resistance during the war, I was feeling pleased with myself. I had come to France to explore the Loire valley. It would have been so easy for me to have lingered in Aix or Nîmes. There is something seductive about Provence. I can dally in that region without much prodding. It is usually disastrous. The sun is strong like the wine, and I find myself only too easily falling into a state of happy indolence, incapable of movement.

I remember seeing a sign Châteauneuf sur Loire, so I must have been only a few kilometres short of my objective, Orléans. I was debating whether to eat at the Auberge St Jacques, famous for its grilled salmon and *quennelles de brochet*, or at La Cremaillère, equally renowned for its peppered venison, both of which had been recommended to me by a colleague on the paper. I came to the top of a hill and as I started to descend on the other side I saw a sign – Les Saules. As I drove slowly through the village I thought what a pretty name. The Willows.

I don't know where the cat came from but it had put its head down and was crossing the road in front of me as fast as it could run. I stepped on my brakes. There was a screaming of tyres. The cat missed my front wheels by a whisker, but I could not hold the car. Luckily I was going slowly or I might not have lived to write this tale. I swung the wheel hard into the skid but could not correct it in time, and the car shuddered its way across the road and brought up with an almighty crash against a lamp-post. I found myself thrown against the door, but again I was lucky and the door held or I would have been hurled out on to the road. I switched off the engine and hurriedly got out. I have a horror of cars catching fire after accidents and I have never fancied being burned alive.

People appeared from all sides and I was more or less carried into a café and made to sit down on a chair.

Someone asked if I needed a doctor.

'Am I bleeding?' I asked.

'No, not that I can see.'

'Then I am probably alive and I don't think I need one.'

'You shouldn't have done that for a cat.'

'I'm very fond of cats,' I said. I must have been lightheaded for I added: 'In fact I like them more than humans. Anyway, where am I?'

'You are in the Cafe des Fleurs.'

I focused my eyes on the woman speaking to me. She was middle-aged and dressed in black.

'You are in the village of Les Saules. I am Madame Morel.'

'Was it your cat, Madame?'

'Yes, I am afraid it was. I am so sorry she should have caused you so much trouble.'

I got to my feet. 'Well, I suppose I had better look at the damage.'

'Don't you think you should sit down for a while?' said Madame Morel. 'Would you care for a glass of cognac?'

'No, I'm fine,' I said, remembering that only hot sweet tea and never spirits should be administered for shock. At least that's what I had been taught in the army.

I walked stiffly across the road to the crowd gathered round the car. It looked a sorry sight with its left side, including front mudguard, well and truly staved in. Even I, with my limited technical knowledge, knew that it wouldn't get me to Orléans.

One of the crowd round the car turned and said, 'I am Georges. I own the local garage a hundred yards down the street.'

'Well, you'd better take charge, Georges,' I said. 'How long will it take?'

'Only a day if it's just a question of beating out the bodywork. But I will have to check the half-shafts. These front-wheel drives can be tricky.'

'Do what's necessary, Georges,' I said. I could afford to be magnanimous. I would not have to pay the bill.

'You should not have done that for a cat,' said Georges. 'You might have killed yourself.'

'I might have killed the cat if I hadn't,' I said.

I went back into the Café des Fleurs, leaving the crowd, which had by now grown considerably, discussing the madness of the English who were prepared to kill themselves rather than a cat.

The problem was what to do. I wasn't feeling all that bright and the prospect of going on to Orléans by taxi did not exactly appeal to me. My dinner at the Auberge St Jacques or La Cremaillère was definitely out. As I accepted the cognac which Madame offered for a second time and drank it quickly, I made up my mind to stay for one night at least in the village. In any case I might have to see the local police, and after all Georges had only made an on-the-spot assessment of the damage to the car, and it might well take more than twenty-four hours to put right, in which case I should have to set about hiring another one.

I asked Madame if she had any accommodation.

'I am sorry. We gave it up years ago. You see, there is plenty in Orléans. Madame Boudin at the bottom end of the village usually has a few rather shabby rooms to let in her café, but her son is getting married tomorrow and of course she is full up with relatives. But there's the château. Very beautiful, very grand and very, very expensive. If you will forgive me, here in the village we say it's strictly for the tourists. I think you would be wiser to go on to Orléans.'

'How far is the château?' I asked.

She turned to a man who had come into the café from a room at the rear. He was wearing a striped apron and was wiping his hands with a dishcloth.

'My husband,' said Madame Morel.

It occurred to me that only in France would a chef have ignored an almighty crash in the road on the principle that food comes first.

Madame Morel explained to him how perilously close to death I had come in avoiding Mimi.

'He should have killed that damned cat,' said Monsieur Morel. Finally in answer to his wife's question he said, 'The château? About two kilometres.'

'Two and a half,' said one of the men who had tired of inspecting the damage to the car and had drifted into the bar to continue discussing my stupidity in avoiding the cat, and to assess the extent of the damage and how much Georges would charge me for making it roadworthy.

'No, no, three,' said someone else.

'Don't be damned silly, two at the most.'

'Gentlemen, give or take a kilometre, it doesn't really matter. Is there a taxi in the village that would take me there?'

'Certainly not,' said Madame Morel. 'My husband will take you. After all it was our fault that you had this accident. You must take no notice of him. He would have been very upset if you had run over our Mimi.'

After I had drunk one more cognac, and transferred my baggage into the back of Monsieur Morel's Renault, shaken hands all round and exchanged good wishes, I was driven off in the direction of the château.

We went down the main street of a typical French village with its butcher's shop, its grocer's, chemist, what looked like a saddler's and blacksmith combined, and its old houses, none of

which was more than one storey high. At the bottom of the high
street to the left up a narrow gravelled track was its church, which
at first sight seemed to be Norman. Then we were out into the
country passing through small vineyards, each with its own farm-
house. About a mile out of the village we came to a bridge, the
Pont de Boeuf, and next to it a café of the same name.

'Not very good food there,' said Monsieur Morel. 'Not a cook
among the lot of them.'

Just beyond the Pont de Boeuf we turned right, leaving the
main Orléans road, and proceeded at high speed down a minor
road. I prayed that nothing larger than a cat might obstruct
Monsieur Morel's progress. A quarter of a mile along the road
we turned left between a pair of impressive lodges and sped up
the approach to the château, which was flanked either side with
limes.

We came out on to the big sweep before the château. As it
was now dusk I could not make out many of its details but it was
certainly not as large as I had expected; more like an eighteenth-
century country house than a château of the Loire. I was rather
pleased. I have never been keen on those Gothic châteaux that
seem popular all over France. But then I do not much care for any
architecture earlier than the 1700s.

There were lights burning in a downstairs room. Monsieur
Morel stopped his car, got out and helped me to take my luggage
off the back seat.

'How much do I owe you?'

'Nothing. It was the fault of our cat,' he said.

I could not help thinking how often the French are maligned,
called greedy, crafty and money grubbing. But then I speak their
language. I like to think that even if my accent is not impeccable,
at least I do my best and that it does make a difference.

After thanking Monsieur Morel, who drove off into the dusk
at high speed, I rang the bell and walked into the château.

I had no trouble in arranging accommodation. It was early
in the year and well before the holiday season. I think the proprietors were surprised to see me, especially arriving out of the
dusk completely on my own. They were greatly concerned for
my health when I explained what had happened and insisted

that I should have dinner in my room. I was feeling tired, in fact I may well have been suffering from delayed shock, so I readily accepted. I cannot even remember what I had to eat that night, so I must have been in a very bad way. But no sooner had I eaten, than I put on my pyjamas, took a couple of sleeping pills (something I very seldom do, save in an emergency) and crawled into an enormous double bed, feeling stiff and slightly miserable.

Luckily the pills were strong. They quickly knocked me out and I fell into a sleep that was somewhat disturbed by visions of cats of all shapes and sizes who seemed to be continually running across the road in front of the car I was driving.

I had breakfast in bed: coffee, croissants and cherry jam. I never eat an English breakfast when I am in France. It does not leave enough room for a full luncheon and dinner. I asked the switchboard to call the local garage run by Georges. When I eventually got him on the line he told me that he had been up since dawn looking at the damage, that it was not as bad as he had feared and that he hoped that by working at it day and night he would have the car ready for me in twenty-four hours. While he knew that my insurance would pay the bill in due course, he would be much obliged if I would settle in cash before taking the car away.

After I had bathed and dressed I made my way down the great staircase. There were in fact two that swept up to the first floor from the hall. The proprietress was arranging tall vases of flowers and when she saw me she came to greet me.

'I hope you slept well,' she said. 'I am Madame Clondel. I think I told you my name last night, but you were in rather a dazed state. I hope you are better after a night's rest, or would you like me to ask the local doctor to come and see you?'

'Thank you, I'm fine. I expect I was a little shocked.'

'A nasty business,' said Madame Clondel. 'People should really try to keep their animals under control.'

'Cats are independent, madame,' I replied. 'Cats are not like dogs.' Changing the subject, I added, 'This is a most beautiful place. Have you been here long?'

'About five years. We ran a hotel in Normandy before the war. Unfortunately during the landings it was damaged beyond repair.'

'I'm sorry.'

She shrugged. 'That's war. We were lucky to survive. Eventually we were compensated by the government, not nearly enough but we are grateful for whatever they could give us. Everyone on the coast of Normandy suffered in the war, many far worse than us. Have you seen towns like Caen for instance?'

'Yes. I am amazed they ever emerged from the rubble.'

'You were in the war?'

'In the desert and in Italy. The worst destruction I saw there was the obliteration of Cassino and the monastery. But as soon as the battle had passed them by its people emerged from their holes and started to rebuild. It's amazing how much resilience there is in the human race. So, how did you come to buy this château in particular?'

'Quite simply, we saw it advertised in a paper. It had belonged to the de Chaumont family for years. I believe they can trace their ancestry back to Charlemagne. But the present count lost his two sons in the disaster of 1940 and with them he lost his heart. He could see no point in keeping on the château and the estate. So he sold the land off to his tenants and we bought the château. You may not think we made a wise decision, but it's early in the season. By the end of this month right through to October we shall be bursting at the seams. We have worked hard and earned our entry in the *Michelin Guide* both for food and comfort. How long will you be staying, monsieur?'

'Two more nights if I may.'

'During that time please feel at liberty to go where you like both inside the house and in the gardens. I would particularly draw your attention to the walled garden to the west of the château.'

I thanked her and made my way out through the heavy doors into the morning sunlight. The large area in front of the château was bordered by lime trees, and on either side of the drive that ran to the road half a mile away there were more limes. Beyond the limes were acres and acres of vines. In fact wherever I looked I could see nothing but lime trees and vineyards. The château faced due south and I turned to my right and skirted the south wall of the garden which Madame Clondel had mentioned to me, following a stone-flagged path. As I turned right again at the corner of the garden, which I estimated must have been two or three acres in size, over to the northwest I could see the spire of the Cathedral of Ste Croix in Orléans. I walked slowly along the west wall of the garden and when I reached its northern corner there were still more vines that stretched away for a couple of miles to the north, right to the banks of the Loire.

As I stood there in that warm spring sunshine I almost felt glad of the accident the previous evening. My only regret was that I had no one to share with me the pleasure and the beauty.

I turned right again and made my way across the wide expanse of lawn that separated the walled garden from the château until I came to the wooden door of the garden. I lifted the heavy latch and pushed open the door whose hinges creaked.

I don't know what I expected. I suppose some kind of a vegetable garden. But there was not a vegetable in sight. I am not a gardener; I have not the patience. I could only describe the walled garden as wild. There was absolutely nothing formal about it. Fig trees, laburnums, lilacs, apple and pear trees and all kinds of flowering shrubs occupied the centre and between them and the gravel path was a strip of carefully mown grass about twenty feet in width.

There were so many roses, so much wisteria, jasmine and honeysuckle of all shapes and hues growing over the walls that it was almost impossible to see the stones through them. Although I am not an expert, I did recognize the deep blood-coloured Guinée, already in full bloom although it was only early May. The scent was overpowering – as if confined within those four walls and unable to escape.

I stood enchanted, absolutely still for a minute, breathing deeply, once again thinking how lucky I had been in my accident the previous evening, before I began walking slowly along the gravel path. Now and again I stopped to examine some particular tree, shrub or rose. Although I was the only person in the garden I had the feeling that there was a tremendous amount of activity going on. There was nothing dead about it and there was a lot more to it than colour or scent. Then I realized that the place was swarming with bees, and there were more butterflies on the wing than I had seen in one place for many years. In the corner diagonally across the lawn there was a summer-house in which there were two wheelbarrows and piles of neatly stacked tools.

I had gone past the summer-house and had stopped to examine a particularly large tortoiseshell butterfly which seemed to be fascinated by the bunches of wisteria flowers that drooped from a very ancient stem at least a foot in diameter. The butterfly was fluttering about at my eye level, or else I would have walked on and noticed nothing. Perhaps the sun, which was shining on the west wall, had more to do with it. Whatever the cause I noticed something white behind the flowers, something white which caught my eye.

As fortuitous as Lord Beaverbrook's call to his villa in the south and the accident in the village of Les Saules caused by a cat, that flash of white was to cause me a great deal of worry, work and introspection for many years to come.

I stepped off the path and, parting the wisteria blooms and roses, saw the plaque for the first time. Set at eye level, about five feet from the ground, it was a rectangular tablet of the whitest marble let flush into the stone wall. The words cut into the marble had been set in gold. For the first time I read those words, little knowing how they were to haunt me, or how many times I was to read them again from the exact spot where I now stood.

IN MEMORY OF
LIEUTENANT ANTONY FITZJAMES RATTIGAN
1921-1942
HE DIED FOR FRANCE
REMEMBERING TOO HIS BLACK CAT WHOM HE LOVED

Apart from my surprise at discovering such a memorial in that garden, it seemed odd to me that Antony Fitzjames Rattigan, whoever he might have been, was born in the same year as myself. What had happened to him? Surely he could not have been killed on that spot? There was no sign of any sort of grave at the base of the wall.

I don't know how long I stood there, but it must have been for at least ten minutes or more.

And who was this black cat he had loved? Cats seemed to be haunting me. A cat had caused me nearly to kill myself the night before in the main street of Les Saules, and now here was a black cat of some kind or another whom Antony Fitzjames Rattigan had loved. Then there was the name Fitzjames. Certainly a grand one. Usually descended the wrong side of the blanket from one of the Stuart monarchs. Why did he die for France and not for England? Finally, who had gone to the trouble of erecting this plaque to his memory? Whoever it was, whether a he or a she, must have had a high opinion of Antony Fitzjames Rattigan. And what was his regiment? A lieutenant in the army, or could he have been a lieutenant in the navy?

I am not by nature an investigative journalist. It's a type of journalism I admire and I think that over the last twenty years it has gone from strength to strength as more and more people have become disillusioned with society and its politicians and are keen to know what really goes on behind the scenes. But I like to pride myself on knowing a good story when I see one. And this was a story that cried out for investigation.

As I spent the rest of the morning wandering around the garden and the neighbouring vineyards and finally exploring the château itself, the name of Antony Fitzjames Rattigan was seldom out of my mind. And his cat, of course. His black cat whom he loved. I am strictly a cat man as opposed to a dog person, so I cannot be blamed if this black cat whom someone had troubled to commemorate on a marble tablet intrigued me equally as much as its owner.

I did not get a chance to speak to Madame Clondel before lunch as she was busy in the kitchen. There were only a few guests at the château, a dozen at the most, and I got the impression that she and her husband did most of the work, no doubt engaging more staff from the village as the season got under way.

I was sitting in a deckchair on the lawn close to the château after my lunch, with a glass and a bottle of brandy on the table within easy reach, when Monsieur Clondel came up and introduced himself. 'I am sorry I did not say "how do you do" sooner,' he said, 'but today I was in the village, marketing. Of course, I heard full details of your mishap. Let me say how sorry I am. But

Georges is a great craftsman and will have your car looking as good as new in no time, even if he will try to overcharge you. But no doubt you, monsieur, with your fluent French will be able to get the better of him.'

I thanked Monsieur Clondel for the compliment and prepared the ground for my questions. 'I hope you will forgive my inquisitiveness, but I am a journalist.'

Monsieur Clondel nodded. 'Yes, I saw from the police form you filled in last night. So inconvenient, but the police are very strict. What paper, may I ask?'

'The *Daily Express*.'

'Ah,' said Monsieur Clondel, which either betokened disapproval of the *Express* or ignorance of its existence.

'I was in your beautiful garden this morning, Monsieur Clondel, and I came upon a rather strange plaque, set in the wall by the summer-house.

'Ah, the plaque. Yes, many of our guests have noticed it, and asked us about it. They are mostly more intrigued by the black cat than the poor lieutenant.'

I picked up the bottle and filled a second glass which Madame Clondel had thoughtfully brought out on the tray and handed it to Monsieur Clondel.

He raised it. 'Your health,' he said. 'I hope you have a happy stay here and will wish to come back.'

I nodded. 'And Lieutenant Antony Fitzjames Rattigan and the black cat whom he loved?' I asked quietly.

'Ah, yes,' said Monsieur Clondel and sipped his cognac. 'The lieutenant and his cat. It is a strange story. A good story for a journalist and I will tell you all I know, which is not much. You must understand that what I can tell you is not all fact – a great deal of it is hearsay. Naturally that plaque did not escape our notice when we came here five years ago in 1946. I think my wife has already told you how our hotel near Caen in Normandy was literally flattened, by the Canadians I fear more than the Germans. Still, we are not bitter about that. Only amazed and grateful that they should have come so far to help in the liberation of Europe. Naturally we made enquiries about that plaque, and discovered that it had been put into the wall on the orders of the count, soon after the liberation in 1945. But when we asked about it in the village, we noticed that the villagers were not altogether happy to talk about it. They behaved like the peasants they are and shut up like clams. Not all of them, but the great majority of them. And let me say straight away that we never did discover anything about that black cat, absolutely nothing. On one thing the two opposing factions in the neighbourhood were agreed. The black cat was a mystery. Only the Count de Chaumont knew the answer, and he was not saying a word.

'Well, what we finally pieced together was this,' continued Monsieur Clondel, after he had sipped his brandy and given me the opportunity, in the hope that the cognac might loosen his tongue, to refill his glass. 'Peasants are peasants the same all over France. Suspicious, clannish, resenting strangers, loyal only to their families so that if one offends someone, one offends all that person's relatives right down to the cousins ten times removed. So when we found, or rather felt, a resistance to our enquiries we did not press them. Still this much we gathered. This Lieutenant Rattigan arrived in this area in the spring of 1942, and it is assumed that he was dropped from the air because in May of that year a plane was heard circling the area, as if it was lost or looking for a dropping zone, which of course was nothing unusual later in the war when the Resistance began to get properly organized. But in 1942, resistance was almost unknown. France was still numb, still feeling the effects of its defeat of 1940. It was rumoured in the village that the count was sheltering a British officer in the château and a great number of the villagers were not at all pleased about this. They had heard horrifying stories of reprisals taken against people who had helped the Allies in other parts of France. Fear of the Gestapo, and indeed of our own secret police, dominated the country, and had reduced it to a state of neutrality. I would hesitate to go so far as to say that France had become entirely pro-German, but the French people on the whole wanted to be left alone. They wanted to plough the land and tend their vines. You could say that the majority did not want to know. There were of course those who were openly pro-Nazi. It was even said that the count himself had once belonged to the French Fascist party. But that hardly matches up with his sheltering a British officer. Mind you, after the liberation those Nazi sympathizers paid dearly for having chosen the wrong side, along with many others who had remained neutral. You cannot imagine the vengeance that took place in this country after the war; in Paris, in all the big towns, and right down to the smallest villages like Les Saules. Old scores, old jealousies were paid off in a bloodbath that some believe exceeded all the brutalities and murders committed by the Nazis. The majority of the atrocities were ruthlessly carried out by the Communist minority who had seized control of the Resistance movement and came within an ace of taking over the whole of France.'

I knew this story well. It makes squalid and nauseating reading in the history of my favourite European country. 'To go back to Lieutenant Rattigan . . .' I said quietly.

'Ah, yes, the poor lieutenant. It seems he stayed in the château for about a month. Then, quite simply, he was killed by the Germans.'

'How and why? There must be more to it than that.'

'Not much. I understand that about the end of May 1942, at about seven one morning, considerable firing was heard in the region of the Pont de Boeuf. You must have crossed it when you were driven here last night.'

I nodded.

'Later that morning, about nine o'clock, one of the Boudin family who owned the café – and still does – went out into the farmyard which adjoins the café, and found the body of a young man, terribly mutilated. No one knows how or why, but the general opinion is that he had been shot to pieces.'

'What was he wearing?'

'Civilian clothes.'

'And this was the body of Lieutenant Antony Fitzjames Rattigan?'

'That is so. But that is not quite all. When the villagers wanted to remove the body and take it to be buried in the churchyard, the Germans arrived and told them that they could not do so; that the body must stay on the dung heap and be allowed to rot.'

'And was the body left there?'

'No. Rumour has it that the count went to see the German

authorities. As I have said it is suggested that he had Fascist sympathies, although these must have been greatly weakened by the loss of his two sons in the defeat of France. Anyway, that's the story. He went to see the German Commandant, I believe in Orléans, and permission was given to remove the body and inter it in the local churchyard at the bottom of the village street.'

'And all that firing in the early hours of the morning?'

'Well, there was some damage to the bridge itself, fresh bullet marks everywhere in the masonry, and what was believed to be a patch of blood on the road, although efforts had been made to wash it away. That's about it. As I have said there was still a lot of argument and bad feeling over the death of the young lieutenant when we came here five years ago. In fact it occasionally still arises, especially when someone has had too much wine. Please don't quote me, monsieur, but we got the impression that the Morels at the Café des Fleurs and the Boudin family who run the Café de Boeuf were strictly on opposite sides of the fence in this affair. The whole thing was a mystery and remains so to this day.'

'You say he is buried in the churchyard?'

'That's right.'

'And the priest who buried him, is he still here?'

'Oh, yes, Father Dominic is still here. But he's more interested in his food and books than his souls.'

'Would he mind, do you think, if I called upon him?'

'No, I'm sure not. Although I doubt if he will say much. Oh yes, there is one more thing. Soon after the war two people came to the village one day and visited the lieutenant's grave. They say one was his grandfather and the other was his mother. They did not stay long. It is said they drove over from Orléans, prayed at the graveside and drove back to the city.'

I refilled Monsieur Clondel's glass. 'It's a sad story. Mysterious but sad. I only wish the count was alive. He must know something more.'

'Whoever said he was dead?'

'You mean to say he's still alive?'

'I'm sure we would have heard if he were dead. He still owns land in the area. Yes, we would certainly have heard. As far as I know, he still owns a mansion in Paris where he lives alone. Since the death of his two boys he has gradually become more and more of a recluse.'

'And is there a Comtesse de Chaumont? You have made no mention of her.'

'No, no. She died before the war, in the early thirties, I believe. They say a terrible death from cancer.'

I continued to talk with Monsieur Clondel for the next hour but, in spite of refilling his glass several times, I failed to elicit further information from him. By four o'clock I was pretty sure that there was nothing more he could tell me.

The story intrigued me. I don't mean that I felt the excitement of a keen journalist at the beginning of some great scoop. It was far more subtle than that. Somehow I felt I wanted to find the links between a young soldier whose body had been shot to bits and whose remains now lay in a churchyard in a small village in the Loire valley, a plaque in the wall in the garden of the local château and, even more mysteriously, a black cat whom he loved.

As I had nothing to do for the next forty-eight hours while my car was being repaired, I decided I might as well make a few enquiries in the village. Clearly my first call must be on the local priest.

By five o'clock I was on my way to Les Saules in a Fiat 500 lent to me by Monsieur Clondel. As I crossed the Pont de Boeuf and passed the café I laughed to myself as I recalled Monsieur Morel's remark of the day before. 'They haven't got a single cook among the whole family.'

At the corner of the main street and the road that led to the right, up to the church, I noticed a grocer's. I stopped the Fiat, went into the shop and bought the best brandy that was in stock. It was a local brew, but I was assured that it was the very best, and only drunk on special occasions in Les Saules. I enquired where I might find Father Dominic and was informed that it was impossible to miss him as he lived in the large house next to the church. I got the impression that my informant felt it was wrong that Monsieur Dominic should be so well accommodated while there were so many French people living in grossly overcrowded conditions brought about by the war.

I left the Fiat in the main street and walked about a hundred yards down the lane. The church on my right was, as I had suspected at first glance the previous evening, Norman and un-adorned. I saw what the woman in the grocer's shop meant. The priest's house next to it seemed unnecessarily large.

I rang the bell. The door opened.

Father Dominic was extremely fat. No, he was more than that. He was gross, and his frame filled the entire doorway. His face was moonlike and I found myself counting the number of chins. His eyes were small and pig-like, but blue. A pair of granny spectacles was perched on the end of a snub nose that nestled between rolls of fat.

He was wearing a black soutane open at the neck. It was badly in need of a wash as down its front were grease stains and crumbs.

Father Dominic was munching.

I was so surprised at this apparition that for a moment I could say nothing. I could only stare.

'Father Dominic?'

'Yes.'

'May I come in and have a word with you?'

He turned and I followed him into his house. The first thing that struck me was the smell of the place. It was a smell that I had only recently encountered. It was the smell of the grocer's shop where I had just bought the bottle of brandy.

Without speaking, Father Dominic led me down a hall. Through an open door on the right I saw a room heaped with books. There were books falling out of the shelves, books piled in heaps on chairs, on tables and on the floor.

I followed Father Dominic into his kitchen. To my amaze-ment, the kitchen, as opposed to the room with the books, was immaculate. Pots and pans hung gleaming on the walls. A large gas-stove shone brightly, and next to it I noticed a charcoal grill. The dresser was filled with plain but solid pottery, and the table in the centre of the room was laid with an immaculate white cloth and heaped with enough food to feed a regiment.

'I'm sorry if I have interrupted a party, Father.'

'You haven't interrupted anything,' he said, 'only me taking a light snack.'

Noticing a whole Bayonne ham, a couple of roast chickens

which appeared to have been carefully stuffed under the skins, a fresh ox tongue lying on a bed of salad and herbs, I must have looked somewhat surprised for Father Dominic said, 'It is my sin. I am both a gourmet and a gourmand. But I have asked my bishop about it and he says it is purely minor, not cardinal.' He crossed himself. 'Thank God for that. Will you join me in a little something?' Father Dominic indicated a chair and I sat down. 'Let me offer you a slice or two of this Bayonne ham. So much better than the Italian prosciutto, don't you agree?'

As a matter of fact I did, and I said so.

'How do you like your snails?'

'In garlic and butter.'

'Ah yes. But may I suggest a different way. Everywhere it is always garlic and butter. You should try to get them the way they cook them in the Jura. Just with double cream and a touch of nutmeg. Nothing more, save a pinch of salt. Rock salt, of course.'

I must have still looked dazed because Father Dominic patted me on the arm.

'Don't worry yourself. I know I must have been a considerable shock to you. One can hardly expect anyone to call upon a simple country priest and be confronted by a monster like myself and not be knocked sideways. Now what about some of that ox tongue? None of that tinned rubbish. Absolutely fresh, allowed to simmer for three hours, cool in its own juice and then dressed with a sauce of tomatoes, gherkins, capers, oil and just a touch of wine vinegar.'

'Yes, I know it,' I said.

'You know it!' exclaimed Father Dominic. 'You mean to say you know it and you an Englishman?' He paused and blushed. 'I do beg your pardon. How rude of me. You are English, are you not?'

I nodded.

'But the English. What food! What horrors are perpetrated by your countrymen. What insults are committed against the Almighty.' He paused and crossed himself. 'And here I meet an Englishman who knows about *Langue de boeuf à la sauce piquante*. Miracles will never cease, dear God.'

He turned his piggy eyes upwards and crossed himself.

I found the situation so amazing, so unexpected that I almost burst out laughing.

'But forgive me,' Father Dominic rattled on, 'I have not offered you a drink. This calls for a celebration. An Englishman who likes snails and appreciates a *Langue de boeuf à la sauce piquante*.'

He went to the sideboard and came back holding a bottle. He put it against his face.

'Yes, just cold enough. I brought it up from the cellar just before you rang the bell.' He held the bottle towards me. 'Do you know it? Quincy.'

I shook my head. 'I'm afraid this is my first visit to the Loire.'

'How disgraceful,' said Father Dominic. 'You must allow me to be your guide as long as you are here. How long do you propose to stay?'

'Well, here in Les Saules, only forty-eight hours.'

'Oh dear, what a calamity.'

'You see, I'm proposing to work my way down the Loire ending up at Nantes.'

'Ah, what a gastronomic tour that could be if I were your guide. But, alas, my parochial duties hold me here. Be certain not to miss the *écrevisses*.'

'Yes, I have been told about them. We call them freshwater crayfish. Do you know we have them in our rivers and streams in England but we never think of catching and eating them?'

'What philistines you English are. But how merciful is the Almighty to produce one Englishman who has even so much as heard of *écrevisses*. What a memory that brings back to me. Years ago I was in Nantua and had placed before me a true dish of *écrevisses Nantua!* He poured a glass of wine, tasted it and then filled my glass. 'Ah yes, *écrevisses* as cooked in Nantua. They came in this large earthenware timbale, tails only, heaped high one upon the other with a garnish of fish *quenelles* and mushrooms. On top was a perfect sauce concocted from a *mirepoix* of vegetables, partly fried with *écrevisse* butter, moistened with white wine and cognac, fresh tomatoes, a touch of tomato purée, fish *velouté*, salt, cayenne and pepper.'

He stopped and giggled, carried away by his own eloquence. There was a faraway look in his eyes as if not only the memory, but even the taste of those crayfish he had eaten in Nantua lingered on. Father Dominic crossed himself. 'Do you know, it is dishes like that which renew my belief in the existence of the Almighty.'

It was not until an hour later, when we had finished what Father Dominic called his snack, that I realized I had never introduced myself. The whole time we talked of nothing but food and drink. Father Dominic had gone to the stove to make coffee when I said, 'I am Michael Nelson.'

'I am Father Dominic.'

We both burst out laughing. I, for my part, had taken an instant liking to this freak of a priest. No, that sounds nasty. I had found him what the Italians call '*simpatico*', a term we do not have in English. There had been a mutual flash of understanding. We both knew that we talked the same language. We might disagree, but our disagreement would not be unpleasant.

'I'm so amazed by that meal and meeting you that I have quite forgotten to tell you why I called on you.'

'Ah, let me guess,' said Father Dominic. 'You wish to confess? That's it. I trust merely a sin of omission. Nothing serious. That presents no problem. We can pop next door right away and get it over with. I shall order you as penance to forgo *écrevisses* for at least twenty-four hours.'

He found the suggestion extremely amusing, and his whole frame and dewlaps quivered as he shook with laughter.

'No, Father, I am not of your persuasion.'

'What a relief,' said Father Dominic. 'Have no fear. I shall make no effort to convert you. Each man and woman must feel his or her own way to God. I have always been amazed at the arrogance of Rome. Do you know, Michael, only the other day my bishop was most upset when I suggested that the Almighty would surely welcome into his arms those savages who have made *pot-au-feu* of our missionaries.'

I was not surprised that Father Dominic had found no preferment in his Church if he had really suggested to his bishop that missionary stew was no debarment from heaven to those that brewed it.

As if he read my thoughts, Father Dominic said, 'I am afraid my sense of humour often gets the better of me. But it really is too ridiculous to expect the whole world to embrace the religion of Christ. What about the Muslims, the Buddhists, the Confucians, the thousands of sects, the millions of people who are searching? Yes, that's the word, searching. Searching for an answer to the riddle of life. But that's enough of that. I really must not draw you into an argument about life's imponderables. Let me ask you instead, now that we have finished our little meal, what has brought you here?'

I decided that it would be best to be open with Father Dominic. I explained to him what had happened to me the previous evening, how I had narrowly escaped death on account of the carelessness of a cat crossing my path. I went on to tell him about my night at the château, my discovery of the plaque in the garden and my subsequent conversation with Monsieur Clondel.

I think that as soon as I got on to the subject of Lieutenant Antony Fitzjames Rattigan I noticed a change in Father Dominic. Or rather I felt a slight tension in the atmosphere, as if he wished I had not mentioned the name.

'So that's why I came to see you. The whole business intrigues me and I thought you might throw some light on it.' I decided to be honest and added, 'I think you should know that I am a journalist, and I suppose that is what makes me so inquisitive. But I give you my word that everything you tell me will be in confidence, if you want it to be.'

Father Dominic thought for a moment. 'What I have to tell can do no harm. But I warn you that there was, and still is, a fair amount of ill feeling in the village over this affair. There is, of course, nothing I can do to prevent you making enquiries, but I think you should step delicately. It would be a pity to stir up old hatreds and feuds. On the other hand I doubt if you will get very far. Shall we go into my library?'

We went out of the kitchen.

'I just want to go to my car for a moment,' I said.

I went out of the house and returned carrying the bottle of brandy that I had bought in the village and went into the library where Father Dominic had cleared two chairs of their load of books and placed them facing one another. I handed him the bottle. He looked at it.

'Excellent. Do you know it? Rather similar to a Burgundian Marc, made from the husks of the grapes after the wine has been made, but I think not so fiery. They say it does not improve in the bottle, but I think it does and it loses its fire.'

He went into the kitchen and returned with the bottle uncorked and two glasses. He pushed some books off a small table on to the floor and placed the glasses and the bottle on it.

'Shall we help ourselves as and when we wish?' I suggested.

'So, you have come here to enquire about the poor young officer, not about myself. You must have wondered, however, what a middle-aged priest is doing in a village like Les Saules talking like Lucullus. The fact is, before the war I was a chef.'

So that was it, an ex-chef priest. An extraordinary combination, certainly the first time I had encountered it.

'During the early thirties,' continued Father Dominic, 'I worked in the kitchens of some of the most renowned restaurants and hotels in Paris, except for a few months when I was at the Pyramide in Vienne, probably the greatest restaurant in the whole of France.'

'What about the Auberge du Père Bise in Talloires? I ate there last year and I've never had a chicken in cream and tarragon like it,' I said. I must be honest. I threw in that remark about the Père Bise to further the common ground I felt existed between myself and Father Dominic and to increase his confidence in me. It was not very pleasant of me, but it was one of those tricks I had learned as a journalist over the years. 'But go on,' I said. 'We can argue the merits of the restaurants of France later.'

'The trouble is that I was restless in the thirties. I was a fine chef, probably one of the best ten in the whole of France, but there was something lacking in my life. In 1935 I discovered what it was. God.' Father Dominic crossed himself. 'There's little more to tell about myself. I was sent here after I was ordained. It was my first parish and I have been here ever since. You can appreciate that in the eyes of my superiors I am a freak, someone they would naturally wish to keep well hidden. After all a gluttonous priest must be a poor advertisement for the Church. But I am not unhappy. I have my books, I have my food, may God forgive me, and I do my duty as a parish priest. My task is not onerous as the

people of this village are divided into two camps. The older ones
believe in God because their parents did, and they come to mass
and the confessional out of habit. The younger ones, if they do
not leave the village, do not come to mass. They are discovering
their own gods. But we get along well enough together, and, if
young, they are still French and appreciate someone who will talk
food to them any hour of the day or night. That's enough about
me. I expect to spend the rest of my life here, until they carry me
out and bury me in the churchyard next door. By then they will
probably have to knock a hole in the wall as I will be even grosser
than I am now. May I take some of your brandy?'

'Of course.'

'I am afraid that what I can tell you about the poor young
officer is not much, but I will tell you what I know. After all a man
with your gastronomic knowledge must be trustworthy.'

I could not help smiling at Father Dominic's somewhat novel
way of estimating human character.

'In the spring of 1942, exactly nine years ago, I knew that there
was a stranger in the area. You mentioned Monsieur Clondel at
the château spoke of a suspected drop from a plane. It subsequently became common knowledge that a young British officer
was in hiding at the château. In those days, the count employed
several servants about the house, not to mention the peasants
who cultivated his vines in the immediate vicinity of the château.

'Not surprisingly the presence of this officer made the villagers uneasy. To be honest, they were frightened of the Germans,
and the word Gestapo brought terror to their hearts. Rumours
of German atrocities kept seeping through to a village even as
small as Les Saules. Men and women were rumoured to have
been executed in Orléans for sheltering Allied soldiers still in
hiding from the time the Germans had overrun France. People
discovered listening to secret radios were hauled off and nothing
more was heard of them. We had come to believe in the existence
of concentration camps, and could no longer refuse to acknowl-
edge that Hitler was out to obliterate the Jews. The people were
terrified of reprisals. There were stories of executions, where
communities had one in every ten men shot because a village or
town had harboured an escaped prisoner or an airman who had

been shot down or landed by parachute. Let me assure you that at that time, we Frenchmen were not at all brave. But you in England were not occupied. You never experienced the fear of the knock on the door in the night. The arrival of the secret police, with the power to take away whomever they wished without a warrant. So I do not blame my countrymen.'

'We had a game in England deciding who of our friends and politicians would have collaborated with the Germans if they had occupied England,' I said. 'It is easy enough to criticize from a safe position. But what I can't understand is what this officer was doing on his own in this area. I mean, he could hardly have taken on the Germans single-handed.'

'There are many theories,' said Father Dominic. 'Maybe he was sent in as a spy, or to join up with an imaginary French pocket of resistance. But the nearest in 1942 was in Orléans, and that's some twenty-five kilometres away.'

'But why was he shot? Why did he come to be found shot to pieces in a farmyard near the Café de Boeuf?'

'You seem to know a great deal already,' said Father Dominic. He smiled. 'But then, you are a journalist.'

'All I know is that his body was found one morning about the end of May 1942, terribly mutilated on a dung heap. I gather too that there had been the sound of firing near the bridge early that day. I have nothing to hide. I got my information from Monsieur Clondel at the château.'

Father Dominic helped himself to another glass of brandy. He placed his hands together as if in prayer. 'Perhaps it would be better if you left it at that. *Requiescat in pace.*'

'I'm sorry if I have embarrassed you,' I said. 'But as I told you, everything that you tell me will be treated in confidence, for as long as you wish; for ever if necessary.'

Father Dominic hesitated before replying. 'There are some things I can never tell you,' he finally said. 'First and foremost are the secrets of the confessional, at which I must not even so much as hint. But I can sense you are a determined sort of person, and mystery will only make you keener to unravel it. There may be people who do not wish this affair to be reopened. You might harm them or hurt them by doing so. I do not know whether this is the case, but, if it is, you must promise me that you will be discreet for as long as they are on this earth.'

'I promise,' I said.

'To go back to the death of the young lieutenant. I was confronted by several hysterical members of the Boudin family at about nine o'clock on the morning of 30 May. One of them had discovered a body in the farmyard adjoining the café. They immediately reported it to the authorities, and soon after a German officer arrived with two soldiers and said that on no account was it to be removed. It was to be left there to rot.'

'But why?'

Father Dominic shrugged his shoulders. 'Who knows? The German officer was an extremely brutal type. He seemed to me to be acting in a most unreasonable manner. He was clearly bent on venting his spleen on the young lieutenant even in death, and I got the impression that he would have done far worse things to him had he been alive. Anyway, I could not leave the poor boy lying out there. I got out my bicycle and went straight to the château and told the count what had happened. To cut a long story short, later that day permission was granted by the German authorities to remove the body.'

'I understand that de Chaumont may have had some influence with the Germans. That he may have even been a member of the French Fascist Party at one time.'

Father Dominic held up his hand. 'You see, that is what I mean about this whole affair. There is rumour, ill-founded gossip, and you must not say such things. At least, not until you have the proof.'

I felt that I had been reprimanded. 'I'm sorry. So you took the body away?'

'Yes. I brought the body into my church on a hurdle carried by members of the Morel family, from the Café des Fleurs. It was not a pretty job. We dug the grave and buried the poor boy.'

'That is all?'

Father Dominic thought a moment, then said, 'I think that is all. Oh yes, I removed the identity discs which were still hanging round his neck. I handed these over to an English officer when we were liberated, together with a report on the whole business.'

'Forgive me if I go into unpleasant details, but have you any idea why the body should have been so terribly mutilated?'

'No. All I can say is that the body had been literally shot to bits. It was the work of a madman or madmen. And that, Michael, is about as much as I can tell you.'

I did not wish to push Father Dominic further, although I felt that he had not told me all he knew by any means.

'Can I see the grave?'

'If you wish.'

The grave was situated in the far corner of the churchyard, apart from the others. At its head lay a plain white marble cross on which were inscribed the words 'Antony Fitzjames Rattigan, 1921-1942'. And that was all.

'I wonder why the body was not removed to an Allied War Cemetery,' I said.

Father Dominic spread out his hands. 'Why trouble? What difference does it make where his mortal remains lie? May his soul rest in peace.' He crossed himself.

Looking at the plain white cross I said, 'And the two visitors who came here to visit the grave in 1946, a woman and an old man?'

'His mother and his grandfather,' said Father Dominic.

'What were they like?'

'They were very sad. His mother, by the way, was a Frenchwoman, most charming. She was born in Tours.'

'And the grandfather?'

'A splendid man. A military man, who introduced himself as a general.'

'They said nothing?'

'No, they knelt and prayed at the grave, at the very spot where you are now standing. Then she thanked me for my trouble, for burying her boy, and departed.'

'And they have never been back?'

'No. But the following year a young woman of about twenty-five or twenty-six came here. It must have been about Easter and I was coming out of the church after hearing confessions. I get a lot of extra work at Easter. I saw her kneeling here praying. I waited until she stood up, and introduced myself. She turned out to be the dead boy's sister. She too thanked me for what I had done, which was very little, and she too went away.'

'Didn't they ask you to say a mass for the dead or anything like that?'

'No, they were Protestants,' Father Dominic smiled. 'But, of course, I did. And I remember him constantly in my prayers.'

'One last thing,' I said. 'The plaque at the château? Do you know anything about that? What does the black cat mean?'

'You will have to ask the count about that. It was placed into the wall by a local stonemason after he went to Paris, on his instructions. Since then he has never been back to the village.'

'It's strange,' I said.

Father Dominic looked at me seriously for a moment. 'My son, it is a very strange affair. May I again plead with you to let this poor young man rest in peace.'

'I will try,' I said. I thanked Father Dominic for his hospitality, shook hands with him, and promised that I would call on him if ever I should pass through Les Saules again. He accompanied me to the door of his house, and as soon as he had gone inside I retraced my steps to the church, went back to the grave and stood looking at the headstone.

For some reason I felt infinitely sad. That white cross, which commemorated the life of a young soldier who had lived for only twenty-one years, suddenly seemed to sum up the waste of war and the stupidity of the human race.

I went back to the car telling myself that it would be sensible to forget the whole business, enjoy a holiday in the Loire valley and get over my unhappy love affair. Indeed, I cursed Beaverbrook for dragging me down to his villa in the South of France for no apparent reason. Had I stuck to my original plan, I should never have heard of a village called Les Saules, or a château with a plaque in its garden, and there would have been no question of disturbing the peace of a certain Lieutenant Antony Fitzjames Rattigan.

Although I had drunk enough with Father Dominic, I decided to drive up the village street and have a beer at the Café des Fleurs and there make up my mind what to do. But just before I reached the café I saw Georges's garage and decided to drop in and see how he was getting on with the smashed Citroën.

Georges was working on the car in the yard at the back of the garage. 'Not as bad as you had feared,' he said. 'Nothing wrong with the half-shafts, which is a bit of luck considering how hard you cracked that lamp-post. By the way, the local *gendarme*, Maurice, was in just now. He tried to get you on the phone at the château earlier but they said you were not in. I hear you have been lunching with our good priest.'

'News travels fast round here,' I said.

'Naturally. This is a village. We have very little to do except to watch one another closely. By the way, you need have no fear of Maurice. He's one of my uncles. The worst he can do is to charge you with damage to property belonging to the Republic. You'll probably find him having a beer at the Café des Fleurs. He's very thick with the Morels. They worked together during the war, something to do with the Resistance.'

I was immediately alert, determined not to show my hand too quickly, remembering that Monsieur Clondel and Father Dominic had both told me how secretive everyone in the village became when the subject of the war and particularly of the Resistance arose. 'Was there much resistance round here?' I asked, trying to sound casual.

'Not much. I don't really know and I couldn't care less. As far as I am concerned it's something that finished six years ago, when I was only fifteen years old.'

Looking at Georges, I was surprised that he was so young, only twenty-one. As if reading my thoughts Georges said: 'I know what you're thinking: that I look older. I don't ask for any sympathy, but I've had a hard time. There was not much food in the war, that I remember for certain. We had no land to live off, only this garage. And when my father had to report for duty I had to work hard at the age of ten helping an old uncle of mine to run the business when my father went away.'

'And your father . . . ?'

'He never came back.'

'I'm sorry.'

Georges shrugged his shoulders. 'Unlike Father Dominic I believe we have only one life so we might as well make the best of it.'

It was clear to me that Georges was not the least bit interested in the war and would not be put off by a direct question. 'When I was lunching with Father Dominic we got around to talking about an English officer who was murdered by the Germans.'

'Oh, him,' said Georges. 'I'm sorry. I do not wish to sound offensive but it's really time people round here stopped arguing over him. He's dead and gone. All the talk and recrimination will never bring him back to life. Personally, I refuse to listen to any of it. Thank God one doesn't hear so much about him now. But when the war ended and the Allies came to liberate us, together with a considerable amount of our furniture, wine, and whatever they could lay their thieving hands on, no one could talk about anything else. But if you want to know anything about him you might try my uncle, Maurice, particularly after he's had a few beers. And now, if you'll excuse me, I'll get back to your car. I'll just give it an undercoat and one of gloss and the hire people can finish it off.'

'When will it be ready?'

'You can take it away tomorrow morning if you wish.'

'You've been very quick.'

'I work hard. I don't propose to stay all my life in Les Saules doing odd jobs, patching ancient bits of farm machinery and putting what petrol there is into tanks. No, as soon as I have enough money in the bank I'm off to Orléans where I have my eye on a small garage.'

I left Georges and drove up to the Café des Fleurs. Georges's uncle, the local sergeant of police, was sitting under the awning sipping a beer. As I got out of the car he called me to come and join him. 'What'll you have?' He asked as soon as I had taken the chair facing him.

'A beer, cold if possible.'

'A cold beer,' he called, turning his head to the entrance to the dining room of the café. 'You have been lunching with Father Dominic. In my opinion, always a little heavy on the salt. After a meal with the good Father one always needs beer – litres and litres of it.'

'It was an excellent meal,' I said.

'A most excellent priest and a superlative chef,' commented Sergeant Maurice.

'I understood that you wanted to see me about my accident,' I said.

'A mere formality.' He drew a document from his pocket and passed it to me. 'If you would kindly fill this up and let me have it before you go.'

Madame Morel came out of the café and placed a glass of beer in front of me. 'I trust you are better. You were badly shaken yesterday evening,' she said. 'Was the château comfortable?'

'Very. Thank you for the recommendation.' As she was about to go I said, 'I think two more beers would be a good idea.'

'Ah, I knew it. He's much too heavy on the salt and spices. I always tell him so, but he will have none of it. And who am I to argue with the greatest chef in the whole of France?'

I picked up my glass, tilted it towards Sergeant Maurice and wished him good health, then took a long drink. I had not realized how thirsty I was.

Sergeant Maurice looked at me. 'So, you are a journalist from the *Daily Express*? You have come from Nice, and you are on holiday?' Noting the look of surprise on my face at this accurate piece of information, he smiled and said, 'No, I am not a member of the secret police. I merely gleaned the information from the form you filled in at the château last night.'

'How stupid of me,' I said. 'That's right. I'm on my way to explore the Loire valley. Rather a roundabout way, but I had to fly down first to see my boss at Cap D'Ail. It was an order.'

I wondered why I found myself explaining my roundabout route to the Loire valley. I suppose because, although I am a journalist, I am always wary of the law. One is apt to judge policemen by the high standard of our English police. It is a very different kettle of fish in other countries. Upset a policeman in the Middle East and you'll find yourself beaten about the head or thrown into a stinking cell for no other reason than appearing to be a bit on the nosey side. Nor, for that matter, are the Paris riot squads exactly selective, but apt to lash out at whoever is nearest to them.

Madame Morel came out and placed two more beers on the table.

When she had gone, to make conversation I said: 'Does one eat well here at the Café des Fleurs?'

'Marvellously. I spend all my meagre pay at Madame Morel's table. I recommend it before you resume your holiday. But whatever you do, avoid the Boeuf by the bridge like the plague. Those Boudins couldn't produce a *pot-au-feu* if they tried. Damned gypsies. Cause me more trouble than all the rest of the village put together. When they are not fighting innocent villagers, they fight each other. I don't worry them. Let them get on with it. With any luck they'll kill one of their own.'

'I get the impression that the Boudins are not exactly popular round here,' I said.

'They have their enemies and their friends,' said Sergeant Maurice. 'It all goes back to the war. Now I'm not accusing the Boudins of anything specific. They were not traitors or anything like that. But they were indifferent. They wanted to be left alone, and so did many other Frenchmen. In a way, the Boudins have some kind of excuse. They're not pure Frenchmen. There's plenty of gypsy blood running in their veins.'

'Yes, I've heard that the village was somewhat divided.' Taking a shot in the dark I added, 'Particularly over the affair of the English lieutenant who is buried in the churchyard.'

Sergeant Maurice did not appear to be at all surprised at my mentioning the subject. 'You couldn't stay an hour in this village without hearing of the affair of the young lieutenant. How much do you know?'

I decided to be frank and told him how much I had already discovered. When I had finished Maurice said, 'Yes, now there's a good example of what I was trying to say about the division in this village. When the body was found on the dung heap and even after the Germans had given their permission for it to be buried after the intervention of the count, the Boudins didn't want to know. It was the Morel family here who helped Father Dominic to carry the body into the churchyard and bury it.'

'And what did you do?'

'No, no, I wasn't here then. I was a mere policeman on the beat in Orléans. I wasn't posted here until 1946, a year after the war finished.'

'But I understand that you were involved in the Resistance in Orléans.'

Sergeant Maurice held out his hand. 'I am glad to say that I did what I could. But it was very little. All I had to do was to keep my eyes and ears open. I was a kind of police informer in reverse. You see, in Orléans there was a collecting centre for escaped prisoners of war and members of the Allied forces who had gone into hiding after the fall of France. At the time I knew very little about the organization. In fact I only had one contact, a butcher in the Rue Pasteur. I regret to say that some of my fellow police were collaborating with the Germans and helping them to pick up the escaped prisoners, and I passed on to my contact any information that I gleaned about police raids and so on. As I say it wasn't much. It wasn't until after the war that I discovered how successful the organization had been. It turned out that I had been part of an escape route known as PAT. It had been organized, I think, in 1941 by a certain Albert-Marie Guérisse. Actually he was a Belgian and I believe a doctor. Eventually he was betrayed and fell into the hands of Himmler's butchers. But somehow or other he survived. After the war your king awarded him the George Cross. I understand a very high honour indeed.'

'Too true.'

As if anticipating my next question Sergeant Maurice continued: 'To come back to the lieutenant. There's not much I can add to what you already know. You are right in suspecting that there was some kind of drop in May 1942, on 10 May to be exact. But what or whom had been dropped no one seemed to know. The Germans were not particularly worried as a plane had been over the area for at least twenty minutes and it was clear that it had lost its bearings, so the Germans did not really know where to look, let alone what or whom to look for. It wasn't until a week later that I heard through Pierre Morel here that there was a rumour going around in Les Saules that there was a stranger in the neighbourhood. Just a rumour, mind you. One of the locals was heard saying in this café that he had seen a young man lurking near his vineyard. Someone else reported seeing a stranger near the Pont de Boeuf. Nothing much. After all, there were plenty of refugees, not to say men who had deserted or were intent on avoiding being transported to Germany as forced labour, lurking in every corner of France. It was, of course, the English lieutenant as we later found out.'

'How and when?'

'The first thing we knew was that towards the end of May there was a flap on at German HQ in Orléans, very early in the morning. Too much coming and going to be healthy. Despatch riders and top brass all over the place. By midday it was all over. But the Germans were very pleased with themselves. One party of soldiers seemed to be celebrating out of all proportion in one of the large cafés in Orléans. I gathered from one of my contacts that they were constantly raising their glasses and toasting a mission successfully concluded.'

'To kill the lieutenant?'

'Without a doubt. When I next saw Pierre Morel a few days later, he told me of the finding of the body of the lieutenant, and how it had been chucked on the dung heap. It wasn't until after the war that it came out into the open that the lieutenant had definitely been in hiding at the château. The count made no secret of it. But as to why or how he was killed we have no exact information or evidence. According to the count he last saw him on the evening of 29 May. The next thing was that Father Dominic arrived at the château the following morning and told him of the body lying in the farmyard. He said that the Germans had forbidden it to be buried and asked the count if he could use his influence with the German authorities to allow it to be removed and given a proper burial.'

'Is there any question of the count having been a collaborator?'

Sergeant Maurice looked shocked. 'Good heavens, no. None whatsoever. A famous member of the Resistance and most highly decorated. A most honourable man and a great loss to the district. If only his two sons had not been killed at Sedan in 1940 I am sure he would have been here still and, what is more, have been of great benefit to the village. You know, villagers need someone to whom they can look for advice and fair judgement. Today it's every man for himself and every man knows best. Hence you see a divided and squabbling France. But then I'm one of the old school.'

'What about another beer?'

He nodded, and I went into the café (not liking to shout like Sergeant Maurice to order the beers) and carried them out myself.

'Is there any point in having a word with Monsieur Morel?' I said as I placed the beers on the table.

'Perhaps. But don't expect him to come out here. You will have to interview him in his kitchen. He is like a duck out of water when he is not there. In fact he's downright miserable.' He picked up his glass and wished me good health.

Ten minutes later Sergeant Maurice looked at his watch. 'I must be on my way. Sometimes I am on duty.' He held out his hand. 'It has been a pleasure to meet you.'

'I hope I have not bored you. I mean, all my questions must seem impertinent.'

'You're a journalist, aren't you?' he said. 'Don't forget to let me have that form back before you go. A mere formality I assure you. If I'm not at the station just leave it on the table. It's never locked. There's nothing to steal there anyway.'

When he had gone I finished my beer, went into the café and asked Madame Morel if I could go into the kitchen.

Monsieur Morel was busy making puff pastry and was not altogether pleased to see me. I tried to appear casual and said that I had been discussing with Sergeant Maurice the plaque I had discovered that morning, and how it had aroused my curiosity.

When I told him, at his request, what I already knew, he said there was nothing more he could add. But his final words were interesting. Rolling out the pastry he said, almost as if to himself, 'It was a bad business, a very bad business. There is no question about it. That poor boy was betrayed. Yes, he was betrayed, without a doubt.'

2

I left Les Saules the following morning to make my tour of the Loire valley. I had firmly made up my mind in the course of the previous evening to put the strange story of the young lieutenant whose body lay in the churchyard out of my mind. But looking back I can see now that I was behaving like an alcoholic who makes up his mind to give up drink for ever, while knowing perfectly well that he is setting himself an impossible task.

I suppose I was not even in with a chance. I was literally on a hiding to nothing. After all I was a journalist and, without being boastful, in those days I was a very good one. I would go so far as to say I was somewhere near the top of my class.

In fact it was only two days later that I found myself sitting down at the table in my bedroom and writing down everything I so far knew about the case.

There is just a chance that I might not have done so had I not been alone; had I had some female company for instance to keep my mind occupied. But I was on my own. I had spent a day and a half sightseeing in Orléans and intended next day to leave for Blois stopping on the way at Beaugency. I had bought a *Michelin Guide* to the châteaux of the Loire and like the true tourist had been reading up my history and deciding which châteaux most deserved a visit.

I had dined very late and too well at the Cremaillère. A bottle of Sancerre had been followed by too many brandies, and by the time I reached my bedroom at my hotel I was in the mood for a party. The last thing I wanted to do was to go to bed. But that is the trouble with being alone in a strange city. I suppose I could have crawled round the bars and cafés and got drunk. I might even have picked up a tart. I know I telephoned the *Daily Mirror* and asked for the girlfriend with whom I had just split, and on whose account I was taking a holiday on my own on the principle that distance makes the heart grow colder. It does to me, except when I'm drunk, when all my resolutions go by the board. When I was told she was not in the building I tried the number of her flat, but without success. Just the sound of that engaged tone.

I felt lonely. I told myself that the so-called holiday was a complete mistake; that next morning I would forget the Loire valley and fly back to England. But the problem was what to do immediately. It was then that I found myself scribbling furiously on the hotel writing paper all that I had so far discovered about the case of Antony Fitzjames Rattigan from the moment I had pulled aside the roses and wisteria that hid the plaque in the garden of the château, to the last words of Monsieur Morel at the Café des Fleurs: 'Yes, he was betrayed without a doubt.'

Looking back I can see that I had succeeded in putting Antony Rattigan out of my mind for less than forty-eight hours. So much for my resolution.

I did not go back to England the following day. I stuck to my original intention and spent a fortnight in the Loire valley. By the end of May 1951, however, I was back in England. My desk at the *Express* had not been taken over and I fell back into the routine of turning out two articles a week and fiddling my expenses. But I felt happier. I was over my love affair. I must have been because about three weeks after I returned I was sitting in El Vino drinking a bottle with Reg Willis of the *Evening News* when she came in with a man whom I particularly disliked on the *News Chronicle* and my heart did not even miss a beat.

It was on that same day that I spoke with Major Sam Wells who was one of the press officers at the War Office at the time. Sam was a regular officer who had been wounded in Italy during the war where he commanded a battalion of the Royal Fusiliers. In those days all three services had their own press officers and it was not until some years later that they were centralized under the Ministry of Defence. The job tended to be looked upon by the professional soldiers, airmen and sailors as one to which the naughty boys were sent for a spell of punishment, or the wounded to recuperate.

Sam had started as an amateur, worked hard, taken advice from his friends in Fleet Street and become highly skilled at handling the press – and was well liked into the bargain. I was

particularly friendly with him, and he liked me, partly because
I had served him in the Italian campaign – if served is the right
word when one considers my trail of thieving, drunkenness and
cowardice up the spine of Italy from 1943 to 1946. Anyway we
got along well together, and later on he was to be of great help
to me at the time of Suez when I was one of the few journalists
to land there on that ill-fated enterprise. He was of even greater
assistance to me during the Cyprus troubles, and later got me
attached to the Black Watch in Aden where Colonel 'Mad' Mitch-
ell was making his last stand and proving that terrorism cannot
be contained by a velvet glove but only by a mailed fist.

I cannot remember why I had gone to see Sam Wells that particular day, but I do remember at the end of our conversation I
suddenly said: 'Would you do me a favour, Sam? Could you find
me any gen on a Lieutenant Antony Fitzjames Rattigan? I don't
know his regiment. All I can tell you is that he was born in 1921,
was killed in 1942 and is buried in the churchyard of a small village called Les Saules, about fifteen kilometres from Orléans.'

'No trouble with a distinctive name like that,' said Sam. Three
days later Sam called me at the office. 'I've got some information
on your Lieutenant Rattigan. Quite interesting. Look, it's my
turn to lunch you. What about today? Say, one at the In and Out.'

I am not one of those people who can wait till the end of the
meal when the coffee and brandy have arrived before getting
down to the serious purpose of the meal. As soon as we were
seated at the corner table I said: 'Right, Sam. What did you find
out?'

'I had an idea as soon as you spoke to me. The Rattigans are
an old and distinguished military family. They fought with Marlborough at Blenheim and Malplaquet in the War of the Spanish
Succession. They distinguished themselves in the Peninsular War
and fought at Waterloo. Prominent in the Crimean War, Boer
War and, of course, the Great War. Picked up a VC or two along
the line, not to mention hundreds of lesser gongs. There is a General Sir Henry Fitzjames Rattigan, still alive and living at a place
called Malplaquet near Kelvedon in Essex. He was born in 1868,
so that makes him eighty-three. He commanded a division in
France during the 1914-18 war. Did no better or worse than all the

other divisional commanders, except that in his case he seemed positively to enjoy being in the front line, and was severely reprimanded by Haig for going over the top with a battalion of Grenadiers. I mean to say, they didn't even do that in the last show.'

I could not help laughing at the thought of a general actually leading a battalion in attack. Sam was right, it had not happened in the last war, nor indeed was it a general's job to die heroically at the head of his men.

'That was the peak of the general's career. At the outbreak of the 1939-45 war he was nearly seventy-one and too old for active service. Seems to have been pushed around at the War Box doing odds and sods. Helped form the Home Volunteers, later to become the Home Guard and so on. I gather from someone who knew him that he was as furious as hell and thoroughly bad tempered over the whole business. There was even a rumour that he dyed his hair and moustache black to make himself look younger and tried to enlist as a private in an infantry regiment. But it may be hearsay. Anyway, he's now out to grass on the family estate, Malplaquet.'

'What about Antony Fitzjames Rattigan?'

'We'll come to him in a minute.'

I did not press Sam. I appreciated the way his military mind was working. He would fill me in with all the available information and intelligence before coming to the objective.

'The general had only one son, born 1901. At the outbreak of war in 1939 he was commanding the 1st batallion, the Dukes. This had been the family regiment since the Peninsular War, in fact you might say it had more or less been their private army since that time. It still has some very strange traditions. No commissioned ranks below that of captain, no NCOs below sergeant. Technically it is still only answerable to the sovereign and need not take any orders from the commander-in-chief unless its colonel feels inclined. Of course, practically speaking, these traditions no longer apply. But it's nice to think that some bureaucrat in Parliament has not had them removed by statute. I don't want to be unkind about Colonel Rattigan. I suppose one could say that the steam had to run out of the family at some time. The fact is that he was not very bright. If he had not been a Rattigan, I doubt if

1939 would have found him commanding the 1st battalion. From what I can gather, to make up for his – how shall we say – lack of brilliance, he compensated by being a martinet, a stickler for complicated drills, discipline and so on.'

'A right bullshitter in other words,' I suggested.

Sam nodded. 'Exactly. He wasn't popular with his officers and was disliked by his men. Anyway, he went to France with his battalion in 1939. Subsequently he moved up with it into Belgium when the Germans started their blitzkrieg the following May, retreated to Dunkirk and was one of the last to leave the beaches where he earned a DSO, together with the undying hatred of the rest of his battalion who christened him Bloody Rattigan. On the other hand without people like him to make that last stand it is doubtful if half the number who got away at Dunkirk would have done so.'

He paused to order our meal.

'To go back to Colonel Rattigan, DSO. In 1944 he was killed within ten minutes of setting foot on a Normandy beach. There was some talk of a posthumous VC, but it came to nothing. I think there were too many proposed VCs in the pipeline after the landings.'

Sam tasted the wine which the waiter had poured. I knew that he was teasing me, deliberately keeping me waiting when he said: 'Not bad for Algerian. I have heard a rumour that they are getting in a consignment of real French wine soon. Just think of it, wine from France at last.'

'Come on, you old sod,' I said.

Up to now Sam had spoken off the cuff and I appreciated how brilliantly he had digested the information that he had gleaned. Now for the first time he looked down at a piece of paper he had taken out from his breast pocket. 'The colonel had two children. First there was Henrietta Marie born in 1920.' He lifted his glass and took another sip of the Algerian wine. 'Not at all bad. Not at all,' he repeated.

I refused to rise to the bait and kept quiet.

'The second child, a son, was born in the following year. He was christened Antony Fitzjames Rattigan. Antony, the one I presume you are interested in, was educated at a prep school called

Lambrook in Berkshire. He went on to General Wolfe College. Wolfe as you probably know is a second Wellington, although of course it considers itself far superior to Wellington. Anyway, in those days they were both still the production line for soldiers to police our Empire. According to Records, Antony went to Wolfe in 1935 and left in 1937, which is a bit odd, but Records assure me that is what is on his file. Then there's a blank until 1939.'

'Only two years at Wolfe, but that's extraordinary,' I said. 'Perhaps he went on to Sandhurst early, or something like that. After all with the Rattigan name behind him he was almost outside the law.'

Sam shook his head. 'No, nothing like that. Your Antony Fitzjames Rattigan goes absent without leave for two years. His name next turns up when he joins up in September 1939.'

'The Dukes of course,' I said.

Sam shook his head again and laughed. 'Not a bit of it. The 3rd battalion, the Southerns.'

'I can't believe it,' I said. In my time in the wartime army I had learned enough about its etiquette and snobbery to know that the Southerns were far from being considered the cream of the army – more like the curds and whey.

'Yes, remarkable isn't it?' said Sam. 'Here is a Rattigan turning up in one of our lesser regiments. I mean, he doesn't even join one of the county regiments.'

'To be frank, he joined a regiment especially created for grammar-school boys and so on, who couldn't, however brilliant they might be, obtain commissions in the posh regiments of the British Army,' I said.

'It still goes on, I'm afraid,' said Sam. 'Only the other day a colonel of the Guards was quoted as saying that he would have only public school boys in the battalion as anyone else would be unhappy, and he did not want unhappy officers. You can imagine what a lot of work that caused me. Telephone never stopped ringing for days, people demanding to know whether it was true, and what we had to say about it. It went right up to the CIGS who gave me a bollocking. It wasn't my fault that idiot of a colonel could not keep his big mouth shut.'

'So Antony Fitzjames turns up in the Southerns. What then?'

Sam consulted his notes. 'The 3rd Southerns went to France, and Lieutenant Rattigan went with them. In the 1940 retreat his battalion came back through Arras where it made a good stand which earned it the grudging admiration of the more élite mobs. It came off in bits and pieces through Calais and Boulogne. Back in England, Lieutenant Rattigan was posted to the 4th Southerns who were forming at Maidstone and subsequently were allotted an area of the south coast to defend in the event of invasion. As far as I know he stayed with the 4th battalion for the next year. Then he turns up again in the summer of 1941 when, in June, he is posted to you'll never guess where . . .'

'The Dukes?' I suggested.

Sam shook his head. 'No, to SOE.'

'Ah, Special Operations Executive. Colonel Buckmaster's outfit. Secret Agents and all that jazz,' I said. 'As a matter of fact I should have guessed. It might make sense. Go on.'

Sam looked embarrassed: 'That's it. That's as far as I could get.'

'What do you mean?'

'Lieutenant Rattigan was reported missing in June 1942. It was subsequently confirmed that he had been shot by the Germans. I'm afraid there is very little information about what happened to the majority of agents who went missing. You see, SOE was disbanded in 1946, by order of the Cabinet, and simply didn't have the facilities to check on what happened to its missing members. It's not just a question of classified information, although that does come into it, of course, particularly where lines and means of communication are concerned. But I haven't given up. I'm trying to find someone who knew Lieutenant Rattigan during his training period. But it isn't easy.'

Sam looked down at his notes. 'By the way, Lieutenant Rattigan's mother is still alive. She lives in the dower house at Malplaquet. For your information her maiden name was Leclerc. His sister lives with her.'

'She is French,' I said.

'Now, no doubt, you'll tell me what this is all about,' said Sam. 'But I'll order another bottle of Algerian first.'

When it had been brought to the table and uncorked I mustered my thoughts and told Sam all that had happened since I had first discovered the strange plaque in the garden of the château. I well remember Sam's first reaction. He did not interrupt me as I told my story, but his first words when I had finished speaking were, 'What's all this about a black cat?'

'If I knew I'd tell you,' I said. 'But you have to admit it adds even more interest to the story, and I simply must find out all about Lieutenant Rattigan even if it means falling foul of the Official Secrets Act. I'll get to the bottom of it even if it's the last thing I do in Fleet Street.'

'Meanwhile, you can do something for me,' said Sam. 'We're getting a lot of opposition to National Service.'

'I'm not surprised. The bloody war has been over for six years . . .'

'We've still got a lot of worldwide responsibilities,' said Sam.

'You're speaking like a Tory politician,' I said. 'OK, I've got the message. National Service is good for the youth of today, teaches them social integration, to be a man and all that crap.'

Sam looked hurt.

'Don't worry, Sam,' I said. 'I'll do something about it. As a matter of fact I believe in it myself, but I don't like the balls that is talked about it. Just you wait till the day when National Service is abolished. I bet you anything you like that our streets will be filled with young gangsters and it won't be safe to go out after dark. Some psychologists once said that men need a war where they can work off their aggressive instincts. So what the hell are they going to do without one?'

Sam looked at his watch, and called for the bill.

As we parted company in Piccadilly, Sam said: 'It's an intriguing story. What'll you do next?'

'Take a leaf out of your book and start at the beginning. By the way, thank you very much for all the trouble you took. It was a masterly briefing.'

Sam smiled with pleasure and crossed Piccadilly. I waited for a cab and asked the driver to go to the *Express* building in Fleet Street. My editor groaned when I told him I proposed to do a piece on National Service and mumbled something about falling circulation and the vital necessity of jazzing the paper up to bring in new readers. I thought this slightly offensive, and when I asked him if he had someone else in mind to take over my desk, he shut up, took me to El Vino and bought me a bottle of champagne.

For the next week I was busy being driven round the country in army staff cars watching national servicemen at work and at play and generally being impressed with what I saw. I must say, too, for the army authorities, that they allowed me to talk with the men without an officer or sergeant standing within earshot. On the whole the servicemen did not seem to be having too bad a time, although there were the usual grumbles about food, lack of leave and shortage of girls. Not much different from the wartime deprivations that I had known only too well myself. Many of them were anxious to serve overseas and I was surprised to find that there were a considerable number who wanted to get to Malaya where there was an extremely unpleasant war being fought against the Communists in the jungle.

On the strength of my meeting Winston Churchill at Beaverbrook's villa in the South of France I rang up his private secretary and was pleasantly surprised to be asked down to Chartwell to have a chat with the grand old man. He was tired, and what struck me most of all was that he still felt bewildered if not downright upset at his rejection by the British people in the 1945 election after he had led them to victory against the Nazis. I formed the opinion then that he would have done far better to go to the House of Lords rather than try to cling to power in the Commons. Naturally I did not tell him so. I got a nice chatty piece out of him. Beaverbrook liked it and telephoned me to say so. So, my star was still in the ascendant.

Needless to say, while I had been involved in these bread-and-butter activities, thoughts of Antony Fitzjames Rattigan were not far from my mind. From whatever angle I studied the affair I came back to my original decision to start at the beginning, which was exactly what Sam Wells had done when he had briefed me so skilfully.

Accordingly, I decided that my order of investigation would be first to get in touch with someone who knew him at Wolfe College and then to go and see his mother. There seemed no point in going back to his preparatory school. As soon as I had filled in his family background and, if possible, those two missing years from 1937 to 1939, I would come to his military career with his joining the unsmart 3rd Southerns in 1939.

The old saying, 'It's not what you know, but whom you know', applies to a great number of professions, not least to journalism. The more contacts you have the easier your work becomes. My advice to anyone entering journalism is to start a contacts book the day they start work. I owe ninety per cent of what success I have had as a journalist to keeping as many contacts as possible on the boil. It may cost a bit, in the way of drinks and meals, but there's nothing more satisfying than, when confronted with a story, knowing exactly where to start.

A few days after I had interviewed Churchill I rang the secretary of the Public Schools Club in Piccadilly and asked him to look up an old Wolfian called Antony Fitzjames Rattigan who had been at the school between 1935 and 1937 and to let me have the name of his housemaster. The information came back in a quarter of an hour. His housemaster had been a certain Philip Hanbury but he was now retired and his place had been taken by a Terence Cobb. Needless to say both had a string of letters after their names.

I put through a call to Wolfe College at six that evening, thinking that would be about the hour Mr Cobb might be in his room taking a glass of sherry or handing out tutorials. I was lucky, and he was most obliging. Without my having to tell a single lie, within five minutes I learned that Philip Hanbury was alive and well and living at Bluebell Cottage, Etchingham, in Sussex. Having obtained it from directory enquiries, I dialled Mr Hanbury's number.

Philip Hanbury answered the telephone and identified himself. 'To whom am I speaking?' he asked.

'Michael Nelson. You don't know me, but I wonder if I could come and see you?'

'Why should you wish to see me if I don't know you?'

I at once got the impression that Philip Hanbury was on the defensive.

'It's quite simple. I would like to have a word with you about one of your old boys.'

'There were so many of them. Which one in particular have you in mind?'

'Antony Fitzjames Rattigan.' There was a pause. 'Are you still there, Mr Hanbury?' I asked.

'I am still here.'

'Do you remember that particular boy?'

'I remember all my boys.'

'Of course you do. May I come and talk to you about him.'

'I believe he was killed in France,' said Mr Hanbury.

'That is correct.'

'Well, there's not much more to be said, is there? Perhaps it would be kindest to let the dear boy rest in peace. Who are you, by the way? What is your interest in Antony Rattigan?'

'You won't believe it, but I came across his grave by accident when I was in France last month. Well, there's more to it than that. Could I come and see you? It would be far easier than talking to you over the phone.'

'But you have not told me who you are.'

'I'm a writer.'

'What do you write?'

'I write for newspapers.'

'Which newspaper?'

I realized that this was a critical point in my conversation with Philip Hanbury. 'It's nothing to do with my paper. I promise you that. It's a purely personal matter. I do in fact work for the *Express*.'

'Not a very nice paper,' said Philip Hanbury crisply. 'I think I have seen your name in it at one time or another.'

'So you read the *Express*?'

'In other people's houses only,' said Philip Hanbury coldly. 'I am strictly a *Times* man myself.'

'I am afraid I do not aspire to such lofty heights,' I said, 'although the editor is a good friend of mine,' I added, throwing in this bit of information as ground bait. My ruse worked and Philip Hanbury became more pliant and forthcoming.

'Very well then. Provided you understand that any conversation is off the record, I would be prepared to meet you.'

'Would you care to come to London and have lunch with me one day? All expenses paid, of course,' I said.

'I never come to London. No, it would be far more convenient if you came down here and had luncheon with me. Now what day would suit you?'

'You name it.'

'I will look in my book.' There was a pause. 'Are you there, Mr Nelson? Now what about this coming Thursday? About twelve-thirty. I see you will fit in very well then. There is a fairly competent train service to Etchingham, and my cottage is not far from a public house which goes by the name of the Sun in Splendour.'

'Thank you, Mr Hanbury. I look forward very much to seeing you on Thursday.'

Two days later I took the train to Etchingham and after making enquiries at the Sun in Splendour I found myself, with no difficulty, at the gate of Bluebell Cottage. I stood for a moment admiring the small front garden with its carefully mown lawn. There was a bird-table and a bird-bath in the middle of it. The first roses were beginning to show and the front of the house itself was covered with a vine and purple clematis.

Philip Hanbury must have been waiting for me for as soon as I opened the gate and began to walk up the path the door opened and he advanced to meet me, holding out his hand for me to shake. 'No trouble in finding me then?'

'It's beautiful, absolutely beautiful.'

'Yes, I like it,' he said. 'Now come inside and drink a glass of sherry. Not exactly what I would drink from choice, but under our communist government one must be content with what one can get.'

I couldn't help smiling at Philip Hanbury's reference to the Labour Party as communists. Mr Hanbury did not miss a thing. 'You may smile, Mr Nelson, but that's what they are. Equality indeed! I was a schoolmaster for forty years, and every year I become more and more convinced that there is no such thing as equality.'

Philip Hanbury led the way into the cottage. I noticed at once the vast number of books. They were packed on shelves along the length of the hall, and there was not an area of wall visible in the sitting room. It was literally papered from carpet to ceiling with books. Philip Hanbury handed me a glass of sherry. 'Well, aren't you going to say anything?' he said.

'I don't understand.'

'But that's too wonderful. Most people who come in here say "what a lot of books". I could scream, yes, scream.'

'It's a pointless remark. You see I collect books myself, if only in a small way.'

'How interesting. What do you go in for?'

'Cookery books.'

'How delightful. I'm afraid I am not so eclectic as that. I cast my net much wider, but I like to think that I have a pretty fine collection of boys' books. You know, school stories, adventure stories and that kind of nonsense. If you are interested, I will show it to you later. It's kept upstairs in my bedroom.'

Philip Hanbury motioned me towards a chair. 'I have prepared a simple cold luncheon, so we have nothing to worry about. Shall we come to the point at once and see if we want to get to know one another better?'

'It's a strange story,' I said. 'Perhaps if I tell it to you, you will understand why I am so interested in Antony Fitzjames Rattigan.'

When I had finished my resumé of the case, in which I was by now word-perfect, Philip Hanbury was almost in tears.

'Oh, what a tragedy. The poor, poor boy. But why and how did it all happen?'

'That's what I would like to find out.'

'And that poor, poor pussy cat. It's too sad. My own darling Toby died just before last Christmas. I still cannot pass his grave in the garden without shedding a tear. I can quite understand how you as a writer must be absolutely intrigued by the whole mournful business. What a waste of youth, and such a beautiful boy too.'

From the moment I had seen Philip Hanbury emerging from his cottage I had had my suspicions. They were fast being confirmed. But I knew I had to proceed with delicacy. One false move and he could dry up and become a desert of information. I decided to approach my target at a tangent.

'How long were you at Wolfe College, Mr Hanbury?' I asked.

'Too long. Too long.'

'I don't understand.'

'To be frank, it wasn't really my sort of place. Shall I bore you with my life story?'

I could see that he was longing to tell me it so I said: 'It won't be a bore, I assure you.'

'You are very kind. Forgive me, but now I live alone after being surrounded by boys for forty years, I confess I do miss someone to talk to, particularly in the evenings. Of course my old boys are always coming down to see me, but it's not the same as having them living in the same house. I'm a kind of decrepit old Chips.'

'You look remarkably well preserved,' I said.

'Do you think so? How kind of you.' I noticed Philip Hanbury turned his head to one side and examined his profile in the mirror over the fireplace. I had to admit that it wasn't at all bad for a man of sixty.

'Some more sherry before I embark on my life story. You will need it,' said Philip Hanbury. 'As I was saying, Wolfe was not really my cup of tea. The trouble was that ever since I was a child, and that's oh so long ago, I have suffered from a dicky heart. The silly thing beats too slowly or too often, I forget which. When I came down from Oxford in 1914, where I must confess that I lived every glorious hour to the full, with the result that my degree was – how shall we say – nothing to be proud of, I found myself forced to take a job at a most dreary preparatory school in Berkshire. I stayed there until 1916 by which time, of course, many masters at our public schools had rushed off to fight for their country. There was a sudden shortage of teachers. By good luck a friend of mine whom I had known intimately at Oxford was teaching at Wolfe and when a vacancy for an English master occurred he put my name forward. Owing to the general chaos existing at the time I was able to slide in quietly.'

'Did you find it very different there?' I asked.

'After I became used to the hustle and bustle it really was most agreeable. Boys are the same the world over. Of course the discipline was positively barbaric. But then it is a military academy and as they say if I did not like the heat in the kitchen I was a free man and could leave. But I like to think that I provided something of a refuge for the more sensitive boys.'

'I had an uncle who went to Wolfe,' I said. 'He ran away. When he was taken back he was given twenty strokes. But that was at the end of the last century.'

'Where did you go to school, Mr Nelson?' asked Philip Hanbury.

'Bryanston.'

'Ah, that modern liberal school. Yes, I've heard lots and lots
about Bryanston. I believe you were all divinely happy there. A
very romantic place I understand.'

'Very,' I said. I felt absolutely on safe ground by now and added:
'Boys were falling in love with one another all over the place.'

'Really! How interesting. But if you will shut little boys up,
romance must rear its fair head, don't you think?'

'Absolutely. I wasn't immune myself.' I thought that was as
far as I need go. I was not prepared to relate the full details of
my sexual aberrations during my years at Bryanston for Philip
Hanbury's delectation.

'Really pleasant to meet a civilized newspaperman,' said
Philip Hanbury. 'I was almost determined not to see you when
you telephoned. I thought you would be all tough and butch. A
great pleasure to meet you indeed, Michael.' Now that he had
called me by my Christian name I thought it was time we got
back to Antony Fitzjames Rattigan.

Reading my thoughts Philip Hanbury said: 'Antony was a
most interesting boy, and let me add a very beautiful one too. I
think we all loved him, by that I mean all of us who were capable of love. I'm not talking of the morons, and God knows they
were everywhere, including the headmaster. An absolute swine.
Antony should never have come to Wolfe in the first place. If
ever there was a boy less suited to the military life it was Antony.
Except possibly myself.'

'I still don't quite understand how you stuck it at Wolfe?'

'In my perverse way I found it rather fun trying to outwit the
system. It was so satisfying trying to help unsuitable boys like
Antony. After a while I came to the conclusion that it was my duty
to stay and try to make life less harsh for boys like him. It was fun
taking on the more brutal of my fellow teachers and sometimes
succeeding into the bargain, particularly as I sometimes sailed a
little too close to the wind for safety, if you get my meaning.'

Philip raised both eyebrows and giggled. 'Mind you I never
gave them any hard evidence, just a whiff of scandal now and

again to tantalize them. Luckily I had a friend on the board of governors who also preferred the company of males to that of the ladies. A most useful ally. Alas he died the year before I retired. But I know it's Antony you want to talk about, not me. Well, as I said, he was most unsuitable material for Wolfe. Far too sensitive to be a soldier. Pushed into it by the weight of all that family tradition, and particularly by his monster of a father.'

'I know the family had been soldiers since the time of Marlborough and beyond,' I said. 'But why do you say his father was a monster?'

'So insensitive to Antony's feelings. He was incapable of admitting that Antony was not military material. It wasn't that he could not see it. He refused to. I started getting bad reports about Antony from his first term in the winter of 1935. He showed absolutely no interest in military history, he was the most slovenly member of the Officer Training Corps, totally incapable of understanding the intricacies of the drill square. On the other hand, he showed an uncanny aptitude for fieldcraft. He was also a very fine shot, but only when he wanted to be. It was this potential that infuriated his instructors. He had an enormous potential which he refused to develop. It all came to a head early in 1936 when Antony came to see me and told me that he had joined the pacifist party and his conscience no longer permitted him to remain a member of the corps. He intended to resign. It's probably impossible for you to appreciate what a scandal that would have caused. He would have been torn to bits by the bully boys and the headmaster. With considerable difficulty I persuaded him to keep his opinions to himself. It wasn't easy I don't mind telling you. Boys can be so stubborn. You see, they believe in absolute right and absolute wrong, and only lose their beliefs as they grow older and come to understand that life is a succession of compromises.'

'The poor little sod. What a bloody position to be in.'

'There was worse to come,' said Philip. 'Oh dear me, far, far worse. For about two years I managed to keep the peace between him and the rest of the school. He spent a lot of time in my rooms reading my books and pouring out his heart to me. He had discovered the Romantics. Do you know, I'm not at all sure it's a good thing for young boys to read the Romantics. Keats and Shelley are all very well, but they give a false view of life as it is lived.'

Philip refilled our glasses.

'Even then all might have been well. It was obvious that war was coming, and Antony, round about 1937, was beginning to lose his pacifist inclinations. He began to be aware of the danger of Hitler. News of the concentration camps, of Hitler's determination to wipe out the Jews, was beginning to filter through and could no longer be ignored. Antony might have been able to hang on until the end of his time at Wolfe and then gone off and joined the wartime forces like the majority of his contemporaries. He could have become a stretcher-bearer or something like that if his conscience had still forbidden him to take up arms as a fighting soldier. But he was not a lucky boy. Do you know what happened?'

I shook my head.

'He fell in love . . . with another boy of course,' said Philip.

'Well, it happens to the best of us.'

'Oh no, this was something serious. Not just a couple of boys fumbling one another in the lavatories or behind the pavilion. The poor boy got it badly, very badly indeed.'

'And he got thrown out of Wolfe,' I said. 'That explains why he only spent two years there.'

'It was a disgraceful business, most disgraceful,' said Philip.

'How do you mean disgraceful? I can't see a school like Wolfe putting up with that kind of behaviour.'

'That's the whole point. There was none of that kind of behaviour, as you so delicately put it. Antony fell in love, but there was nothing physical about it. It was all too romantic and pure for that. He would have been shocked if you had suggested to him that he might have wished to touch the object of his adoration. And what a pretty boy his beloved was too. I can see them together now. Oh, what a picture those two angels made. Antony with his fair hair falling across his forehead and his friend Tom with dark hair and a complexion that literally glowed. It had a kind of peach-like quality. You know, what is called the bloom on the fruit.'

Philip looked upwards under his hooded lids and sighed a long, sad sigh.

'Oh, Antony was so silly, so tiresome. There was nothing I could do to save him from himself. You see I knew that Tom, that was the boy that he fell for, was not as pure as he would have Antony believe. Now he had been behind the pavilion, he had fumbled in the lavatories, he had in fact been a very naughty boy indeed. What is more, he didn't love Antony one little bit. He took Antony's love for granted. He led him a pretty dance I can tell you.'

'So what happened?'

'Alas, one day Tom fumbled the wrong boy. The idiot went and complained to the head prefect of the house, and that wretch bypassed me and went straight to the headmaster. That was the end of Tom. You know, the telephone call to his home, the arrival of an irate father, and the departure of Tom midst much speculation and gossip.'

'And Antony?'

Philip thought for a moment. 'He was heartbroken. There is no other word for it. In all my years as a schoolmaster I have never seen anyone hurt so much, and I have come across a few disasters I can tell you. It was terrible to watch. He began to pine away. He withdrew completely into himself. His work, which had been bad, became atrocious. He was so miserable that even the bullies left him alone. I don't think he would have cared even if they had set about him. They could have kicked him to bits and he would have thanked them for putting him out of his misery.'

'Poor little sod,' I said again.

'I was at my wits' end, I don't mind telling you,' said Philip. 'But there was little I could do. He would not even confide in me. He withdrew completely. Looking back I can see now that all he wanted to do was to get away from Wolfe. It was much too closely associated with his beloved Tom. He still refused to listen to me when I suggested to him that Tom might not be altogether the person he had come to believe in. Oh dear, poor Antony was in a mess. Do you know it would have been better if he had had some physical relationship with Tom. It might have brought him down to earth, he might even not have liked it. That happens sometimes with boys, you know. They can be incurably romantic, but when it comes to practicalities they can become all puritanical and disgusted with sex.'

'What happened in the end?'

'He committed a kind of suicide. He went to the headmaster and told him what he felt about Tom, that he was in love with him. I told you the headmaster was a bounder, an absolute barbarian. He hadn't a clue what Antony was talking about. As far as he was concerned there was no sex at Wolfe, and the idea of love between the boys was anathema to him. I'm afraid the horrible fellow was not at all well versed in the Classics. Do you know what the shit did? Forgive my language but I still boil when I think of him. The shit telephoned Antony's father, who I think was a major at the time. That same day Antony was removed from Wolfe.'

'And he'd done nothing?'

'Exactly. As far as I know they had not so much as kissed one another. Monstrous, wasn't it?'

'What happened then?'

Philip held out his hands. 'That's the end of my story. I never heard from Antony after he was expelled, nor from Tom for that matter. Antony went out of my life. I wrote to him at his home, most discreet letters, of course. But they were returned marked Address Unknown. It was all very peculiar. The next thing I knew about him was when we were compiling our Roll of Honour of those who died in the last war. His name turned up on a list from the War Office. What a waste of a beautiful boy, what a waste.'

Philip sighed.

'Nothing more?' I asked.

'Just one small point. Tom became a priest after the war.' He went to one of the bookcases and pulled down a volume that contained the names of boys who had been at Wolfe College. 'Here we are. Thomas Ruthen Makepeace, born 1920. Wolfe 1935 to 1937. Ordained priest 1948. Present address: St Mary's, South Ascot, Berkshire. That's all. You notice there's nothing about him having been chucked out. We never admit to our failures, naturally.'

Philip Hanbury stood up. 'I would suggest this is a good place for us to break for luncheon. Afterwards perhaps you would care to see my collection of boys' books.'

'There's nothing I'd like more,' I said. But my thoughts were far away. Certainly I would get in touch with Thomas Ruthen Makepeace, ordained priest in 1948.

And what happened in the years 1937 to 1939 to Antony Fitzjames Rattigan? Presumably his family had disowned him if Philip Hanbury's letters to him had been returned marked Address Unknown.

As we walked along the hall lined with books to the small dining room, Philip Hanbury said: 'I do wish you knew more about that black cat whom Antony loved. Oh, he was a beautiful boy. But cats always show such good taste, don't they?'

3

A few days later I took one of the pool cars belonging to the *Express* and drove down to Kelvedon in Essex. There was no traffic on the roads as the country in 1951 was still in the throes of petrol rationing. That is, petrol was rationed for everyone except for those who could buy it on the black market. I had not told my editor that I had any particular story in mind. As I have explained, my star was very high in the sky at the time and I had more or less carte blanche to do what I wanted to do and to go where the fancy took me. I'm not at all sure that the editor was very happy about this, but he was clever enough to realize that I was Lord Beaverbrook's blue-eyed boy, even if a few of my fellow journalists had another word for it. But at least the editor knew I wasn't after his job. I have noticed over the years that eyeing the editor's chair always makes an editor uneasy; sometimes it can turn him positively vicious. It's just as well to remember that there is no such thing as an honest sheet of expenses in Fleet Street. Close examination of a journalist's expenses can always turn up some blatant dishonesty, and put him in line for the axe.

It was a beautiful June day, and as I drove through the green countryside I went over my previous day's homework. The new edition of *Who's Who* which I had consulted in the library of the *Express* had supplied me with enough basic information to be going on with. General Sir Henry Fitzjames Rattigan, KCMG. KB, DSO and bar, MC, had been born in 1868. He had served in the Boer War, India and the Great War of 1914-18. His MC had been awarded to him for gallantry in the Burma uprising of 1931, a campaign I had not come across before. In the war just over he had been shuffled around at the War Office, at various times being involved in the Directorate of Transport, Eastern Command and the Home Guard. Too old for active service, as Sam Wells had explained to me, the old fire-eater must have suffered torture at his undignified postings by people who had just wanted him shuffled on to the sidelines. At present he was Colonel in Chief of the Dukes. There were no hobbies or names of clubs listed in the general's entry. Just the name of his country residence, Malplaquet, near Kelvedon, Essex.

As I drove towards Kelvedon I had no particular plan of action drawn up. I had not telephoned either the general or his daughter-in-law and her daughter to announce my arrival. I do not know why. I just had a hunch that it might pay me to arrive out of the blue. Telephoning can be a tricky business. It can put people on their guard. They can, at worst, refuse to see you; at the best they are given the time to muster their defences and have all the answers ready. One is not always as lucky as I had been with Philip Hanbury, but then he had been an extrovert, the kind who is always only too anxious to talk to the press, however much they may protest their dislike of it. People like Philip are usually vain into the bargain. They love to be the centre of attention.

I was not feeling particularly thirsty that morning, although I often did in those days because in the evenings I would spend far too much time in the Fleet Street pubs, particularly in El Vino, gossiping and drinking, with the result that about eleven the following day I usually felt like a few glasses of beer to counteract the dehydration. I had cut down on my drinking considerably since my discharge from the army where I had been more or less drunk for five and a half years without let-up. One of my rules was to keep off spirits until six o'clock in the evening and stick to beer at lunchtime.

I had driven through Witham and was about two miles from Kelvedon and Malplaquet when a pub on the left side of the road caught my eye. In fact it was not the pub that attracted me, but its sign hanging outside. It bore the words 'Malplaquet

Arms'. Immediately I swung hard left into the forecourt causing a car which was close behind me to brake violently and almost skid into my rear. There was the sound of prolonged hooting and the driver went past, shaking his fist and hurling justified abuse in my direction. A sign saying 'No Beer' was hanging on the front of the pub, but the door was open and I walked into the public bar, not knowing what to expect. I suppose it was the first time I had come across traces of Malplaquet and the army had taught me that time spent in reconnaissance is seldom, if ever, wasted.

A middle-aged man looking as if he had had a rough night out was washing up glasses in the sink behind the bar. He looked at me and glared. 'Can't you read? Got no beer.' I had never ceased, since returning from the war in Italy and being demobbed, to be amazed at the old-world courtesy landlords extended to their potential customers in the English pub. I determined there and then to do an article about it – no doubt headed, 'How do they earn a living?'

There was no point in antagonizing my host. I had learned to bite back the sharp retort when in search of information. 'I'm sorry. It can't be easy trying to run a pub with nothing to sell.'

'You can bloody well say that again.'

'Any cider?' I asked.

'Might find you half a pint.' He bent down and came up holding a pint bottle which he proceeded to unscrew. He poured the contents into a half-pint glass.

'Thanks,' I said. I picked up the glass and tasted the cider. It was flat and extremely unpleasant.

'Stranger round here, aren't you?' said the landlord.

I nodded. 'I suppose it's no good offering you a drink if you've nothing to sell.'

'Well, I wouldn't say no to a Scotch.' Seeing the look of surprise on my face he added, 'Have to keep it under the counter for my regulars. And I'm one of my regulars, aren't I?'

I could not argue with his logic.

He took a whisky bottle from behind the counter and poured himself a measure, looking at me suspiciously. I had noticed too that post-war publicans did not like strangers in their pubs. I think they were too busy trying to satisfy their thirsty regulars without having to put up with the moans of outsiders.

'Must make life difficult for you, all these shortages and rationing too?' I had touched on a sore spot.

'Difficult! Bloody impossible, and to think we won the bloody war. Why, those bloody Germans are better off than we are. Mark my words, in a few years' time they will be cock of the walk and we shall have sunk deeper and deeper into the shit. Don't talk to me about the Labour Government. The worst thing that ever happened to this country, except possibly winning the war.'

'Sometimes I feel I would have done better to stay in the army,' I said.

'What was your mob?'

'RASC,' I said.

'Same as mine. At least we didn't go short in the good old Corps. Bags of booze and plenty of the other, especially in Italy.' I recognized the glint in the landlord's eyes. I could just see him paying for sex with the starving refugees with a tin of filched bully beef.

'I served in Italy,' I said.

The landlord was not much interested in my military career. 'God, what a bloody cock-up that Italian campaign was. Sheer waste of time and effort – and lives. The soft under-belly of Europe indeed! Old Churchill must have been off his rocker or else he had never been there. Nothing but bloody great mountains, one after another, and all the time they were taking away division after division to land them in the south of France. A fat lot of bloody good that did.'

'I couldn't agree more,' I said, trying to sound sympathetic. In fact, what the landlord was saying had a lot of truth in it. Now that he had softened up a bit I thought it opportune to make a few enquiries. 'Is Malplaquet, General Sir Henry Rattigan's place, near here?'

'You're almost there. The gates are half a mile down the road. You aim to see the silly old bugger? Watch out, he's right round the bend. Used to drop in here for a drink when I first took over the place. One night we had an argument about the Italian campaign and he stumped off in a hump and has never been back.

Stuck-up old bugger. I thought we had fought the war to get rid of people like him.'

I found it difficult to equate his hatred of the Labour Government with his dislike of the English gentry. He was clearly one of those chippy people who are incapable of approving of anything or anyone.

'What about his granddaughter and daughter-in-law? I believe they live in the dower house at Malplaquet.'

'They live in a bloody great house, if that's what you mean,' said the landlord. 'Bloody disgraceful. There's the old general in one palace and those two women in another. Disgraceful, with our terrible housing shortage and decent folk round here living in conditions not fit for pigs.'

I was becoming more and more confused as to the landlord's political convictions.

At that moment the door opened and a man of about fifty to fifty-five came into the public bar. He carried himself upright. He was wearing thick corduroy trousers, a heavy tweed jacket patched at the cuffs and elbows with leather, gaiters and a flat check cap.

'If you want to know anything about Malplaquet this is your man,' said the landlord. 'Worked there man and boy until the war. Head keeper.' He pointed at me. 'This gentleman has been asking about the general and his family, Jack. What'll it be? The usual?'

Jack nodded and the landlord bent down behind the bar and produced a bottle of Guinness.

'Let me pay for it,' I said.

'That's kind of you, sir.' The new arrival filled a glass and lifted it towards me. 'Your good health, sir.' He carried his glass to a table in the corner of the bar, sat down and removed his hat.

'Do you mind if I join you?' I said.

'Not at all, sir.'

I sat down at his table and found myself being stared at by a pair of bright clear eyes. 'So, you were the general's head keeper.'

'That's right. I was his head keeper, until the war that is.' I noticed that he pronounced the word keeper more like kipper.

'You don't work for him any more?'

'No, sir.'

I felt I was not getting very far. 'So you were pensioned off?'

'In a manner of speaking, sir.'

The landlord came to my rescue. 'What Jack means is that the general sold off the estate after the war, that's to say after his son and his grandson were killed. He just kept the two houses.'

Jack nodded. 'That's about it, sir. But I have nothing to complain of. Sir Henry treats me well, very well.'

'So you work for the new owners of the estate?'

'How could I? Not after working for Sir Henry. No, you won't find me working for one of those syndicates. All they're interested in is the number of birds they can kill. Presentation means nothing to them. They couldn't shoot the skin off a rice pudding let alone hit a cock pheasant screwing down wind at eighty miles an hour. All they want to do is to shoot the birds up the backside, blow them to bits at twenty yards' range. Ah, you should have seen the general in action fifty years ago. Used to shoot with the king in those days at Sandringham and his majesty came here for the odd day. King Edward VII I'm talking about, sir. The old general wouldn't go out of his way to please him. Always gave him the most difficult stand and wasn't above wiping his eye. The king didn't much like that, I can tell you.'

For the first time he smiled, at the recollection of the general taking the birds that the king missed. I could sympathize with his majesty not being best pleased.

'What about the colonel, the general's son?'

'A fine shot, sir, but took it too seriously. Then the colonel took everything seriously, God rest his soul. He was a funny bugger. Always getting at the general to move out of the big house into the dower house. But the general wasn't having it. "I'm staying here till they carry me out in my wooden box, Pullen," he would say to me. That's my name, by the way, sir. Pullen, Jack Pullen. The general always called me Pullen. And that's how it is today. The general is still in the big house, and his daughter-in-law and Miss Henrietta, that's his granddaughter, live in the dower house. The colonel was killed in Normandy. Funny thing that. I reckon I was on the same beach about the same time as the colonel caught it. Very funny coincidence you might say.'

'Who were you with?'

'Lovat Scouts, sir.'

I was impressed. 'So you were among the first ashore on the beaches,' I said.

'We weren't exactly the last,' he said modestly.

'How did you come to join the Lovat Scouts?'

'It was the general's idea, sir. When the war came along, Sir Henry called up Lord Lovat and says, "I've got just the man for your mob – reliable, sober and all that kind of thing." Mind you I used to take the occasional drink in those days, but only at weekends or when the birds flew badly and Sir Henry was in a bad temper. He could get angry too, very angry if they didn't fly properly. "If I want tame birds, Pullen," he used to say, "I can always spend a day in Windsor Park." This was a crack at His Majesty George V. The general used to reckon that the birds at Windsor were tamed so that they didn't fly away at the sound of a shot and the king could be sure of killing a few. Not a fine shot like his father, whatever you may read about him. I loaded for him when he was performing here one year and he shot like a right duffer.'

I realized that I was on the right tack – that shooting, good shots, bad shots and game birds were subjects Jack Pullen was willing to talk about. 'And his grandson, young Antony Fitzjames Rattigan. Was he a good shot like his grandfather and father?'

I detected a look of sadness on Jack Pullen's face.

'That was a bad business. Nearly finished off Sir Henry that did. You know, sir, he was killed in France. In 1942. Dropped on some crazy scheme by some idiots who should have known better. Perhaps I shouldn't say that, but he was too young, too young by far. He would have done better to have come into the Lovat Scouts with me and I could have kept an eye on him.'

'He would have fitted in well then?'

'Like a glove. He was magnificent at fieldcraft. I'm not at all ashamed to say he was my best pupil. Never seen anyone like him either before or since. He could move like a cat. It was out of this world. Talk about using the ground. It was uncanny. He had a natural gift for it. Yes, he would have done better if he had stayed with me.'

'I saw his grave in France last month,' I said.

'Did you now, sir? Always wanted to go and pay my last respects myself, sir. But the general says it's a waste of time, though he did go himself. Perhaps I'll slip over there one day on the quiet. What's the name of the place where he's buried?'

'Les Saules. A small village in the Loire valley about twelve miles from Orléans. If you do go you must pay a visit to the local château. It's a hotel now. In the walled garden there's a plaque in his memory. It's got rather a strange inscription on it. It gives his name and the dates of his birth and death and at the bottom it reads: "He died for France. Remembering too his black cat whom he loved."'

Jack Pullen looked surprised. 'You did say black cat, sir?'

'Yes, what's odd about that?'

'Thought I knew everything about Master Antony, sir. After all he almost lived with me during his holidays from school. But I never knew he cared for cats. You see the colonel wouldn't have one on the estate. Reckoned they were sinister animals. He even gave me orders to shoot all cats on sight. I didn't do so, of course, except for the odd ferals when they started playing havoc with my birds. I don't think I can even recollect seeing young Master Rattigan with a cat or even speaking about them. That's very odd, sir, very odd indeed.'

'Why didn't Antony Rattigan go into the family regiment, the Dukes?' I asked. No sooner had I spoken than I realized that I had made a mistake and moved too fast. I should have stuck to guns and game birds.

'I wouldn't know, sir.'

'Funny that he should join the Southerns,' I said.

Jack Pullen looked down at his glass and made no comment.

I knew I had made a mess of things and I didn't expect any answer when I said: 'By the way, what happened to him after he left Wolfe College in 1937?'

I found myself looking into those bright eyes again. There was a pause. 'I wouldn't be knowing, sir,' he finally said. 'If you want to ask any more questions, sir, may I suggest you call on Sir Henry or the colonel's widow? Now if you'll forgive me, I must be on my way.' He rose from the table, wished the landlord a good morning and walked out of the bar.

'Funny old bugger,' said the landlord. 'Can't understand people like him. Still calls them the good old days. A right snob if you ask me.'

I stood up. 'They didn't sound such bad old days to me,' I said.

'All right if you were born in the right kind of bed,' sneered the landlord.

I could not think of a suitable answer. I left the stale cider in its glass and walked out of the pub.

As I drove towards the entrance to Malplaquet I cursed myself for making such an elementary mistake. Still, I had gleaned some useful information. Jack Pullen had talked about Antony's superb fieldcraft. I knew too that his mother was French. So presumably Antony could well have been bilingual. I knew that very few agents had been dropped into France unless they were fluent in French. Fluency in French together with a high standard of field-craft made Antony a highly eligible agent.

Just before the village of Kelvedon, I turned left between high iron gates and a lodge. On the top of the gates were lions rampant with what looked like flaming torches. But time and weather had eroded the finer details of the Rattigan family's coat of arms.

I drove through half a mile of thick woodland, no doubt the very woods where Jack Pullen had reared his pheasants in happier days – in the good or bad old days, depending on which side one had been on. At the far end of the wood I came out into a park, liberally dotted with large oaks which I judged, by their size, to be a couple of hundred years old or more. After another half-mile the road bore sharply to the left and the house came into view.

I am not an expert on architecture but I knew I was looking at a perfect example of an early Georgian country house. It was all the more impressive because no later generation had considered it insufficiently grand and set about so-called improvements – like the addition of porticos and classical columns – and as a result it was quite unspoiled.

The gravelled area in front of the house was separated from the park by a low balustrade. As I got out of the car I noticed for the first time that haymaking was in progress and the smell of freshly cut grass was blown in my direction. I pulled the bell. It was one of those bells that operate on wires as opposed to electricity and

I heard it jangle far away inside the house. As I stood waiting, breathing in the scent of the freshly cut grass and gazing down at the park that was vividly green in the June sunshine, I couldn't help feeling saddened that the lucky person who should have inherited this idyllic place lay buried in an obscure village in France.

The door was opened by an immaculately dressed butler. I was not surprised. There was an aura about Malplaquet, something indefinable. It seemed to have got stuck in the past. Even the tractor in the park in front of the house was out of place. I could visualize horses in its place and hear the shouts of their driver as he urged them on.

'Yes, sir?'

'Is Sir Henry at home?' I asked.

'Would you be having an appointment, sir?'

'No'

'In that case, sir, may I suggest that you write to Sir Henry stating your business and requesting a meeting.'

I sensed at once that I would not get past such a watchdog, but repeated my question: 'Is Sir Henry at home?'

The butler looked at me sternly. 'As I have said, sir, I would suggest that you write to Sir Henry.'

He was courteous, but at the same time determined that I should not pass. Nor was he giving any information away. I had not the faintest idea whether Sir Henry was at home or not. I had not so much as got a toe in the door.

I was about to turn away and admit defeat when a voice called from the hall, 'What the devil are you nattering about, Jarman?'

'I am not nattering, Sir Henry,' said Jarman, turning to face the figure who was walking across the hall towards us as we stood confronting one another in the doorway. 'I am merely pointing out, Sir Henry, that it is not your custom to receive visitors without an appointment.'

'Quite right, Jarman, quite right,' said Sir Henry.

I could not help smiling to myself at the way Sir Henry had accepted the admonition from his butler. Sir Henry joined Jarman at the doorway and stood looking down at me from beneath a pair of grey bushy eyebrows. I had expected to see an older-looking man. Like his one-time gamekeeper Pullen, whom I had just met, he held himself upright in what is commonly termed a soldierly manner. As far as his dress was concerned, he was wearing much the same as Pullen, although I could appreciate that the cut was considerably superior. 'Well, young man, what the devil are you doing disturbing my morning nap? That reminds me, Jarman. The Madeira decanter is nearly empty. Don't let it happen again.'

'No, sir,' said Jarman.

There was nothing obsequious in the way he spoke. Clearly Jarman had been in the wrong in allowing the Madeira decanter to run dry and he was not going to argue about it. In the same way, Sir Henry had not been the slightest bit upset when he had been reminded that it was not his custom to admit anyone without a prior invitation. They were both strong-willed men who respected one another.

Sir Henry looked down at me. 'Well, young man, since you're here, what do you want?'

'I've come to see you about your grandson, Antony . . .'

'He's dead.' Sir Henry spoke without any undue sign of emotion.

'I know,' I said. 'But I'd still like to talk to you.'

'Let him in,' Sir Henry said, turning to Jarman.

I walked past Jarman who showed no trace of annoyance or surprise, and followed Sir Henry across the carpeted hall into the library. Unlike so many libraries, it was not a dark room. The windows were tall and looking through them I could see the hay-making in progress in the park and faintly catch the noise of the tractor. Where there were no shelves every vacant area of wall was crammed with pictures of men in uniform, covered with medals, sashes and ribbons of bright hues. I noticed that one particularly distinguished soldier, with his plumed hat under his arm, was wearing the Most Noble Order of the Garter.

Sir Henry must have followed the direction of my eyes for he said: 'My great-grandfather. Absolute idiot. Can't think why the old queen gave him the Garter.'

I wished I had done more homework and could have a put a name to the figure who stood there looking into the distance, and thus impressed Sir Henry with my knowledge of his family background.

'What's all this about my grandson?' Sir Henry said abruptly.

'I came across his grave in France, sir. In a village called Les Saules.'

'Not surprising. He's buried there.'

'Forgive me, Sir Henry, but I also unearthed some rather strange facts about him. I know he died nine years ago, but his death is still a bit of a mystery and seems to have caused quite a lot of argument in the village.'

'Can't think why. The boy was dropped into France, captured by the Germans and shot out of hand.'

'I suspected something like that,' I said. 'But it's not the whole story. Did you know that at the château outside the village there's a plaque to his memory?'

'What's so odd about that?'

'Didn't the local priest mention it to you when you paid a visit to your grandson's grave?'

'No.'

I decided to make no mention of the cat. Sir Henry, like his son the colonel, may have had a strong aversion to cats.

Sir Henry looked at me closely: 'You seem to know a great deal about my movements. Of what interest can they be to you? It's over and done with. Nothing can bring my grandson or my son back to life.'

The door opened and Jarman came in carrying a silver tray on which stood a decanter of Madeira and placed it on the table.

'Care for a glass?'

'Thank you.'

Sir Henry poured out a glass and handed it to me. 'Splendid drink. Only to be drunk at eleven. Like champagne. Never after luncheon and never with it. Certainly not in the soup. Not that I much care for soup. As my father used to say, why build a good meal on a lake?'

I sipped my Madeira while Sir Henry glowered in my direction. I felt I was floundering and getting nowhere fast. 'I'll be honest with you, Sir Henry.'

'About time. Never could stand beating about the bush.'

I must say the old general was a good listener. He only interrupted me three times as I related the story of how my interest in his grandson had been aroused, and each of his questions was very much to the point. When I had finished the story I said, 'There you are, Sir Henry. My cards are on the table. If you tell me to get out now, I'll go, and you can forget that I ever called. But I can't promise that I will be able to put your grandson out of my mind. There are too many questions to be answered.'

'You newspaper boys are all the same. Dig, dig, dig, until you get at the dirt.'

'Or the truth.'

Sir Henry accepted my reprimand. 'Quite right, my boy. Still I don't understand why you should be so interested in how my grandson died.'

'I am not sure myself. Maybe because I'm a journalist by nature and information is my life. I'm not happy about the whole business. The division of people in the village of Les Saules is strange, particularly as the war has been over for six years.'

'So you want to publish the story of how and why my grandson died?'

'No, sir, not as long as anyone might get hurt.'

'Can't see how anyone could be hurt. Don't suppose the idiots at SOE would be exactly pleased. The boy should never have been dropped in the first place. Mind you, I don't know a great deal of what they were up to. What little I know I can't tell you. Official Secrets Act, you understand. But I assure you it's not much. Were you a soldier?'

I was somewhat taken aback at the abruptness of the question. 'I don't know if soldier is the right word. You see, I don't come from a military family like you.'

'Don't make excuses. What did you do?'

'I was called up as a driver in the Royal Army Service Corps. I ended up as a captain.'

'Well done. Came across your mob in the Boer War. Called themselves the Waggoners in those days. A good crowd. Wiped the eye of the Gunners, didn't they? Went in and pulled out the guns. That's why you can wear the lanyard, isn't it?' I was amazed that General Sir Henry Rattigan, Colonel-in-Chief of the Dukes, should know of the battle honours of a corps as lowly as the

Royal Army Service Corps. 'Terrible war, that one. Bad generals, bad climate, but good soldiers,' said Sir Henry.

'But you won your first DSO there, Sir Henry, on the Modder River,' I said, hoping I did not sound too sycophantic.

'Came up with the rations, no doubt carried by the Waggoners,' said Sir Henry. 'Damned stupid battle. Lord Methuen's show. Couldn't have commanded a platoon of lead soldiers if he'd tried.'

'While on the subject of decorations, what was the Burma uprising of 1931?' I asked. 'Where you won your MC.'

I could see that Sir Henry was pleased that I had done some homework on him.

'Lot of damned natives being led astray by a damned lot of revolutionaries. That MC? Another gong that came up with the rations.'

'Is it true that you led an assault in the 1914-18 war at the head of a battalion of Grenadiers, although you were a general at the time, Sir Henry?'

'Lost my sense of direction. Let's leave it at that, my boy. But old Haig was cross, very cross indeed. Not much of a general, Haig. Lost too many men.'

So the story was true after all.

'Anyway we're not here to discuss my military career,' said Sir Henry. 'What can I tell you about my grandson? I suppose you want to know why he was thrown out of Wolfe?'

'I know already.'

'Oh,' Sir Henry paused. 'Damned unkind thing to do. Blame my son for that. Rupert, that was my son, had no sense of humour. That's why he would never have got beyond the rank of lieutenant-colonel. Commanded my old battalion. Got himself killed in France, but I expect you know all that. No, if Rupert had had any sense, which he hadn't, he would have refused to take the boy away and the headmaster could have done nothing. That headmaster was a fool too. Did you know he got removed from Wolfe himself in the end?'

'No.'

'Messing around with one of his senior prefects.'

Seeing the look of amazement on my face he added: 'Oh, yes.

It's true enough. Never came out. All hushed up. I was in India at the time my grandson was turfed out. Would never have happened if I had been in the country.'

I was surprised that Sir Henry should have taken so liberal a view of his grandson's behaviour. As if reading my thoughts, Sir Henry said: 'Lock a lot of randy young fellows in a monastery and what the devil do you expect? Used to get a lot of it in India. In my brigade I gave orders that a blind eye should be turned to it. Of course we had our brothels there, but the girls were so damnably dirty. No sulphaminamide or penicillin in those days either.' I warmed to Sir Henry. Having expected to meet a relic of the past, instead I found myself talking with a highly civilized man. 'Of course, my daughter-in-law was upset. And my granddaughter. Have you met them?'

'No.'

'You must go and see them. They're only a few minutes from here. I'll give them a call and tell them to expect you. Now, where was I?'

'Your daughter-in-law was upset?'

'Ah yes, Marie Louise. Pretty woman. Still is. French, you know. One of the Leclercs. Not at all suitable for Rupert. Scared stiff of him, which was the worst possible thing for him. Shouldn't have married her so young. Damned silly, a young subaltern of twenty marrying. Wouldn't have been allowed if he hadn't been a Rattigan. I would have stopped it except he had made her pregnant, the idiot.'

'What happened to Antony after he left Wolfe?'

'Ask his sister about that, or his mother. They know more about him than I do. I believe he got a job on a newspaper. Something in your line. Never came near me, the young idiot. I suppose he thought that I was upset and didn't want to see him. Probably thought I was like his father.'

'You mean your son chucked him out of the house.'

'More or less. I told him not to be such an idiot. But he wouldn't listen to me. He wouldn't listen to anyone. I've told you. He was a rotten soldier. Oh, all right on the square. Good at set exercises. Never a speck of dust on his field boots, and if there was, his servant was for the high jump. But he didn't understand men. No sense of man management at all. That's the secret of a successful army, officers who understand man management. It goes right through from platoon to army command. Look at Montgomery. Knew exactly how to lead his men, even if he did make a number of mistakes. Arnhem for instance. Wasn't flexible enough. Knew that two German divisions had moved into the dropping area, but refused to change his plan of attack. But you don't want to hear an old general, who was put out to grass, expounding on the errors of generals more successful than himself. Let's get back to my grandson.'

'Why did he join the Southerns in 1939? Why not the Dukes?'

'That son of mine again. Nothing wrong with the Southerns, mind you. Put up a fine show at Arras. I imagine Rupert didn't want him in my regiment, and Rupert commanded the 1st battalion so I suppose what he said carried weight.'

I liked the way Sir Henry referred to the Dukes as 'my regiment'. 'Didn't Antony ever come to see you?'

'No. Never after he left Wolfe. I tell you that son of mine behaved like a bloody fool. I suppose the wretched boy thought I didn't want to see him.' Sir Henry looked away. 'I'd have given anything to have seen him here at Malplaquet before he was killed.'

'What will happen to the place now?' I asked.

'Happen to Malplaquet? It will die, like the Rattigans. When they carry me out in my box that is the final curtain for Malplaquet. It goes to the National Trust on my death. I've got to endow it, of course. That's why I've sold off the land, all one thousand acres and four farms, to set up a trust fund.' He paused and added in an almost childlike voice, 'Sad, isn't it?'

'Very,' I said. I looked through the window. The tractor was passing in front of the house. Through the half-open window of the library I smelt the scent of the grass. Yes, it was sad. In a few years General Sir Henry Fitzjames Rattigan would be dead and Malplaquet would be turned into a museum.

'I never thought it would happen. After Antony was killed, there was always the chance that Rupert might produce another son. After all my daughter-in-law was only forty when he died. I've tried not to think about it too much. What makes me so sad is that Antony would have suited Malplaquet. I know he wasn't cut out to be a soldier. But he loved this place, he was never happier than when he was staying here when my wife was alive. Of course in those days it was naturally assumed that Rupert would take over when I had gone, and Antony when he died. A funny thing. We soldiers never think of ourselves as likely to be killed in wartime. It's always the other man that dies. Anyway, enough of that. Another glass of Madeira?'

Sir Henry did not wait for me to answer but filled my glass.

'Perhaps you would like a Bath Oliver. It brings out the flavour of the wine,' he said. He pushed a silver biscuit barrel in my direction. 'When were you born?' he asked. Again I was surprised at the way his line of questioning suddenly altered.

'In 1921, sir.'

'Thought as much. If Antony had been alive he would have been your age. I would have handed Malplaquet over to him.'

Sir Henry sounded wistful and, in an attempt to revive his spirits, I said, 'Tell me something about Malplaquet. It's got a feeling about it. I sensed it the moment I drove through the park.'

Sir Henry nodded and smiled. 'Yes it is a lovely place, the most beautiful place in England. There are quite a few stories about Malplaquet. Would you like to hear some, or would it bore you?'

'Certainly not.'

'Help yourself to Bath Olivers. Good aren't they?' He stood up. 'Perhaps you would like to have a look round. I'm afraid the pictures aren't up to much. They all need cleaning anyway. Don't know who half of them are, so don't trouble to be polite and ask me. Except the Gainsborough. Everybody seems to like it. Bit too quiet for my liking. Like something with a bit of action in it myself. Let's start in the main hall and I'll tell you something about it.' He paused and looked me up and down. 'Something strange about you, my boy. Yes, I suppose it's because Antony would have been your age.'

It was a long time since I had been called 'my boy'. But it wasn't just that that made me warm to the old general. He had what so many people were conspicuously lacking in since the war. I think it could best be described as style.

'Of course everyone will tell you that the Battle of Malplaquet was won by Marlborough, but that wasn't so. It was my ancestor's victory and Marlborough took the credit for it. The thing about Marlborough is that he was a past master at using other people. Women in particular. As early as 1665 he was making eyes at the Duchess of Cleveland, the king's mistress. He was shipped off to Tangiers a couple of years later, with five thousand pounds of her money in his hand to keep him happy. He used his sister Arabella – she was the mistress of the Duke of York – to secure his colonelcy. And so on and so on. But of course it was his wife's friendship with Queen Anne that really made the fellow. My ancestor hated his guts, couldn't bear to be in the same room as him. Considered him greedy and only capable of furthering his own interests. I'm proud to say my ancestor built Malplaquet with his own money. Not like Blenheim, a perfect monstrosity if you ask me, except that Winston was born there. Blenheim was paid for by the taxpayers. That really got under the skin of my ancestor. He walks the long gallery at night. They say he won't rest in his grave until Blenheim is burned to the ground.'

'Have you ever seen him?' I asked.

'Frequently.'

We climbed the stairs to the gallery in question and paused to admire the portrait of the ghost.

'He looks decidedly sour,' I commented.

'That's what Antony used to say, young man,' said Sir Henry. 'Ah, here's the Gainsborough. That's the second baronet.'

I noticed that the second baronet, who was standing with his wife, two children and a dog, with Malplaquet in the background, was in uniform, which made the scene look slightly less rustic than I would have wished.

'Forgive me for asking,' I said, 'but why did your family not go to the House of Lords?'

'None of them wanted to. Too many upstarts there. Like Marlborough. Winston hasn't gone there either, has he?'

When we had finished our tour of the house and returned to the library, where Sir Henry insisted I drink a final glass of Madeira, I said: 'It seems terrible that the place should be going out of the family. Isn't there anyone who can inherit it?'

'Too many wars, my boy. Too many damned wars. Killed too

many of us off. Rupert and Antony were the last in line. There are some French in-laws somewhere, but they wouldn't be the same, and in any case who wants a lot of Frenchmen at Malplaquet? Hardly suitable, considering my ancestor beat the backsides off them there anyway.'

Suddenly Sir Henry looked tired. He was an old man and he had been talking more or less non-stop for more than an hour. I decided that it was time to take my leave. I stood up. 'I'll let you know if I find out anything more about your grandson, sir,' I said.

'Ah, yes. Antony. If you find anything of interest I would be glad if you would let me know. But don't stir anything up. Better to let sleeping men lie, don't you think, my boy?'

'Don't worry, sir. I promise no one is going to be upset.'

'Tell you what. Give me a day or two and I'll have a word with an old friend of mine who served with the SOE. High up in the French section. Don't know how much he'll tell you or even how much he knows. But he might be useful. His name's Lennox Birdham.'

I knew the name immediately. 'Major Lennox Birdham, one of the most highly decorated men for his work with the Resistance, at least a George Cross to his name and every foreign decoration available,' I said.

'That's the fellow.'

Once again I felt that the general was on my side. 'You'll probably have to go and interview him on a racecourse. Horseflesh is all he thinks about these days, you know. Otherwise you will probably find him at the Turf Club. Now what about my granddaughter and daughter-in-law? Would you like to see them?'

'That's kind of you, sir.'

Sir Henry picked up the telephone and dialled a number. 'That you, Henrietta? Listen. Have a young fellow with me who wants to ask you one or two things about Antony. Yes, our Antony. No, no, it will be all right. Nothing to worry about. This afternoon? Right then. No, no, it's nothing serious. Yes, come on over later if your mother's away, and have some supper. See you later.'

He put down the receiver. 'My granddaughter will see you this afternoon.' He turned to me. 'Been a pleasure to meet you, my boy. Can't think why you are so interested in my grandson. By the way, would you care to stay and have something to eat with me? It must be nearly time for luncheon and I am sure Jarman can rustle up enough for two.'

'No, thank you, sir.' I felt that Sir Henry had had enough of me for one session and I did not wish to jeopardize the future.

I set off down the drive but parked the car at the edge of the wood and walked back to the parkland where I stood and gazed at Malplaquet. I found an oak, sat down with my back against it and continued to stare at the house. The hay cutting was still in progress and the air was still very sweet. I must have dozed off, for when I woke and looked at my watch it was four o'clock. My throat felt on the dry side, no doubt due to Sir Henry's fine Madeira. I got back in the car, turned it, and drove back in the direction of the house, taking a right-hand turn before reaching it which led to the dower house about two miles away.

The house was sheltered from the road by a belt of trees. It was nowhere near as large as Malplaquet but just as beautiful and had probably been designed by the same architect, certainly by one of his school. Before I had stopped the engine Henrietta Rattigan came round the side of the house. As I stepped out of the car she came towards me and shook my hand. 'I was beginning to wonder what had happened to you,' she said.

'I'm sorry. I have no excuse. I fell asleep in the park looking at Malplaquet.'

'Never mind. I've got some tea waiting for you on the lawn.'

I followed her round the house and settled myself in a garden chair which had been padded with cushions.

She looked at me closely. 'I've been racking my brains. Now I know who you are. You work for the *Express*, don't you?'

I detected a note of unease in her voice so I said quickly, 'That's right. But I'm not here on anything to do with the paper. It's entirely a personal matter, I promise you.'

'I hope you haven't been upsetting Grandfather, talking about Antony,' she said. She paused to pour out a cup of tea, which she handed to me. 'Perhaps you had better tell me all about it.'

'It's probably all about nothing, if one can call the death of your brother nothing. Shall I start at the beginning?' Once again I went through my story. How I had come across the plaque, how

I had met Father Dominic, how I found the village divided. I did not omit to tell her of the mention of the black cat on the plaque, nor of the fact that I knew that her brother had left Wolfe prematurely.

'Why on earth didn't Father Dominic say anything about the plaque at the château?' was her first question when I had finished speaking.

'I don't know. It's one of the many things that fascinates me about the whole business.'

'As for the cat, we were never allowed cats in the house when we were children. Father couldn't stand them.'

'I know. I ran into Jack Pullen when I was having a drink in the Malplaquet Arms earlier and he told me. To be honest that cat fascinates me so much now that one of the things I will have to do very soon is go and pay a visit on the Comte de Chaumont.'

'You know, considering how influential Grandfather was I was always a little surprised we did not find out more about Antony's death,' she said. 'I know of course that he was working for SOE but what he was doing in France was never explained to us. Did you know we were not officially informed of Antony's death until after the war, and then we were only told that he had been executed by the Germans in the village of Les Saules? We knew something had gone wrong because we never heard from the French section of SOE, who were supposed to inform us that he was safe and well once a month. We always prayed that he might have been a prisoner of war, although there was not much hope of that. After all, agents dropped into France weren't usually afforded the status of prisoners of war.'

'I don't even begin to understand what he was doing in the SOE to put it mildly,' I said. 'From what I can gather your brother was a most unmilitary type of young man. Why, even at Wolfe he tried to get out of the Officers Training Corps. If you will forgive my saying so, that must have been a nasty shock to your father.'

'You can say that again,' she said. 'Father was absolutely furious. He couldn't begin to understand how a Rattigan could be averse to charging around with a bayonet and sticking it into the first belly in sight. Of course, it was careless of Antony to get thrown out of Wolfe. He should have shown more sense. He was too demonstrative though. He never could hide his true feelings. I mean to say, I had a crush on my gym mistress, but I didn't go round telling everybody about it and looking as if the end of the world was at hand.'

'It must seem impertinent of me probing into your family affairs,' I said. 'But I hope you will understand that I can't help it. I am intrigued, that's the only word for it. How well did you get on with your brother?'

'Marvellously. I don't think there were any secrets between us. Take that ridiculous business at Wolfe, for instance. From what I could make out, Tom Makepeace didn't care a bit for Antony. He was one of the school tarts and was rightly chucked out. Antony was always in trouble with Father and I did my best to protect him. Father went out of his mind when Antony was expelled from Wolfe and when Antony went and joined the Southerns that was the end. Do you understand enough about the military hierarchy to know what joining the Southerns meant?'

I nodded.

'Father never knew that Antony had joined the SOE and even when he heard that Antony was missing in France he didn't change his opinion of him. Antony had let down the Rattigans and Father never forgave him. Of course he was killed himself in 1944. But from the time Antony left in 1937, my father never spoke to him.'

'Not a word?'

'Not a single word.'

'What about your mother?'

'She doesn't like to talk about Antony. In fact we seldom mention his name even now. I'm so glad she's not here. She's in France with her family. Did you know she is French?'

'Yes, she's a Leclerc.'

'That's right. Like me she adored Antony. When she heard that he was missing she nearly died. Have you ever seen anyone die of a broken heart? Oh yes, believe me it can happen. My father was of no help to her. She was terrified of him. It was a totally unsuitable marriage because in her funny kind of way she loved him. Her sense of duty was split between the two of them. She felt she must be loyal to her husband; she could understand why

Father did not want to see Antony again. At the same time she loved Antony. After all he was her only son, and however badly he had behaved in my father's eyes she did not love him any the less.'

'How did you get on with your father?'

'I never saw much of him. He spent a great deal of time with his regiment. You could say he lived for it, and had few interests outside of it.'

'Not even Malplaquet?'

'Not even Malplaquet. Unlike Antony, who adored the place. That's one of the great regrets of my life. Antony would have suited Malplaquet down to the ground and vice versa. God, that bloody war, that bloody war.' She must have noticed the look of surprise on my face on hearing her swear. 'I won't apologize,' she said. 'Not only did I lose Antony and my father, but my fiancé too. He was killed at Salerno in that useless Italian campaign. He wasn't even a professional soldier which infuriated Father when we became engaged. I'm afraid my father spent his life being angry.'

There was a pause in the conversation. I leant forward and helped myself to a cucumber sandwich.

'Did you see much of your brother between the time he left school and the time he joined the Southerns?'

'The odd day here and there. After he left Wolfe he worked in Rochester on the local newspaper. He joined the Southerns when the war broke out. But he was miserable in Rochester. It wasn't the right job, and he never had enough confidence. He was very lonely. He missed his family, his mother and me, and in a funny kind of way his father whom he thought he had let down. When we did meet I felt he had changed. We were no longer the friends we had been as children. It was as if he was holding something back and was unable to communicate with me any more. It wasn't very nice I can tell you. He wouldn't even come and see his grandfather, and he would have been welcome at Malplaquet at any time in spite of what Father might have thought. My grandfather didn't think much of my father, you know.'

'Sir Henry is a remarkable man. Not at all what I had expected.'

'What had you expected?'

'Oh, someone spitting fire and brimstone. It was a lovely surprise to meet someone so civilized and courteous. Considering I came barging in on him without even troubling to call him first, he behaved marvellously.'

'He tried to forget Antony,' she said. 'But I believe there isn't a day goes by that he doesn't mourn him, just as Mother does. He was probably delighted that you showed such an interest in Antony. You know, it's very strange you turning up here and talking about him. After all, he's been dead for nine years now, and you seem to have brought him to life very vividly.'

'I'm sorry if I have upset you.'

'No, no. And if you do find anything more about him, don't hesitate to let me know. It would be wiser though if we met somewhere else, say in London. I don't think Mother would care to have the wound reopened, that's assuming that it is closed, which I very much doubt.'

'I'm seeing someone who was pretty influential in the SOE, thanks to your grandfather. I may turn up something else.'

She came round to the front of the house and saw me into the car. Just as I was about to drive off, she leant down to the front window and said: 'I'm intrigued about that cat. I really would like to know more about that.'

4

The day after I called on Sir Henry I was back at my desk in the *Express* building looking at a blank sheet of paper in my typewriter, thinking about Malplaquet and wondering if I could do a piece about the decaying ancestral homes of England, when the telephone rang.

It was Sam Wells at the War Office. 'Listen, Michael, I've got some news for you which may be of help. That's to say if you're still interested in the Rattigan boy.'

'Very,' I said.

'Well, you know he served with the Southerns in France. I think I told you that the battalion, or rather what was left of it, came out through Calais and Boulogne in 1940. I happened to be speaking to the colonel of the 1st battalion yesterday, and he was one of the survivors from the 3rd. He was a platoon commander at the time. Just off the cuff I happened to mention the name of Antony Rattigan and he said he knew him well. What is so extraordinary is that he knows you as well.'

'Knows me? What's his name?'

'Colonel Peter Smith.'

'That's very helpful. Such an unusual name.'

'Apparently he met you in Italy. Says you were always drunk.'

'There were a lot of drunks in Italy, and a lot of Smiths.'

'Seriously, he does know you. Says he came across you on the Anzio beachhead. Apparently you had several truck loads of mines to deliver to his company, and he remembers the incident very well because you left him several gallons of army rum. He was most impressed. He reckons the rum did more to boost the morale of his men than the mines.'

'I vaguely remember the incident.'

'Anyway, if you telephone him he would be very pleased to see you. But not before the weekend as he's got some kind of exercise on. He's stationed at Colchester.' Sam gave me the telephone number.

'Pity I didn't know about this yesterday. I was at Malplaquet yesterday. I had a most illuminating chat with General Sir Henry Rattigan. He's putting me in touch with Major Lennox Birdham.'

'Well, I wish you better luck with the SOE than I had,' said Sam. 'Let me know if there's anything more I can do. I shall want you to do some more PR for the army in return, of course.'

'Get stuffed, Sam,' I said and put down the phone.

I did my piece on the country houses of England, the prospect of their decay due to high taxation and the age of envy created by the post-war Socialist Party. I never referred to the Labour Party in those days. I knew that Lord Beaverbrook thought the word Labour dishonest and deceptive. I think he would have liked to have called it Communist. Then I telephoned the number Sam had given me and left a message that I would come down on Saturday morning and that there was no need to call me back if the date was suitable.

I was still mystified as to why Antony should have gone off and joined the Southerns at the outbreak of war. And there was still that gap of two years between 1937 and 1939. All I knew was that he had worked on the local newspaper at Rochester, which was clearly on my visiting list.

I had started what I called the Rattigan File, rather a grand name for what was no more than a few notes. Antony's sister had told me that after leaving Wolfe College he had worked on the local paper in Rochester. I rang the library and found that it went by the name of the *Echo*.

I had made a note too of what his schoolmaster, Philip Hanbury, had said – that Tom Makepeace, the probable cause of Antony's trouble at Wolfe, had been ordained in 1948 and was now at St Mary's, South Ascot, in Berkshire. I found his telephone number in the directory without any difficulty and put through a call. I was not very hopeful that it would prove fruitful, but it seemed to me that I might as well try to fill in the gaps before learning more of Antony's army career. I had by now found myself thinking about Antony Fitzjames Rattigan as plain Antony. I was, I think, just beginning to understand something about him as I started to draw the threads together. I heard the ringing tone, the receiver was lifted and a voice said: 'Father Makepeace speaking.'

I gave my name and said that I would like to come and see him that same evening, if it was possible.

'Is it urgent?'

'Not exactly. It's about an old friend of yours. Antony Fitzjames Rattigan.'

'Is this some kind of joke?'

'No, no, far from it. Your old housemaster, Philip Hanbury, at Wolfe gave me your name. I assure you it's nothing to worry about. It's just that I have become interested in the life and death of Antony and I thought you might be able to help me.'

'I don't know who you are, nor do I care. If it's blackmail . . .'

'For Christ's sake,' I began and checked myself, realizing this was hardly the way to talk to a priest. 'I'm so sorry. It's nothing to do with blackmail. I could explain it to you on the telephone, but it would be far easier if I came down to talk to you.'

'Very well. Would six o'clock this evening suit you?'

I said it would suit me very well. As I replaced the receiver I thought how lucky it was that I had not mentioned the *Express*. If I had, Father Makepeace might have refused to see me at any price.

I caught the train from Waterloo at five o'clock and reached Ascot about forty minutes later, where I was lucky enough to find a taxi on the rank which ran me down to St Mary's at South Ascot which was only half a mile away.

Father Makepeace had given me the address of his house and when I rang the bell the door was opened immediately so that I got the impression that he was waiting for me in the hall. 'Shall we go into the study?' he said after I had introduced myself.

He offered me a chair and sat down at a desk facing me. I could sense that he was nervous. He kept clasping and unclasping his hands. He was extremely good looking and well preserved and I estimated about two or three years older than myself, somewhere in the region of thirty-two. Unlike Father Dominic's soutane, his was immaculate and I noticed that as he sat down he folded it in such a way around himself that it would not crease. His shoes were highly polished and sported silver buckles.

As he stared at me, clearly waiting for me to speak, I found myself alternately watching his twisting hands with their well-manicured nails and his eyes which were fixed on me.

'About Antony . . .' I began.

'Yes, about Antony. I have thought hard during the last few hours since you telephoned and as I have nothing to conceal I have decided to be honest with you.'

'Don't you want to know who I am, or why I wanted to talk with you?' I said.

'What does it matter?' he said. 'I pray constantly for Antony's soul and that he may rest in peace. God, in His infinite mercy, will forgive me.'

'Has He much to forgive?' I was finding the conversation embarrassing and added: 'Look, you've got to let me explain why I have come here.' I found myself reddening under Father Makepeace's stare. It was really nasty being taken for a common blackmailer.

'As you wish.' He leaned back in his chair.

'It all started in France, about three weeks ago,' I began.

Father Makepeace did not interrupt me once as I unfolded my story. When I had finished speaking I noticed that he had stopped twisting his hands and had perceptibly relaxed, leaning back in his chair.

'I said just now that I prayed for him daily and that God in His mercy may forgive me.'

I nodded.

'Is there nothing odd about that? Does it not strike you as peculiar?'

'Not really. After all as a priest it is your job to pray for the dead.'

For the first time he smiled.

'But why do you think that I pray God will forgive me?'

'You will have to tell me. All I know is that according to your faith if you pray to God and are genuinely sorry, He will forgive you.'

'You are not a believer, are you?'

'No, I'm afraid not.'

'Do you know about guilt?'

'I think so.'

'Guilt is the most terrible punishment that God can mete out. However much we have sinned, and however much we believe that God forgives us, He does not always take away from us the burden of guilt. For it is with guilt that He punishes us.'

I did not feel like entering into a theological discussion. 'I take your word for it,' I said. 'But why are you so guilty?'

'Because I killed Antony,' said Father Makepeace.

'Come off it,' I said. 'Antony was killed by the Germans in a village called Les Saules in the Loire valley.'

'Yes, I know. I wrote to his sister for details when I read his name in the special supplement to the college magazine that Wolfe College brought out after the war naming all those who had been killed.' He paused and smiled. 'It was rather funny that I should have even received a copy of the supplement. I would have imagined that my old school would wish to forget me. Did you know they threw me out? The usual offence common to public schools.'

'Yes, I knew.'

'That makes it much easier then. Were you at a public school?'

'Yes, just about the same time as you and Antony were at Wolfe. It was as queer as hell, if you'll forgive the expression. Half the masters were queer, I suspect a few of them actively.'

'I suppose Philip Hanbury told you about me at Wolfe.'

'Yes, I'm afraid he did.'

'He's a gossipy old queen, but very urbane,' said Father Makepeace. 'Anyway, to go back to Antony's death. I had a short note from his sister, I might say almost a curt note, just stating that Antony had been killed in France while working for SOE and was buried in the churchyard of Les Saules. I got the impression that she knew I had been the cause of Antony's death, and that she didn't want to know me.'

'I'm still not sure what you mean when you say you killed him.'

'I don't want to sound dramatic when I say I broke his heart.'

'That's what Philip Hanbury said.'

'Philip Hanbury was no fool. Antony fell deeply in love with me. The trouble was that I did not fall in love with him. Oh, he was very beautiful but so were lots of the other boys. I was having too much fun and games all round to put up with Antony's attentions. He was far too intense. I don't even think he knew what it was all about. I would go so far as to say that if I had laid a hand on him he would have run a mile. Looking back it might have been better if I had done so. All he wanted to do was to write poems to me. I didn't think them very good, although I never told him so. When I was caught *in flagrante delicto* with a boy whom I can't even remember now and was thrown out, Antony went completely to pieces.'

'I'm still mystified,' I said.

'I'll explain. When I was chucked out of Wolfe I received very different treatment from my father from that which Antony received from his. You see my father didn't really approve of Wolfe. I had only been sent there because my grandfather, who was a distinguished soldier, believe it or not, had been there and subsequently become one of the governors. I am sure my father, God rest his soul, thought he'd better ingratiate himself with his father by sending his own son there. Frankly he thought it would be beneficial to his inheritance. So when I was chucked out my father didn't mind one little bit, because grandfather had died by then and left him what there was to leave.'

'Your father must have been a unusual man. What did he do?'

'He was an actor. Not a very good one, I'm afraid. Of course the acting profession has more than its fair share of queers, so they are much more readily accepted in the theatre than in other spheres of society. I might add that my mother wasn't unduly upset either. She positively disapproved of Wolfe with its anti-quated traditions. Anyway there was a family conference as to what should be done with me, and to my delight my father suggested that the best thing for me was that I should be shipped off to Paris to study at the Sorbonne. So off I went to Paris, and what a time I had there. In those days, compared with London, Paris was a paradise for all deviationists. I shall never forget my first visit to Montmartre, and my sheer amazement at seeing men actually dancing together without anyone thinking it odd. To put it crudely I had what I then considered to be a ball. I was young and beautiful and besieged on all sides by men of all nationalities.' He paused. 'I trust I'm not shocking you.'

'Not a bit.'

'All the time, of course, I knew deep in my heart that I had done Antony irrevocable damage. Had it not been for me he would never have been thrown out of Wolfe.'

'I really can't see that you can blame yourself for that,' I said.

'Can't you? I can. You see, when he was chucked out he used to write me letter after letter telling me how much he loved me and enclosing great chunks of romantic poetry. I should have ignored them and never answered them. In that way he would have got me out of his system. But, being a bitch, I always gave him the impression that there was a ray of hope; that one day I might be able to love him as he loved me. Although I was having affairs right and left I was not willing to let him go. It seemed a good idea to have as many strings to my bow as possible, and as I have said Antony was very beautiful and the possibility of sex with him one day was not lightly to be thrown away. Does that make sense?'

'Yes.'

'So I kept him stringing along. I knew from his letters that he was having a bad time with his father; that he had been thrown out of home. When he managed to get a job on the Rochester local paper he still continued to write me reams and reams telling me how much he loved me and how miserable he was without me. His one idea was to get to Paris to see me. He had very little money and was saving every penny to pay the fare. Then one day he wrote to say he had enough to come. This put me in a panic as I was in the middle of an affair with a successful ballet dancer. Do you know what I did? I sent him a telegram saying that I should be out of Paris, and that it would be a waste of time if he came over. I did something even worse. I read aloud his letters to my friend, who found them extremely ludicrous.'

'That wasn't very pleasant.'

'Pleasant! It was disgusting, unforgiveable,' said Father Make-peace. 'But even after I had put Antony off, he kept on writing to me. To keep him on the hook I sent him the occasional line, more often than not just a postcard, telling him how hard I was working when in fact I never did a stroke and lived entirely for pleasure.'

'What finally happened?'

'Just before the war started I returned to England to join up, but to my utter amazement I was rejected as unfit for military service. Antony continued to write to me at my parents' home, so I knew that relations between him and his father had not improved. Soon after war was declared he wrote to tell me he had joined the Southerns and would be going to France. He begged me to let him come and see me, but again I refused. I had picked up an artist at the Café Royal and was having too much fun to want to put up with Antony's romantic ramblings.'

'What a bitch,' I said almost involuntarily.

'I was. Anyway, Antony went off to France and suddenly he stopped writing to me. I was surprised at first, and believe it or not, rather annoyed. I actually wrote to him after Dunkirk to find out if he was all right. I received a very incoherent letter in return saying that he was alive and well, that he had made a mess of his life, that he had been a complete failure, that he had let his family down and that he didn't blame me and I was always to remember that. He must have been drunk at the time he wrote that last letter to me for he repeated three times that bit about not blaming me. It was so badly written, almost illegible, that he must have been drunk.'

He paused. 'That's the end of the story. After that he went out of my life. It wasn't until I read that he had died in the war – by which time I had become a priest – and wrote to his sister to ask what had happened and received that cool note back in which she told me he had died working for the SOE, that I became aware of the enormity of my sin, of my wickedness towards Antony. You see, I could have helped him, I could have given him at least the love and affection he so desperately needed. Because of me he lost his career, his family and his life.'

'It's debatable,' I said. 'I honestly don't think that feeling guilty is going to be of much help to you, or to him for that matter.'

'I told you guilt is one of the ways that God punishes us.'

'That's a matter of opinion.' I could not make up my mind what I thought of Father Makepeace. In some ways I admired him for his honesty, but I have always found all that guilt stuff incomprehensible and boring. To change the subject I said: 'Why and when did you become a priest?'

'My rejection for military service was a terrible shock. I had seen myself in one of the smarter regiments, wearing a well-cut uniform and on Christian-name terms with the cream of the aristocracy. You know, of course, that most queers are snobs. I was at my wits' end as to what I could do. It's just possible that I might have got into one of the corps, the Royal Army Service Corps, for instance.'

I could not help smiling.

'What's so funny about that?'

'It was my mob,' I said.

For the first time Father Makepeace looked embarrassed. 'Oh dear, I am sorry.'

'Don't worry yourself. Antony's grandfather, General Sir Henry Rattigan, thinks we did a splendid job, in the Boer War anyway. But go on, what happened?'

'It was very simple. God took over.'

'How do you mean?'

'It was on Christmas Day to be precise. Christmas Day 1941. I went to church with my mother and father, more in the course of duty than anything else. While I was at church God came to me and I knew that I must become a priest.'

'Just like that?'

'Just like that. I hesitate to compare myself with St Paul. Do you know about his conversion?'

'Yes, the road to Damascus,' I said. ' "Saul, Saul, why persecutest thou me? It is hard for thee to kick against the pricks." What is more I know what is meant by pricks. They were goads for keeping the oxen moving.'

'Very good, very good indeed,' said Father Makepeace. 'But you didn't come here to hear about my conversion. Is there anything more I can tell you about Antony?'

'I don't think so,' I said. 'I think you may be indulging in excessive self-flagellation.'

'It is my cross to bear, not yours.' I got the impression that he was slightly annoyed with me.

I stood up and held out my hand. 'Thank you very much.'

He conducted me down the passage and opened the door.

'By the way, I shall not be here much longer but my successor will know my whereabouts if you want to get in touch with me again.'

'Where are you going?'

'The time has come for me to go and work where I am really needed. You see, I had another vision today, or whatever you like to call it. Just after you telephoned I knew I must leave this too-comfortable, middle-class life I am living here and go and live and work with the sick and needy. I shall be applying to my bishop tonight for a suitable parish, or maybe a hospital. God bless you, Michael.'

Father Makepeace smiled at me and closed the door.

I still did not know whether I liked him or not. In the recesses of my nasty mind I wondered what he did now about sex. Not that it was any of my business.

The following morning I called my secretary at the *Express*, and when I had checked that there was nothing demanding my attention that could not wait, I put through a call to the *Echo* in Rochester, gave my name and asked to speak to the editor.

'Bill Wheatley. What can I do for you, Michael?'

I knew when he used my Christian name that I would get all the help possible from the editor of the *Echo*. I have always found fellow journalists remarkably helpful. It's said to be a cut-throat business and I suppose there is an element of competition, but in my experience that exists more between the newspaper proprietors than the rank and file. I have seen reporters pooling all their information when working on the same story – which would have given their bosses kittens had they been present at the time.

'Listen, Bill, I wonder if you could do me a favour? It's nothing to do with my paper or yours. You might call it a piece of long-term research that I've got entangled with. How long have you been with the *Echo*?'

'Too long. Since 1935. Never had the desire to set the world on fire. Preferred a steady job with a pension at the end of it instead of plunging knives into other people's backs in Fleet Street. How's yours, by the way?'

'Sore sometimes. Seriously, do you remember a kid who joined you, probably in the late summer of 1937? Antony Fitzjames Rattigan?'

'Remember him well. How is he? Can't say I ever thought he would make a newspaperman.'

'Dead. Killed in France in 1942.'

'I'm sorry. So what do you want to know about him? He was the grandson of some famous old general, you know.'

'Yes, I know. I'm more interested in what he did while he was with you on the *Echo*. Did he have any friends, what did he do, did he work hard? Anything you can rustle up on him.'

'No problem,' said Bill. 'Shall I call you back?'

'Would it be all right if I came down?'

'Be pleased to see you. When?'

'Lunchtime today if you're not too busy.'

'This paper runs itself,' said Bill. 'How about the Victoria at one o'clock? It's in the High Street. You can't miss it. Do you look like your picture on your column in the *Express*?'

'Older.'

'They're always older,' said Bill Wheatley. 'See you at one.'

I have always believed in punctuality, or it may have been the one thing that was instilled into me during my wartime service in the army. If a parade was called for seven in the morning one was there at five minutes before seven, and all hell was let loose if one turned up at one minute past. So at five minutes to one I walked into the bar of the Victoria in the High Street, Rochester.

I had no difficulty in recognizing Bill Wheatley. He was a beefy man, wearing country tweeds, and had positioned himself at the end of the bar nearest the entrance where he could scan all new arrivals.

We shook hands.

'What would you like, beer? It's not bad at all.'

'Pint of bitter.'

We carried our glasses to a table.

'I've booked a table for lunch at half-past if that suits you,' he said.

'Thanks. It's on me.'

'I'm not proud when it comes to paying,' he said. 'I dare say your expenses are better than mine.'

'I told you that it has nothing to do with the *Express*.'

Bill roared with laughter. 'Come off it. Do you mean to say you take your girlfriends out to lunch and dinner and pay for them yourself? If you do you are the first newspaperman I've met who does.'

'If it makes you happier, Bill, I'll put you down to expenses. Interviewing editor Rochester *Echo*. What about?'

'Vice in Chatham. High incidence of VD in Royal Navy. How's that?'

'I'll buy it,' I said slipping into the matey jargon I found myself adopting when talking with members of my profession. 'But it's a fact that this is a private investigation, nothing to do with the paper.'

'I believe you if you say so.'

'I'm investigating the life of one ordinary soldier from the time he was at school until the time he was killed at the age of twenty-one. It's research in depth to discover what he felt, why he acted the way he did and whether ultimately his early death was worthwhile.' As I spoke I realized that I was vaguely expressing what I was trying to do, although as yet I had not the slightest idea how the story would finally come together.

Bill took out his pipe and started to fill it. 'Sounds an awful lot of research to me. Rather you than me. Hope it all pays off.'

'It might do,' I said. 'It's still all very much in the air. Do you want to know anything more?'

'No, that's fine. Shall I tell you what I know about Antony?'

I nodded.

'Antony joined us in the late summer of 1937, on the 27 June to be precise, and worked on the *Echo* until he left on 20 August 1939. I was senior reporter, that's to say the senior of a total of three reporters, when he came to us. I left the paper a week before him when I had to report to my territorial unit just before war was declared. So he was with me all the time he was here.'

'How did he come to join the *Echo* in particular?'

'Out of the blue. One day we had a letter from him asking if we could take him on in any capacity, preferably as a junior reporter. It so happened that our editor at the time was looking for a junior. He was bit of a snob and was impressed that in his letter of application Antony mentioned that he was the grandson of General Sir Henry Fitzjames Rattigan. So Antony got the job. As a matter of fact there were no other applicants as the pay was only £80 a year. On the other hand you could get digs with morning and evening meal and laundry for twenty-one shillings a week in those days.'

Bill Wheatley paused to get his pipe under way.

'I well remember that day in June when Antony turned up. I don't know what I expected, but certainly not anyone who looked less likely to make a newspaperman. When he walked into the reporters' room I nearly told him not to waste his time but to turn about and go and look for a career elsewhere.'

'What was wrong with him?'

'Everything. To begin with he was far too good looking. More like a bloody Greek god than a cub reporter. Fair hair, blue eyes, slim, well built, you name it he had it. Quite honestly there was something positively girlish about him. Don't get me wrong. All the time he was here he never stepped out of line – and it's unfair to accuse the boy of being queer just because he was so good looking. But that wasn't the only thing. I've never met anyone so shy. When he came into the room I could sense that he had been steeling himself for minutes to pluck up courage to knock on the door. He was red in the face with embarrassment and could hardly speak. He just stood inside the door and said, "I'm Antony Rattigan." Anyway I introduced him to the other two reporters, and I could see that they were as amazed as I was. Finally I said I would take him in to meet the editor and do you know what he said? He said, "Do you think I should go and put my best suit on first?" I mean to say, what answer is there to a bloody silly question like that? The other two, Tim Pearce and Mick Shanly, just burst out laughing. I can't blame them. It was funny, if rather pathetic. I told them to get out of the office. I think later on they were ashamed of their behaviour and went out of their way to be kind to Antony. When they had gone I sat Antony down in a chair. For one moment I thought he was going to cry. I got one of the girls to bring him in a cup of tea and all the time I was thinking how the devil can I ever make a reporter out of someone as shy as this. He was like a bloody deer, terrified of human contact. The idea of him getting a foot inside anyone's door was ludicrous.'

'What happened then?'

'I asked him where he intended to get digs. Would you believe it, he hadn't the faintest idea. I don't think he'd even thought about them. No doubt he imagined that they would turn up like manna from heaven. I actually got a bit bloody-minded with him at that point – or I suppose it was really the editor I blamed for taking on such an absolute twit – and I told him that he was no longer a mollycoddled schoolboy and was joining one of the toughest, nastiest professions in the world, and hadn't he better think again. Do you know what the little sod said?'

I shook my head.

' "Give me a chance, sir. Please give me a chance, sir." I bloody ask you.'

I picked up the empty glasses, took them to the bar and brought back two more pints of beer. 'But he stayed,' I said, 'for two years less a couple of months.'

'That's right. As a matter of fact he didn't turn out badly at all. But he would never have made a good newspaperman, not in a year of Sundays. He was too shy. He gradually got better, but he was positively embarrassed when it came to interviewing strangers. I don't care what they say about this business but you've got to be brash and heartless. You've got to be prepared to cash in on private grief, to force your way in where you're not wanted. Oh, I know not so much on a local paper as on a national. But it's no good being soft and apologetic. I'll say one thing for Antony, he was a worker. He could never put in enough hours.'

Again Bill paused, picked up his glass and took a long drink.

'I never got to know Antony, Michael. I never knew him better than I did that first day in June when he walked into my office scared out of his bloody mind. He had to force himself to knock on that door, and I honestly believe he had to force himself to carry out every assignment I gave him, from piddling things like interviewing the grower of the biggest leek of the year to chatting up the local mayor or asking some pompous councillor what his policy was. He had guts if nothing else. As a matter of fact Tim and Mick, the other two reporters, noticed this too and respected him for it. He was so bloody helpless, so willing to please, that you wanted to help him one moment and kick him up the arse the next. But you could never dislike him, poor little sod. He was so bloody lonely. We did our best to help, but the three of us were all older than he was. We were in our mid-twenties and he was only seventeen. Another thing, he had this posh accent and we had all come up the hard way. It didn't really matter but that accent cut the air like a knife and at times Mick in particular couldn't help taking it off.'

'Didn't he make any friends?'

'Not really. I asked him out to dinner once or twice, and so did the others. But we all found the same thing. He had nothing to say and I'm afraid all our wives found him a crashing bore. Even my wife remarked that she had never met less suitable newspaper material in all her life. Anyway, after a bit we grew accustomed to having him about the place and I'm afraid we used him. Work! He would positively leap at the chance of going to evening functions. You know, attending the dinner of the local football or rugby club, the meetings of the Oddfellows and the Round Table and so on, although he must have steeled himself every time to make the effort.'

'No girlfriends?'

'Not that I know of. The girls in the accounts department thought the world of him. I think they all wanted to mother him, always telling him what beautiful long eyelashes he had and all that balls, which he absolutely detested. Incidentally, I've arranged for you to meet one of the girls who was in the department when he was here.'

'That's kind.'

'Well, she may be able to tell you more about his social life than I can. Frankly all I connect him with while he was here was work, work and more work. It was pathological, almost as if he was working to forget – I can't imagine what. Another thing, he was so bloody miserable-looking and hardly ever seemed to smile.'

'I see what you mean about his not being newspaper material. Why the hell did he apply for a job on the paper?'

'I asked him once,' said Bill. 'He told me he had to get a job of some kind, and writing was the only thing he knew anything about. When I asked him what he wrote, he said: "Poetry". Bloody poetry, I ask you! Fat lot of good poetry does you when you have to be down at the court at ten each morning listening to the most boring cases and making sure you get the names spelt right. What the hell has poetry to do with the fact that our local drunk was up in front of the beaks again for being pissed outside the Victoria at half-past two in the afternoon and was fined five shillings for the umpteenth time?'

'Did his family ever come to see him?'

'Once or twice. A sister. Occasionally he used to ask me for a few hours off to meet her. He was always apologetic as if he were asking me an almighty favour. Considering he was putting in never less than eighty hours a week, I ask you. As a matter of fact I once saw them lunching together in the dining room here. I suppose she was a few years older than him, twenty or twenty-one and an absolute smasher. When he saw me looking at them, he turned scarlet as if he had no right to be eating in the same room as myself.'

'He doesn't seem to have had much fun.'

'Bloody little,' said Bill. 'I wish I could have done more. At least I got the editor to give him a rise after three months and by the time he left to join the army he was on to forty-five shillings a week. What did he join by the way?'

'Didn't he tell you?'

'No. One day early in August 1939 he came to see me and told me that he was off to the army. A couple of weeks later he was gone. What happened to him?'

'He joined the Southerns.'

'And was killed in France?'

'Yes, he was killed in France,' I said, 'but not with the Southerns. He was dropped by the SOE, captured and killed by the Germans.'

'Fucking Hell!' said Bill so loudly that the drinkers at the next table stared disapprovingly in our direction. 'A bloody secret agent! Antony a secret agent! I'll never believe it. Tell me more.'

'I can't, Bill,' I said. 'I haven't got as far as that in my research.' I looked at my watch. 'Ready for lunch?'

As we went into the dining room Bill was still muttering to himself.

We were back at Bill's office shortly before three. Bill rang through to the accounts department and asked for Mrs Adams to join us. After Bill had introduced us, he said, 'Right, there you are, Michael. I must be off to my golf.'

'A good healthy life you live here,' I said.

'When Fleet Street has knifed you to pieces why not try it?' he said. 'If there's anything more I can do just give me a ring. Thanks for the lunch.'

'Thank the *Express*,' I said.

When Bill had left the room, I said, 'I'm making some enquiries about a boy who worked here – Antony Rattigan.'

'I know,' said Mrs Adams. 'Mr Wheatley told me. Is it for the *Express*?'

'No,' I said. 'It has nothing to do with my column. I may be writing something about his life.'

'How is he?'

'I'm afraid he's dead, Mrs Adams. He was killed in France in 1942.'

'Oh dear, poor Antony,' she said. I could see she was genuinely upset. 'He didn't have much of a life, did he? He couldn't have been more than twenty-one.'

'That's right.'

'What a bloody shame,' she said. 'Oh well, it's no good crying over spilt milk, is it? What is it you want to know about him?'

'Anything you can remember. What sort of a boy he was, how he got on with the crowd here, any particular incidents, Mrs Adams.'

'Call me Janet, Michael,' she said. 'Well, let me think. It's a fair time ago isn't it. Getting on for fourteen years since he came here, and I wasn't much older than him at the time. I wasn't married in those days either. There were three of us about the same age in the accounts department and an old fogey in charge. Looking back, the first thing that struck us about Antony was the fact that he was so good looking. He made us all swoon just to speak to him. Of course, we were just silly girls in those days and we did silly things like drawing matches to see who should take him in a cup of tea. Not that he was often in. He spent most of the day and night working. He must have been out of his mind. I know because I looked after the pay packets, and when he first joined us the mean so-and-sos only paid him twenty-one shillings a week. It was less than we were getting. Some days we got worried that he wasn't getting enough to eat and we would offer him bits of chocolate.'

'Was it always like that? Did you ever get to know him better?' I asked.

'Yes, but not till the following summer. By that time we knew a little more about him. Not much, but just a little. It must have been Tim or Mick, they were the two reporters at the time, who told us that his grandfather was some bigwig in the army and owned some stately home in Essex called Malplaquet. I'll always remember it because it's such an odd name. But none of us knew what Antony was doing here. It was not any of our business. You might say we were intrigued but it was his affair and we left him alone. It would have been rude to have asked him, wouldn't it? Anyway, that summer of 1938, after Antony had bought his bicycle, I knew that he wanted to ask me something. It was the way he kept hanging around me, especially when I was on my own. My goodness, Michael, I've never met anyone so shy and backward.'

'That's what Bill told me,' I said.

'Finally I couldn't stand it any more. It was a Friday evening and I was about to go home with nothing in particular in mind for the weekend. I hadn't started to go steady then. I found him hanging around the corridor at the top of the stairs, and as I passed him he said, "Good night, Janet. Have a nice weekend." So I said, "I don't expect I shall." "Oh dear, why not?" he said. "Because I shall be bored out of my mind." We just stood there looking at one another and he started to go red. Then he managed to say, "Have you got a bicycle?" As a matter of fact I didn't own one, but I knew where I could borrow one, so I said, "Yes. What have you in mind?" I had to ask the question because I knew he never would. "Would you care to come out with me on Sunday?" he said. "We could have lunch at a little pub I've discovered." ' Janet smiled at the memory, as if the incident had taken place only a few days ago. 'That's how it started,' she said.

'What started?' I asked.

'Not what you're thinking. Oh, nothing like that, Michael. Just a series of bicycle rides around the countryside, on Sundays when he was not working. Absolutely harmless, but they were fun. We'd go to pubs, walk on the weald, in the woods and through the orchards. Do you know, Michael, he was fantastic at finding his way about. It was more than that, it was uncanny. And what he didn't know about the countryside wasn't worth knowing. He knew every bird and beast by name, every butterfly, every insect. He once showed me a fox and its cubs in a clearing in a wood. We had to approach them in a certain way, I think it was downwind or something like that. I tore my dress to bits and my stockings were ruined, but it was worth it.'

'Did he tell you where he learnt it all?'

'Once or twice he mentioned Malplaquet, but he never would say much about the place except once he told me it was the most beautiful place in England. I asked him if it would ever be his and he looked upset and said that it might be, but nothing in this world was certain. Quite honestly, I don't know much about his family, but whoever they were they gave him a right raw deal.

One day he mentioned the name of a man called Jack Pullen. He told me this Jack Pullen was the greatest man in the world. Do you know who this Jack Pullen was, Michael?'

'Yes. He was Antony's grandfather's head keeper at Malplaquet before the war. I believe he could charm the birds out of the air. Were you happy with Antony, Janet?'

'Only when we were in the country. When we were back in the office he always withdrew into himself. It was only in the countryside that he could forget whatever it was that was on his mind. In my opinion there was plenty. Oh, I remember another funny thing that happened that summer. You see, Antony knew everything there was to know about nature. He said that if he had to feed off the countryside that was no problem. He didn't know just about wild strawberries and blackberries. He said you could eat most things and he kept making me taste all kinds of horrible things. I was a bit scared, I don't mind telling you. It was the same with all those toadstools. He said that only three or four were poisonous, and one day we collected some monstrous toadstools that were growing on a rotten tree stump and he said that they were delicious fried with a little butter, salt and pepper and that I should take them home and get Mum to do them.'

'Did you?'

Janet laughed. 'Yes. Mum went out of her mind and the toad-stools went straight into the dustbin.'

She paused. 'Would you care for a cup of tea? Here am I doing all the talking and I'm getting a bit dry.'

I nodded. She picked up the telephone and asked for two cups of tea to be brought in. After the tea arrived we talked in a desultory fashion for about five more minutes without anything vital emerging. I think by then I must have gained her confidence for she suddenly said, 'There's one other thing. Well, two. I wasn't going to tell them to you, but I don't think you're out to harm Antony. You're not, are you?'

'I promise you I'm not,' I said.

'It was the Christmas of 1938. The last Christmas before the war. As I've said, all the girls were mad about Antony. Some of them even had the cheek to ask what we did in the country. When I said we just looked at the birds and the beasts and the flowers, they didn't know how to take it. As a matter of fact my going out with Antony made me something of a celebrity. Silly isn't it? But that's how offices are and young girls' minds work. Well, it was the custom in our department to give a Christmas office party for our fellow workers. We didn't ask the heads of departments, not Mr Wheatley for instance from the reporters' room because he was the chief reporter, just Tim, Mick and, of course, Antony. One of the girls in our department was called Pearl. Very pretty she was, with masses of boyfriends, and she wasn't over particular whom she went with. I forgot to say that Antony once or twice asked me about her and I got the impression that he was interested in her. But I never thought much of it because I knew Antony would never make a move, and if there was going to be one it was going to be in my direction if I had anything to do with it. Sounds silly, doesn't it, Michael? It's all so long ago and as I've said I think we were all in love with Antony in one way or another, some more than others.'

'Anyway, I think some time before Christmas, Pearl must have made a definite pass at Antony. Quite the worst thing to do. He would have started to run and not stopped running until he had put several miles between himself and her. This really made Pearl mad. She wasn't the kind of girl who liked to be turned down, and she was jealous of me because of my Sundays with Antony. So she hatched up a plot with the other girls and I think with Mick and Tim. It was all very childish. We had hung mistletoe in our room, and it was arranged that the first man to arrive there after all the girls had collected would be Antony. So Tim and Mick told him to go on and join the party and they would come along in a minute. It was all so silly.'

'Go on,' I said.

'It was about six. We had all had a few drinks at midday, you know what office parties are, especially at Christmas.'

'Hell,' I said.

'So into a roomful of tipsy girls comes Antony on his own. The moment he stepped into the room I could see that he was terrified, him being just the only man. But before he could retreat, someone switched off the lights and he was seized and dragged under the mistletoe where the girls started to slobber all over him, laughing and shouting. Some of the things they said were pretty obscene. Pearl in particular mauled him about. She had drunk more than the others and was well away. She actually grabbed him, if you get my meaning, and tried to take down his trousers.'

'What did Antony do?'

'Nothing,' said Janet. 'Absolutely nothing. Pearl told me afterwards that he just stood there shaking. Shaking with fear, she said. I don't believe it was fear. I would say it was sheer embarrassment.'

'And then?'

'Suddenly he let out the most almighty shriek. I mean a real cry like an animal caught in a trap. It was awful. It stopped everything. Someone put on the light. He was still surrounded by girls and Pearl still had her hands down his front. He just froze and stared at her. Before anyone could say anything he kind of pulled his clothes around himself and ran out of the room. After that the party went flat. I think everyone was ashamed of what had happened. It was never mentioned afterwards and no one took the micky out of him again.'

'I must ask you one thing,' I said. 'Do you think he didn't like girls?'

Janet answered quickly. 'No, I never thought that. He was just afraid of them. In fact quite the opposite. I honestly believe if Pearl had paid more attention to him and forgotten all her other fellows, it would have been a different story. He just couldn't stand the vulgarity of it. It had to be something private, it wasn't anything he could rush in to. That's why I never made a pass at Antony myself. I knew I could easily scare him off and the kind of relationship we had was better than none. Looking back I would say I was falling in love with him. Of course nothing would ever have come of it. We were miles apart. It's so funny to think of him now. I mean, you coming here today brings back that awful party so vividly. What a shame his being killed like that. What a waste. I wonder what happened to that place Malplaquet he talked about. Would it have been his?'

'Yes,' I said. 'His grandfather still lives there, and when he dies it goes to the National Trust. Antony's father was also killed in the war, on the Normandy beaches, and that's the end of the family.'

'What a shame,' she said.

'What was the other thing you were going to tell me?' I asked.

'Well, when Bill Wheatley told me this morning that you were coming down to ask about Antony, I remembered something that Pearl told me a few years ago. By the way, she left here soon after war was declared.'

'What did she do?'

'I suppose you could say she became a barmaid. Anyway what she did was her own business. We still pass the time of day when we meet in the street, but you couldn't say we are in and out of one another's houses.'

'What did she tell you?'

'I think it's something she should tell you herself,' said Janet. 'What's more if you hear it from her, you'll be able to judge for yourself whether it's the truth or not.'

'How do I find her?'

'I called her this morning and I said that when we'd finished chatting you would give her a ring and go over and see her. She said to be sure to bring a couple of bottles of gin.'

'What does that mean?'

'Take it any way you like,' said Janet.

I decided that Janet was a very decent person.

Half an hour later I had collected a couple of bottles of Gordons from a wine merchant in the High Street and was ringing the bell of Pearl's flat in a modern block on the outskirts of the town. I don't know what kind of person I had expected to find. Pearl was very much better looking than Janet's description of her had led me to suppose. The flat was comfortable and simply furnished, and as she led me past the open door of the bedroom I noticed a large double bed, strewn with multi-coloured cushions. I handed her the bottles of gin.

'Very generous,' she said. 'Would you care for one?'

'Yes please. Tonic if you have any.'

'Sit down, Michael,' she said.

After she had filled two glasses with an enormous quantity of gin she came and handed one to me. It was when she was very close up that I noticed how thick her make-up was. I also thought I could detect a slight glassiness in her eyes together with a touch of moisture which more often than not betrays the heavy drinker. You can see it in my own and in a great many others in Fleet Street any day of the year.

When she had sat down on the sofa next to me she took a long drink and said, 'Ah, that's better. I believe you want to hear about our Antony.'

'That's right. But first I must tell you that he was killed in the war, in France in 1942.'

'Poor little sod,' she said. 'He didn't have much of a life, did he?' She lifted her glass and emptied it in one gulp. 'Do you mind?' she said, and crossed to the table where the gin bottles were standing and refilled her glass.

'Nothing like a glass of the hard stuff to get over a shock with,' she said.

'I'm told hot sweet tea is the right medicine.'

'Balls,' she said. 'So, he's dead. I often wondered what happened to him. Funny little sod he was. So you want to hear about him do you?'

'That's right. I'm writing his life story, but not for my paper.'

'You're welcome,' she said. 'But he didn't have much of a life, did he?' she added, repeating herself. She took another mouthful of drink and I thought I had better get on or else she was going to become either incoherent or hostile. I've noticed over the years that drink takes people in three ways. There are the touchy drunks, the loquacious happy drunks and the morose drunks who close up like clams.

'Did Janet tell you about the office party?'

'Yes.'

'That was a right cock up, if you'll excuse the expression. I made a right mess of it, didn't I? It was all so silly really, because I knew that Antony was mad about me, but like the silly little fool I was, I wanted to be hard to get.'

'How did you know?'

'I can tell when I turn a man on,' said Pearl. 'As a matter of fact it excited me to know I was driving Antony mad. The trouble was that I had too many boyfriends in those days. Aren't men bloody fools, Michael? All they can think about is sex.'

'I don't know,' I said.

'Don't be so bloody prudish. I bet I can turn you on. Would you like that?'

'Maybe later,' I said.

'Proud, aren't you?' she said.

Again I had that feeling that I was losing my grip. I edged closer to her and put my arm around her.

'That's better,' she said. 'Never could stand fellows who pretend they don't care.' She looked up at me and winked.

I leaned over and kissed her gently on the forehead. She smelled of expensive scent. 'About Antony.'

'To hell with Antony,' she said. 'Didn't have much of a life, did he?'

'Not much of a life. But what happened? Janet said something happened between you and him. Here, let me give you another drink.'

'Trying to get me tight, are you? Not necessary, Michael.' She kissed me very expertly. 'I can fancy you without a drink. Not like some of the buggers who maul me about.' She took another sip from her glass. 'Poor Antony. What a beautiful boy he was too. Do you know something, Michael? He is the most beautiful man I have ever known in my life. I mean he was the most beautiful man. Poor little sod. Still I'm glad I had one night with him. Just one night of love, just one night of love,' said Pearl. 'And not all that bloody good at that. Still, I did my best, I did my best.'

'What happened?'

'What happened? Not much. It was after Dunkirk. You know, Dunkirk when we were thrown out of France.' She paused and took another drink. 'Oh, what the bloody hell, it's all so long ago now. It doesn't matter.'

'Go on, Pearl, darling.'

'So, it's darling now, is it? Watch your step, Michael. I'm a nice girl, I am.'

'I know. What about Antony?'

'Oh, he was much nicer than you,' she said and giggled. 'He had beautiful skin. Soft as a baby's bottom. Soft all over was our Antony in more senses than one.'

'So you had an affair with him?'

'I went to bed with him, if that's what you mean. I told you, didn't I? Just after Dunkirk.'

'Here?'

'Don't be so bloody daft. I hadn't made any money in those days. Hadn't learnt how to extract it out of silly buggers like you. No, I don't mean you, Michael. You're not too bad looking. Not that you're beautiful.'

'After Dunkirk?'

'Dunkirk. Was it a great victory? Mr Churchill said so, didn't he? After Dunkirk. That's right. Look I'll show you something.' She disengaged herself from my arm, walked across the room to a cupboard, took out an old wooden tea caddy, brought it back to the sofa and tipped it up. Regimental badges, flashes, stripes, pips and crowns of all shapes and sizes cascaded on to the cushions and some fell on to the floor.

'Just a few mementos of my friends,' she said and giggled. 'Mind you, only a few.' She raked them over until she found what she was looking for. 'Here you are. This was his,' she said, handing me a cap badge.

I looked closely at it and saw that it was the regimental badge of the Southerns.

'Read what's written on it.'

I looked closely at it. '*Semper fidelis*'.

'That's right. *Semper fidelis*. Do you know what that means, Michael? That means "Always faithful". Always bloody faithful. Do you know, Michael, of all the bloody men I've known I think Antony was the only one who could have been always bloody faithful. Didn't have much of a life, did he?'

'So it happened after Dunkirk?'

'That's right. Not here. In a grotty room I had in those days before I went up in the world. I was still at the *Echo* and just beginning to learn my trade as it were, when one day Antony turned up. Defending the south coast or something like that. Very handsome he was in his officer's uniform.'

'What happened?'

'We just ended up in bed together. That's about it. No, it's not. The whole point is that it was his first time. I mean his first time in bed with a girl. Oh, a lot of them tell you that. I think they imagine they are flattering you. But in Antony's case it was the bloody truth. Do you know how I knew, Michael? He just hadn't a clue. I don't even think he knew how a girl was made. He was scared out of his wits into the bargain. To begin with he couldn't even get a hard on at all. I had to do all the work if you get my meaning. But I'll tell you something else, Michael. By the morning he was a different person. It was a funny thing. He was like a dog whose mistress had been kind to him. Silly little bugger kept on telling me how much he loved me, that he would never forget me and so on. I asked him why the hell he hadn't done something when he had been on the paper before the bloody war. That wasn't fair, was it, Michael? I never gave him the chance. What a bloody fool I was because I really did fancy him, I promise you I really did fancy him.'

'Did you ever see him again?'

'No, never. I left the paper. I had found more profitable employment. Do you understand what I'm getting at? No one at the *Echo* knew where I was living, so I don't suppose he could ever have found me even if he tried as I kept moving from flat to flat. I did a few months at Chatham but those sailors were too much for me, especially when they'd been to sea for a month or two. Talk about wanting their money's worth! Poor little Antony. Not much of a life was it?'

'No,' I said. 'But you gave him one night of love.'

'Here, you take it,' she said, holding out Antony's cap badge. 'It doesn't really fit in with the others. Perhaps his family would like it. He came from a posh family didn't he?' She giggled. 'If you give it back to them, tell them it came from a tart with a bloody heart of gold. But there's no such person, is there, Michael?'

'Only you, Pearl,' I said.

Pearl put her arm round me and pulled me on to her and started to kiss me. She tasted sweet. 'Do I turn you on?'

'Yes, Pearl.'

'Let's be comfortable in the bedroom,' she said. She stood up. 'Bring the gin with you,' she said. 'But first give me a couple of minutes in the bathroom.'

I looked at the cap badge, once again read the inscription, *Semper fidelis*, and slipped it into my pocket.

5

Petrol rationing was still very much in force in 1951, and, as a piece of paper had been circulated at the *Express* threatening all and sundry with instant dismissal for using the company's cars unless on urgent and strictly official business, I took the train to Colchester on Saturday morning to keep my appointment with Colonel Peter Smith, the commanding officer of the 1st Southerns.

I showed my credentials at the guardroom to the depot and a few minutes later found myself following the provost sergeant at a brisk pace across the square to battalion headquarters. I could not help noticing the prevalence of whitewash, highly polished fire buckets and a general atmosphere of bull, which made me feel nervous. I have never recovered from the shock of my five years in the army. That's what comes of being subject to military discipline when one is very young.

The colonel was waiting for me, and stood up from his desk the moment I came into the room. The provost sergeant announced me as if he was introducing the Lord Mayor at a City banquet.

'Well, we meet in somewhat different circumstances,' he said, shaking my hand and indicating a chair.

'I understand from Sam Wells at the War Office that it was at Anzio,' I said. 'You will have to excuse me but my recollections of the days on that appalling beachhead are decidedly hazy. I understand that I gave you some much appreciated rum.'

'That's right. You turned up with a couple of three tonners loaded with mines and gallons of the hard stuff.'

'I must have been out of my mind.'

'Just drunk, Michael.'

'How disgraceful. I'm told anyway that the rum if not the mines inspired the remnants of your battalion and saved the day for Britain.'

'Just about it,' said the colonel. 'By the way, would you care to walk over to the mess and have one?'

'Could we discuss the business first?'

'No problem. I understand that you are making enquiries about Antony Rattigan. He was killed in France. Something of a mystery, but we understand that he was dropped by parachute. Poor fellow.'

'Yes, he joined the SOE after leaving the Southerns. Do you want to know why I'm interested in him?'

'Sam Wells just told me to pass on to you anything that might be of use to you.'

'Roughly speaking, I'm just trying to find out why and how he was killed.'

'That's fine by me,' said Colonel Smith. 'He was a funny boy. Sometimes I felt he wasn't cut out to be a soldier. I don't mean he was inefficient or anything like that. He always seemed to me to be trying too hard.'

'Perhaps you would begin at the beginning, at the start of the war?'

'Well, I hope it will be of help, but there isn't all that much to tell. Now let me see. I joined the 3rd Southerns here in Colchester within a few days of war being declared. In those days it was a territorial battalion, not a very smart one, I must admit. You see, I was a mere bank clerk and I had to join a regiment that would take me. Had no public school education or anything to help me along.'

'I understand. It's still a bit that way, isn't it?'

'It is, but it doesn't worry me. I've come quite a long way in my life. After all I can go anywhere I like now. My commission has conferred on me a certain status.' Colonel Smith smiled and I began to warm to him.

'I only mention this business of class or what have you, because it was so extraordinary that Antony turned up at the same time as myself as a subaltern in the Southerns. I mean to say, with a name like Rattigan, a famous general for a grandfather, and his old man more or less owning the Dukes, you would have thought he would have done a lot better for himself.'

'Did you ever discover why he joined the Southerns?'

'Not really. I think our commanding officer at the time was a bit of a snob and was only too pleased to have a Rattigan in the battalion. Felt it gave the battalion a bit of class and all that balls.'

'Did Antony ever say anything about it himself?'

'Well, I did ask him once. It must have been one evening after a boozy session in the mess. I was only a lieutenant at the time and Antony a second lieutenant. When I say boozy I don't mean Antony was drunk, because he only took the occasional glass. But I think that the wine, or what have you, had loosened his tongue. When I asked him what had made him join a mob like the Southerns he told me that it was the only regiment that would have him and that any regiment was as good as the other when it came down to the actual business of fighting. As a matter of fact I felt pretty guilty about questioning him. Only a couple of days before he joined us the colonel had told us informally in the mess that he would be coming to us with the rank of second lieutenant and we were not to ask him why he had chosen our crowd. We gathered that he had received a direct commission, no doubt on account of his name being Rattigan. It was strange, but we had a great deal of other things to worry about, not least putting the battalion into some kind of order so that it could go to France.'

'Was Antony a keen soldier?'

'Keen? He never stopped working, and he expected his platoon to work as hard and conscientiously as he did. Quite frankly they didn't like him. It wasn't that he was a bull-shitter. It was that he expected his platoon to be better than all the others, and himself to be better than he was. It wasn't a question of currying favour or licking anyone's arse. I suppose you could say he was a perfectionist, and that didn't go down well, I don't have to tell you, during the weeks of the phoney war. But I do remember there was one thing about him that was almost uncanny. That was his fieldcraft. Do you know what is meant by that?'

'More or less. Ability to move without being seen, to live off the land and so on.'

'He was uncanny, Michael. That boy could approach a sentry at night and be on him before the chap knew there was anyone near him. I can tell you when he was duty officer and had to make the rounds of the sentries at night, every bloody one of them was on his toes, but still they couldn't stop him surprising them. One night there was a nasty incident when one of the sentries took a lunge at him with his bayonet. But Antony was prepared for him and just took a small grazing on his left side. I suppose he could have put the sentry in question on a charge, but he wouldn't even consider it. In fact, I got the impression that he thought the whole thing a bit of a joke. After that the chaps respected him a lot more though they could never bring themselves to like him. He was never a popular officer.'

'I understand the 3rd battalion did pretty well in France.'

'I thought we were the unsung heroes,' said Colonel Smith. 'Who told you that?'

'No less an authority than Sir Henry Rattigan. His actual words were that the 3rd battalion put up a damned fine show at Arras.'

'That's praise indeed,' said Colonel Smith. 'I don't know how much you know about the 1940 campaign in France.'

'Enough to know it was a right cock-up.'

'You can say that again. I won't bore you with the details. In fact those days are still extremely confused as far as I am concerned. If I said we moved up to the Belgian frontier and then came skeltering back that would be about the whole story. Anyway, at the beginning of May we found ourselves north of Arras across the highway that runs up to Lille. Confusion was absolute. The roads were clogged with refugees, and I don't think anyone in the battalion had much hope that we would extract ourselves. One and all saw an inglorious future as prisoners of war. Anyway we received orders to hold the road north of Arras to allow the remnants of our division to pass through on the road to the south-west which ran to Cambrai. A classical example of sacrificing a small force for the good of the greater. A kind of Thermopylae, but I'm afraid our men didn't see it like the Spartans.'

'Who shall blame them?' I said.

'Exactly. But we did put up a good show. Our division, or what was left of it, was able to pass through Arras and ultimately reached Dunkirk where it was taken off. You can read all about it in the official histories, and we are proud of the number of gongs we picked up. Two DSOs, two MCs, three DSMs and six MMs. A considerable achievement, you must admit. Anyway, after about three days' non-stop fighting there came the problem of getting what was left of the battalion out. We were down to about two hundred men and four officers by then. In other words we were by now at less than a quarter strength. Once again came the problem of sacrificing the few for the benefit of the majority. The colonel called for volunteers. Now don't laugh.'

'Why should I?'

'There was only one. Antony Fitzjames Rattigan. You mustn't blame the men. They had fought hard and well. They had done their bit and they were morally and physically exhausted.'

'He couldn't have covered your falling back on his own,' I said.

'No. He ordered the remains of his platoon to stay with him. It was as simple as that. The colonel didn't have much option but to agree as everything was in a state of utter confusion. You'll appreciate we were under heavy fire the whole time and communications had completely broken down. So the remains of the battalion pulled out and passed through Arras in the rear of the division leaving Antony and about eight men to cover the retreat.'

'Only eight men?'

'Give or take one,' said Colonel Smith.

'What happened?'

'Now we enter the land of conjecture. No, no. I'm not trying to be mysterious. The fact is the truth will never be known. You see nothing more was heard of Antony or his men until three days later. By that time we had reached the coast and turned north towards Dunkirk, when it was decided that we should be taken off at Boulogne. Then out of the blue Antony turns up.'

'With his men?'

'With just one. His platoon sergeant.'

'The rest were killed or taken prisoner?'

'All killed. They were posted missing to begin with and later presumed dead when they failed to turn up as prisoners of war.'

'But Antony and his men had achieved what they set out to do.'

'Yes, you could say that,' said Colonel Smith. 'The battalion let the division get away to fight another day, and Antony's platoon did the same for the battalion. But that's not the end of the story. Division was delighted with the battalion and there was talk of giving Antony some kind of a decoration. I should say here that the poor fellow was in a dreadful state when he caught up with us at Boulogne. He was suffering from battle fatigue, shell shock, call it what you like. Anyway when we got back to England and had started to form up again at these barracks here, there was not much to be got out of him. If it hadn't been the question of the possibility of handing out gongs to him and his sergeant, the matter would probably have rested there.'

'I don't get it. What was the problem? He seems to have put up a good show, as they say.'

'As soon as we got back here at the end of May 1940 I was promoted adjutant of the battalion. If I remember Antony went on sick leave. Anyway, he came back at the beginning of June looking physically better but seeming more withdrawn than he had ever been. I think I've made it clear that he was not exactly an extrovert. Then rumours started to float around the depot. Nothing much, but enough for the colonel who had come out of France safely to ask me as adjutant to make some discreet enquiries.'

'What sort of rumours?'

'Rumours about Antony's behaviour. His sergeant had been very badly shaken like Antony, and had taken to the bottle. Quite a common reaction as you probably know among men who have undergone some particularly unpleasant battle experience. Anyway, his sergeant, Sergeant Griffiths, started to put it about when in his cups that Antony's behaviour under fire had not been all it had been cracked up to be.'

'But you said that Antony never claimed anything; that he kept whatever had happened to himself.'

'That's right. It was only the question of gongs that brought the affair to the forefront.'

'I understand,' I said.

'One day the Regimental Sergeant Major came to me in a hell of a state. He didn't know what to do. You know, although we weren't, and still aren't, a smart regiment, we have our pride. The honour of the Southerns is as precious to us as theirs is to the Brigade of Guards. Apparently the previous night Sergeant Griffiths had got particularly pissed and more or less accused Antony of running away in the face of the enemy.'

'Very tricky,' I said.

'You can say that again. I went immediately to the Colonel who nearly had kittens on the spot. He had just been put up for the DSO and indeed he deserved it for the way he had covered the division's retreat, although I doubt if the poor sods under the ground would have felt the same. So there is yours truly having to investigate a very nasty rumour concerning an officer of the battalion put about by his own sergeant.'

'How did you set about it?'

'With great discretion. I had Sergeant Griffiths into my office and asked him if it was true that he had been spreading this rumour. He was very taken aback, and what is more he was genuinely sorry. He blamed the drink for anything he might have said and promised that he would keep quiet in future. That wasn't good enough. I had to get to the bottom of the affair. After all it was far too risky to have a sergeant prone to booze spouting malicious gossip every time he was in his cups. I could not exactly threaten him with a court martial, and at the same time I just could not let him roam around free. But he wasn't forthcoming. I thought of getting him posted to one of the other battalions, but that would not have solved the problem. So I just worked on him. I had him in day in and day out questioning him.'

'What did you discover?'

'Quite a lot. By the way, Michael, this must be in the strictest confidence. I finally did manage to get what I believe to be the truth out of Sergeant Griffiths. Very interesting it was too. Antony had been incredibly brave. He had also been incredibly cowardly, if one can use that word about someone who loses control of himself. Let's start with the brave bit. According to Sergeant Griffiths, at first, after the rest of the battalion had withdrawn through Arras, Antony's platoon had come under heavy attack – by at least a company of the enemy, Sergeant Griffiths estimated. We had left Antony with plenty of bren-guns, one to each of his eight men, and Antony had sited them extremely well. He managed to hold off the attack for twenty minutes to half an hour until the Germans brought up some kind of armoured vehicle. We had also left him with a Boyes anti-tank rifle. It's not much of a gun, a .55 which gives a hell of a flash and a kick when you fire it. It can just about deal with an armoured vehicle, but would be very unlikely to stop a tank. Anyway, this AV starts coming down the road. Antony and his sergeant are dug in to the ditch and Antony lets this AV get within twenty yards or less before stopping it with the first shot from his anti-tank rifle. As the crew bailed out, Sergeant Griffiths knocked them off with his bren.

'This put a brake on the Germans' advance and they quietened down a bit, until they got a mortar into position and then they let all the shit in hell drop round Antony and what was left of his platoon. Sergeant Griffiths estimated that by this time there was only Antony, himself and a couple of men left. Then, according to Sergeant Griffiths, Antony went out of his mind. He ordered Sergeant Griffiths to fix bayonets and charge. Yes, to bloody well charge. Sergeant Griffiths said he was completely raving bonkers. He generously attributed it to the heavy mortaring, but quite rightly he wasn't having anything to do with a Charge of the Light Brigade, and told Antony as much. Whereupon Antony pointed his pistol at him and ordered him to charge or he would shoot him for cowardice. Sergeant Griffiths knocked the pistol out of his hand and slapped him hard in the face for good measure. He swore he had no alternative; that Antony's nerve had failed him, and that he was a gibbering mass of jelly. No sooner had he struck him, than Antony completely broke down and burst into tears. Before he could stop him Antony was out of the trench and legging it back down the road for all he was worth. By some miracle he was not hit.'

'And Sergeant Griffiths?'

'Seeing that everyone else in the platoon was killed and his officer had fucked off as he put it, there seemed no point in hanging around. He crept away from the road, secured some cover in a small wood and was able to make his way back to the coast without further trouble. He says it was a matter of good luck.'

'He sounds like a good man, Sergeant Griffiths.'

'He was. He died last year. He became one of our best Company Sergeant Majors. What was more, he kept his mouth shut. He was a regular soldier and he didn't want the battalion to be brought into disrepute. He was the first to admit that Antony had behaved with outstanding gallantry. He reckons he just could not stand up to the heavy mortaring. Also there was a hell of a lot of carnage about the place, blood, limbs and God knows what else. I discussed the matter with the colonel, who agreed with me that the matter should be allowed to rest there; that no useful purpose would be served by holding a court of inquiry.'

'Did you believe Sergeant Griffiths?' I asked.

'There was no reason why he should lie. Yes, I believed him all right. The colonel and I thought it would be a good idea to get Antony posted away from the battalion but the problem was solved for us. Our 4th battalion was allocated a stretch of the Kentish coast to repel the Germans when they threatened invasion in the summer of 1940, and Antony was sent to join it, having a record of fine fighting service in France and being just the kind of young officer any battalion would be glad to have on its strength.'

'Did you ever see him again?'

'Never. I stayed with the 3rd battalion here until August 1941 when I was shipped via the Cape to join the 8th Army. After that Salerno, Anzio, the whole cock-up of the Italian campaign. Shortly I hope to be going with my battalion, as it is now, either to Aden or Cyprus.'

'Let me recommend Cyprus. You'll get shot at in both places but the climate in Cyprus is more friendly,' I said. 'Now, what about that drink? Then I'll buy you lunch at the best hotel in Colchester and perhaps we might go over some of the finer points. It's a strange story. No one except you, the colonel, Sergeant Griffiths and Antony himself knew what took place outside Arras?'

'No. The rumours died away after Antony was posted to the 4th battalion.'

'So the people at the SOE would never have heard of the incident?'

'Never. Though they may have heard that Antony had put up a fine show in France. His prowess with that anti-tank rifle became quite a legend. After all, most soldiers were frightened to fire the bloody thing it had such a kick. As for putting an AV out of action with it, why that was nothing less than a bloody miracle.'

6

I left England at the beginning of July 1951 to make a tour of the Middle East, taking in such godforsaken spots as Aden and the Gulf States – Kuwait, Oman and Saudi Arabia. I went on into Iraq and Persia and everything I saw boded ill for the future.

America in those days seemed intent on removing British influence from that part of the world without having any intention of taking over the responsibilities herself. It had something to do with an inbred dislike of the British Empire, or rather what was left of it. I came back towards the end of July having sent home a series of gloomy articles at which a great many people scoffed.

During my time abroad I had little opportunity to consider what my future researches into the life and death of Antony should be. I was too fully occupied with meeting presidents, prime ministers, governors, generals and sheiks of various degrees of importance while trying to cope with the appalling climate. The Middle East has never been my favourite spot. It always upsets my stomach.

A few days after my return I was sipping my early morning tea and going through the rival papers when the telephone rang. 'Hall porter of the Turf Club here, sir. Is that Mr Nelson?'

'Yes.'

'Message for you from Major Birdham, sir. Says will you meet him at the entrance to the members' enclosure at Goodwood today, a quarter of an hour before the first race? For your information the first race is at 2.15. He presents his apologies for not telephoning himself.'

I had already done my homework on Major Lennox Birdham although I had not discovered much. In fact, the press cuttings in the *Express* library were decidedly on the thin side where he was concerned. They basically came down to the fact that he had been an agent in France during the war and had been awarded the George Cross for his outstanding bravery. Unlike some of his fellow agents whose memoirs were now beginning to appear, in so far as the Official Secrets Act permitted, Major Birdham had not as yet seen fit to put his own into print.

I rang my office and as usual received a telling off from my secretary for not letting her know what my next piece was to be about, as the editor wanted to know. 'Tell him I'm doing something on racing,' I said. 'I haven't quite decided on the angle yet. Possibly: How does the British working man manage to spend a day at the races in the middle of the week when the country is in such dire straits? Or the managerial class for that matter. I don't really know. Possibly something on gambling. I'll play it by ear when I get to Goodwood.'

'It's all right for some,' she said.

'It won't last for ever, sweetie,' I said. 'My star is in the ascendant right now, but it can sink without trace tomorrow. I only have to fall foul of Lord Beaverbrook.'

'There's quite a faction moaning about you in the building,' she said.

'You don't have to tell me. Jealousy will get them nowhere. It's the biggest arse-creeper who wins in Fleet Street!'

'There's no need to be crude,' she said. 'If the editor wants you, where can he get hold of you?'

'The members' enclosure at Goodwood.'

'Grand, aren't we?'

'Yes, very. But only for the moment,' I said and rang off.

I am not a racing man. It seems to me that racing and gambling are the same thing, and the latter has never appealed to me. I am not against it on moral grounds. The fact is, anything that runs on four legs carrying my money on its back invariably comes in last. I decided long ago that I might as well give the money to charity as to bookmakers.

But I had to admit, as I took the special bus from Chichester station to Goodwood racecourse shortly after one o'clock, that Glorious Goodwood lived up to its name. It was still early July and the trees had not developed that slightly dusty and dried look that they get towards the end of the summer. It was a bright day with a cooling wind blowing off the Downs. There was a growing crowd and everyone seemed to be in a thoroughly good temper.

I presented myself at the members' entrance at five minutes to two. At exactly the same time Major Lennox Birdham came to the gate and shook me by the hand. 'I see the old military habit dies hard,' he said.

'How do you mean?'

'Five minutes before parade and not a minute later, captain,' he said. Seeing the look of surprise on my face he laughed. 'I've been through your file. Quite a distinguished career, from driver to captain in five years. Middle East, Persia, Iraq, the desert, Italy, Austria and finally home to Civvy Street. See, too, that you were training on amphibious craft to go to the Far East. Spared that on account of the dropping of the atom bomb. Bet you were relieved. But enough of that. Soon time for a glass of champagne, but first we must get our bets on.'

'I don't bet, major,' I said.

'But you must. You see I have a horse running in the first race that's going to win. A racing cert, I promise you.'

'What's its name?'

'Soldier Lad.'

'It must win then,' I said. 'How much shall I put on?'

'Say ten per cent of your weekly salary. Yes, I think ten pounds would be the right amount for a non-gambling man.'

Major Birdham had certainly done his homework on me, even to the extent of knowing how much the *Express* paid me.

'Where do we bet?'

'On the rails. If you don't mind I won't put our money on until just before the off. You see, I am proposing to have quite a substantial bet, and I don't want the word getting about or the odds will come tumbling down.'

I knew enough about the racing game to appreciate the major's tactics. I was also impressed by his cool-headedness. Literally thirty seconds before the runners came under starter's orders he leaned across the rails and whispered into the ear of one of the country's leading bookmakers. Then they were off.

It was a five-furlong sprint. Soldier Lad got away to a good start, led all the way and came in with two lengths to spare.

'Easy, isn't it?' said Major Birdham. 'We'll just slip down to the unsaddling enclosure and congratulate Gordon Richards for earning me enough money to keep my horses for another month. Then we'll celebrate with a glass or two of champagne.'

I had never been into the hallowed unsaddling enclosure before, but I could appreciate what fun it was to be a member of the élite on the inside of racing. In the back of my mind I decided on my piece for the paper the next day. I would write about how easy it was to make a living at racing provided one was in the know. How many people beside the major, the trainer and the jockey, were sufficiently well informed to know that this was Soldier Lad's race?

The voice of the course announcer informed us that Soldier Lad had been returned at odds of six to one.

'Better than I had dared to hope,' said the major. 'Here are your winnings.' He counted out twelve white five-pound notes and handed them to me. Seeing the look of embarrassment on my face he said: 'It's all right. My bookmaker will be paying me by cheque.'

'It's all too easy,' I said. 'I think I will change my job.'

'It isn't always like this, believe me, Michael.'

'It's very impressive, major,' I said. 'Let me buy the champagne.'

We went in to the members' bar and the major led me directly to a corner table where already seated was an extremely attractive woman. I somehow assumed she would be Major Birdham's wife, until he introduced her to me as Sally Adams. 'Or rather I should say former Flight Officer Sally Adams,' he said.

I shook hands wondering what an ex-Waaf had to do with Antony Fitzjames Rattigan.

'Go ahead and order the champagne. May I suggest the Krug non-vintage,' said Major Birdham.

'Delighted,' I said and placed my order with the waiter who was hovering near the table.

After the waiter had poured the champagne, the major started to expound on the intricacies of the racing game, giving me a great deal of useful copy for my article on racing. It was not until the bar began to empty as the members left to follow the fortunes of the horses in the second race that he said, 'Enough of that.

As I do not have the winner of this race, I think we can now get down to business. First of all about Sally. She was Antony Rattigan's "mother" during his training for the SOE. It was her duty to watch him from start to finish, and finally to decide if he was the right material for the tasks that would be allotted to him. Unusual job for a woman. But she was the best in the business, the very best that we ever had in Baker Street. Before I go any further I'll put my cards on the table. As you must be aware I have done my homework on you, no doubt as you have done the same on me, though I suspect you could find out precious little.'

'That's right.'

'I know that you have been screened by MI5 and in the course of your job you have access to classified information.'

'Correct. And I have never abused the privilege.'

'If you had, you would be in the Tower,' said Major Birdham. 'We understand from General Sir Henry Rattigan that you are interested in the death or murder of his grandson Antony. So are we. You have already been told by Major Sam Wells at the War Office that the SOE was disbanded in 1946 by a special order of the Cabinet. I won't go into the reason for that order. As a result our organization was completely dismantled, and we literally did not have the personnel to investigate every case of those of our agents who went missing in France. All we know about Antony is that he was shot by the Germans in the village of Les Saules in the Loire valley and is buried in the churchyard there. He was dropped in France on 10 May 1942 and according to our information died on 30 May. We know nothing of what happened during those three weeks he was in France. Nor did we ever hear from his wireless operator who was dropped with him. He literally disappeared from the face of the earth. We can only assume that he came down in the River Loire and was drowned. There are several possibilities, but the fact remains that his body has never been discovered.'

'It's the first time I've heard about a wireless operator,' I said.

'I may be able to tell you a lot of other things you don't know about. To be frank with you, Michael, in return for supplying you with all the information at our disposal, we expect you to keep us informed of anything you may discover. Is that fair?'

'Perfectly,' I said. 'Let's get something else straight. I am not investigating the life and death of Antony Fitzjames Rattigan for the *Express*. It is purely a personal matter. It was the plaque that set me off. You know about the plaque, do you, and the strange mention of a black cat?'

'Yes, we know about the plaque. We know it was put up by the Comte de Chaumont. We've had our opposite numbers in France question him, but he is saying precious little. The only thing that emerged was that he was extremely sensitive about the whole business and gave the impression that it was a subject he did not wish to discuss. Have you seen him yet?'

'No. He's on my visiting list,' I said.

'Right. Now that's settled I think I had better fill in the background and then Sally will take over and give you details of Antony during his training period. As you know, after the fall of France the SOE was set up under the Ministry of Economic Warfare with the purpose of what Churchill called setting Europe ablaze. A rather optimistic phrase, but then the old man was given to rather flowery language which had little to do with reality. To begin with I was involved with an organization known as MI9, whose purpose was to set up evasive routes for ex-prisoners of war and those who had been left behind after we had been pushed out of France. My particular route was the one known as PAT which came down from the north to Paris, and passed through Orléans on to Toulouse, then across the Pyrenees from Perpignan, finally on to Barcelona and then to Madrid. This route was originally set up by Albert-Marie Guérisse, who was actually a Belgian. He was eventually captured, incidentally by Himmler's men, but incredibly survived. For his services he was decorated with the George Cross after the war. PAT was one of the most successful of the evasion routes and in fact by 1944 it had expanded so that a steady flow of men were coming through a place called Châteaudun to the west of Orléans under the code name of Sherwood. That is by the way.

'I came out of France in mid-1941 when I severed all connection with MI9 and transferred to the SOE in a more aggressive role, one that Mr Churchill would appreciate. I joined Colonel Buckmaster in Baker Street with the special task of training agents in sabotage, assassination, and aggression in general. To be honest it is doubtful whether my section was worth the cost in human lives. The real value of the SOE was in encouraging the French Resistance and supplying it with arms, so that it could play a useful part when the time came for the Allies to invade France. That, of course, was not to happen until 1944. Any questions so far?'

'First of all why couldn't you have moved over to a more aggressive role in the Loire valley instead of returning to England?' I asked.

'Two reasons. First of all they wanted me back in England in the role of instructor. Secondly I knew far too much about the operation of the escape route through Orléans which MI9 had set up. Had I fallen into the hands of the Gestapo they might have got too much information out of me. It is impossible to assess the limits of pain which one human being can withstand. We found that some people gave in instantly. A few went to their deaths, dreadfully mutilated, taking their secrets with them.'

'You mentioned the Comte de Chaumont. Was Antony meant to contact him?'

'That was the purpose of the mission. His objective was to set up a cell based on the château. Our information from our opposite numbers in the Free French here in England was that the Comte was very pro-English and particularly anti-German. Both of his sons had been killed in the fighting of 1940.'

'I believe he was something of a fascist in the thirties?'

'Quite true. So were a great many other people of his class, including a number in England. Our information was that he had changed sides.'

'Was it good information?'

'I had no reason to suspect it,' said Major Birdham. 'Anything else?'

'Did you ever return to the Loire valley? As an agent, I mean.'

'No. I've told you I knew too much. I was too great a risk. I went back to France, but to the south and not until just before the invasion. I don't see what that has to do with Antony. Shall we go back to him?'

I nodded.

'One of our main problems with our agents was that they had to speak perfect French, and by perfect I mean just that. They were usually bilingual. I had a French mother, like Antony, just in case you should wonder about me. In the summer of 1941 a top-secret order went out asking that anyone who spoke fluent French should forward their names to the War Office where they would be considered for one of the commando units that were being organized for raids on the coast of France. This was the cover story at the time and no mention at all was made of the SOE. In fact security was so strict that a number of men trained for the SOE and were found unsuitable and returned to their units still under the belief that they had been training for the Commandos.

'In that summer of 1941 we received an application from Antony, who was serving in the Southerns. Immediately his name struck a chord, and sure enough a few discreet enquiries revealed he was indeed the grandson of General Sir Henry Rattigan and the son of Lieutenant Colonel Rattigan, the commanding officer of the Dukes.'

'No doubt you also discovered that he left Wolfe College under a cloud.'

'Of course.'

'Didn't that worry you?'

'We took it into consideration, of course. But not for one moment did we ever consider him to be a homosexual. Frankly, if everyone who had shown such tendencies while at public school was barred from office, there would be a great shortage of people in high places including the Cabinet and the Church. As a matter of fact one of our very best agents was a fully fledged practising homosexual. Alas, he never came back. He received a posthumous GC for his work.'

Major Birdham paused. 'One other point that may interest you. Although we had hundreds of applicants to join us, or rather the commando unit, we actually chose a mere dozen. Either they were not sufficiently fluent in French, or unsuitable material. Recruiting by asking for volunteers was generally speaking a failure.'

'How did you recruit then?'

'I'm ashamed to say on the Old Boy network. It sounds horribly clannish but the fact is that it worked. A great many of our agents came from the City, stockbrokers, bankers and so on. The smarter London clubs too proved a fruitful recruiting ground. I'm afraid we encountered a great deal of hostility, especially from the professionals at MI5 and MI6. They had some justification I must admit. A great many members of the Firm, as we were known, were products of the British public schools. Although it has never been officially admitted I think this is why the Labour Government were so keen to disband us immediately after the war. They did not like to have an élitist underground movement in the country on the whole opposed to their socialist policies.'

Major Birdham picked up the bottle of Krug and refilled our glasses. 'I think this is where Sally takes over. Although I had overall control of the training of our agents in F section of the SOE . . .'

'F section?' I interrupted.

'F for France,' said Major Birdham. 'From the moment Antony was considered as potential material for the SOE, his training came directly under Sally.'

'I know it's easy to be wise after the event, but in fact I was not quite as sure as the major was about Antony's suitability for our section,' said Sally. 'Don't get me wrong. I had nothing against Antony for being chucked out of Wolfe College. The queer agent the major mentioned just now was one of my products, and almost certainly the best agent I was ever to train and put in the field. But one of our golden rules was never to train anyone with an emotional problem, in particular men or women suffering from unhappy love affairs who didn't care whether they lived or died. They were a menace not only to themselves but to everyone operating with them. What worried me in Antony's case was the tension within his own family. He made no secret of the fact that his father had refused to speak to him after he was thrown out of Wolfe. What I suspected had maddened his father even more was Antony's reluctance to show any interest in a military career. After all his family had produced hero after hero for hundreds of years and it was assumed that Antony would carry on the tradition.'

'I happen to know that he was a bit of a pacifist during his time at Wolfe,' I said.

'I didn't mind that either,' said Sally. 'There were a great many of them in the thirties whose war records were subsequently of the highest order. No, what worried me was Antony's concern at his rejection by his family, particularly by his mother. Not that she did not love him. She adored him, but she adored and loved her husband as well. What he said carried the day. Poor woman, she did not know what to do. In fact the only member of his family who kept in touch with him was his sister. Even with her he did not feel quite the same as he had done as a child.'

'That's what she told me.'

'So you know her then?'

'I've met her and Sir Henry. At Malplaquet. What a place! And what a splendid man the old general is. A pity Antony could not have gone to him. He was very fond of him. He still is.'

'You're so right,' said Sally. 'I should have realized that at the time and made him go back to Malplaquet. There we are. I didn't. I'm not excusing myself, if in fact I have anything to excuse. But there was this doubt in my mind about Antony, and looking back I would say the slightest doubt was sufficient reason not to take him on as an agent.'

'I think you are being unfair to yourself, Sally,' said Major Bird-ham. 'There is no reason to suppose that you didn't put anything but an efficient and highly trained agent into the field. The fact that he was killed had nothing to do with you.'

Sally shrugged her shoulders. 'It makes little difference to the poor boy now, does it?' she said. 'There's one other point, Michael. During Antony's training period I gradually became aware that he was considerably attracted to me.'

'Everybody was. I mean every male,' said Major Birdham. 'Including myself. But she was untouchable, Michael. Absolutely virginal. No that's unfair. She was a dedicated worker, totally committed to producing one-hundred-and-one-per-cent efficient agents. She had no time for sex.'

'One day I'll reveal the sordid truth,' said Sally. 'But I'm still bound by the Official Secrets Act, you know. As a matter of fact I wasn't worried too much about Antony feeling attracted to me.

It was, as the major knows, quite a common event. A kind of mutual like or dislike can grow between trainer and trainee. As far as Antony was concerned there was something sweet and slightly pathetic about him. In some ways he seemed younger than he was. He was only twenty when he came to us and twenty-one when he was killed. But he was more like an eighteen-year-old. This may have been due to his incredibly good looks. He was very blond, with a perfect physique and a schoolboy freshness about him which he never lost even when I had finished turning him into a thug. I know it's a strange thing to say about a man, but the truth is he was beautiful. That's the only word that describes him.'

'What made you finally accept him?' I asked.

'Two things. No, three things. First of all his determination to make his own way in the world after his family had more or less disowned him. In other words the almost two years he spent on the Rochester paper carving out his own career. That needed guts. Secondly, when the time came for him to join up, the fact that he picked a regiment like the Southerns where he would be free of family ties, inhibitions and pressures. Thirdly, the report of his bravery in the retreat in France.'

I decided to keep quiet. There seemed no point, certainly at this juncture, in revealing what the colonel of the Southerns had told me concerning Antony's behaviour outside Arras. But what Sally had revealed to me was beginning to build up a firmer picture of Antony.

Sally had paused as if aware that I had something in the back of my mind. 'Is this useful?' she said. 'Do you want me to go on?'

'Yes, please do,' I said hurriedly.

'Would details of his training interest you?' she asked. 'It's routine stuff, but you may be interested in my reactions.'

'Yes, go ahead,' I said.

'Well, in the summer of 1941 Antony joined F section at Warnborough Manor, near Guildford, ostensibly to undergo commando training. Here he went through the very tough course of four weeks of military and physical training which he passed with flying colours. Those not weeded out were then let into the secret: that in fact they were not training to be commandos, but agents to be dropped in France. The very few who declined to go on with the course were not posted back to their units, but to fresh units, under threat of instant court martial and death by firing squad if they so much as breathed a word of what they had learned.'

Sally paused and took a sip of champagne. I was so engrossed in the story that I was surprised to hear in the background the voice of the commentator announcing that the runners in the second race were on their way down to the start.

'Again, looking back, I am not quite sure if I had been right over Antony,' Sally continued. 'He was just too good at everything. Whatever he put his hand to had to be perfect. It didn't make any difference whether it was pistol shooting or work with the sten gun or the Chicago piano – as the Thomson machine gun was affectionately called before we abandoned it as being too heavy and liable to stoppages. His instructors were amazed at his pistol shooting, whether from his pocket or lying in a bed. He was far above average. The sten was a very tricky weapon to fire in those days. As you know it was manufactured to take British and German ammunition, but a hard slap on the butt could some-times cause it to fire, and a lot of the men didn't like the damned thing at all. Not so in Antony's case. He completely mastered it and by constant nightly practice could assemble it in the dark in a matter of seconds.'

'Would you say he was over-keen?' I asked.

'I think so. Again, looking back it's easy to say so. But at the time I wavered between admiration for his dedication and a nagging doubt as to why he tried so hard. In fact I had to have him in on one occasion and more or less reprimand him.'

'What had happened?'

'He had damn near killed one of the instructors. It was during his course of unarmed combat when he was learning to stab properly.'

I grimaced.

'It was a tough course, Michael. I was there to turn out killers, you know. Now, the technique of stabbing is never to stab down-wards but up through the ribcage. Exactly what happened never came out, but apparently the instructor told Antony to come at him. Antony did just that, but was far too quick for the instructor, and as I say he was very nearly killed. Luckily it was a dummy wooden knife, but the wretched fellow was in hospital for several weeks and was finished as an instructor as far as we were concerned.'

'After that incident we seriously considered getting rid of Antony,' said the major. 'We discussed the case endlessly. You see, we wanted to have as much confidence as was humanly possible in the agents we would be putting into France.'

'Actually, what turned in Antony's favour,' said Sally, 'was the PE exercise. Yellow Plastic Explosive to you, Michael. We set Antony the task of breaking into an RAF airfield and placing PE on the planes. Antony was allotted Tangmere, a fighter base in Sussex. God, what an almighty rumpus that caused. Antony went in and out like a dose of salts, unseen, unheard, completely undetected. The wretched station commander nearly had kittens when he was informed by us that if he inspected his planes, he would find a number of them decorated with PE, and the real stuff into the bargain, without, of course, the detonators. It really wasn't very kind of us.

'After his course at Warnborough Manor, Antony went up to our country house near Arisaig on the west coast of Inverness. Here again it was his superb fieldcraft that made us forget any doubts about him that we may have entertained. Here he perfected the art of silent killing, as we called it, practised his rope work and had still more pistol and sten training together with a course of factory and railway demolition. To lighten what was after all a grim and grinding course we set the trainees the problem of poaching a salmon, not so easy as you might think and few of them were successful at it. Antony excelled himself. In one night he came back with six superb fish, which were much appreciated by everyone. They made a pleasant change from army rations. He explained to us how he did it, it was a technique he had learned during holidays in Scotland. But none of our subsequent trainees ever mastered it.

'At the end of his course at Arisaig I suppose you could say that Antony was our star pupil. On the surface at least he was way ahead of the rest. From Arisaig he went with the others who had stuck it out so far to Ringway Airfield near Manchester where he did the five requisite drops from a Whitley bomber through a hole in the floor of the aircraft, including one by night.'

'I'm glad I served in the Royal Army Service Corps,' I said.

'Finally he ended up in our country house near Beaulieu, in Hampshire, where we taught him how to spot a follower and so on, how to conceal a personality and above all what to expect in the way of interrogation. We even went as far as seizing our would-be agents in the middle of the night and subjecting them to intense and extremely rough handling verging on brutality. But we told them if you don't like the heat, stay out of the kitchen. I suppose, though, the main point of Beaulieu was teaching them how to look ordinary. That's what I mean by concealing a personality. That is about all I can tell you about his training. I should add that before he went to Beaulieu he spent several weeks at our school near Bedford where his name was changed and he started to memorize his cover story. He also familiarized himself with the behaviour and use of reception committees in France in so far as they existed in those early days. I should add that during this long period of highly intensive training, Antony, like his fellow trainees, was never allowed to communicate with anyone in the United Kingdom, except through F section of the SOE.'

'I think you have missed one thing out, Sally,' said the major. 'The second-in-command at our place near Bedford was a Frenchman. We were amazed to receive his report to the effect that he did not consider Antony suitable material.'

'But from what you say he was your star pupil,' I said.

'Exactly. The second-in-command wrote on his report "Why does Lieutenant Rattigan try so hard? What is he trying to prove?" ' said Major Birdham.

'That's about it then, Michael,' said Sally. 'I hope in that welter of material you may find something useful.'

'What happened after Beaulieu?' I asked.

'He came to our place in Harley Street where we perfected his cover. We also sent him to a French dentist to make sure that his British fillings were changed for French ones. This was the only time he was afraid. He was terrified of that French dentist and said he was a sadist who deliberately tortured his customers.'

'Finally, on 10 May 1942, we sent him into France with all the training that we had been able to give him. On the surface a potentially brilliant agent. After that you know as much as we do.'

'What were his specific objectives in France?'

'To set up a Resistance movement in the Loire valley around Orléans. In the first instance to contact the Comte de Chaumont. After that he would be very much on his own.'

'It seems to me to have been an almost impossible task for someone so young.'

'You are probably right, Michael,' said Sally and I detected a note of regret in her voice. 'Sometimes I think we sentenced him to death.'

'Were you ever in love with him, Sally?' I asked.

'I suppose I could have been. But there wasn't much time for love in those days. By the way, Michael, if you do find anything out, I would be interested to know about the black cat.'

The members started to pour into the bar and I realized that the second race was over.

'A second bottle of Krug, I suggest,' said Major Birdham. 'Then a stroll to the paddock to inspect the form for the next race.'

'Any more winners for today, Major?' I asked.

'Just be satisfied with what you've won, Michael.'

The next day I produced my piece for the *Express* on the art of successful gambling. Lord Beaverbrook telephoned me from his villa in the South of France to tell me how much it had amused him, and to caution me against the evil of betting on horses.

7

I spent the greater part of August 1951 in New York on behalf of the *Express*, hating it. I just could not stand the heat. There was at the time some talk of making me the paper's permanent correspondent there and I was very relieved when the idea was abandoned and I was recalled to England at the beginning of September.

During my time in New York, between the consumption of

devilish dry martinis which consisted of ninety-nine per cent pure gin stirred in ice with one per cent dry vermouth, which always left me with a violent hangover, I managed to get down some notes on Antony while investigations into his death were still fresh in my mind.

My first assignment on my return to England was to go to Paris to do a series of stories on Charles de Gaulle, who was proving on the surface to be extremely anti-British. It was Churchill who had said, referring to the Free French emblem, the Cross of Lorraine, that it was the one cross he could do without. But as far as the French were concerned, de Gaulle was just what the nation needed. He gave them back their pride in their own country, which had been shattered by the defeat of 1940 and the knowledge that they owed a great debt to the Americans and the British for their liberation. I still think one of the great tragedies of Britain in the years immediately after the war was that our sense of pride was gradually eroded. Patriotism became unfashionable. Any part we might have played in the shaping of the post-war years was prohibited by our insistence that we were an impoverished third-rate power. By thinking that, we became one and have continued as such until this day, except that by now we must rate as a tenth-rate power or a banana republic.

No sooner had I arrived in Paris and booked in at the Ritz than I telephoned Duff and Lady Diana Cooper. He was our ambassador at the time to the French Republic. I had known them through mutual friends. I was unable to speak to the ambassador, but Lady Diana was delighted to hear from me and invited me to dine at the embassy the following night. I did not mind one little bit when she said, 'Full rig and medals. You've called at the right time. One of my guests just had to drop out with flu and I was racking my brains for someone to fill the gap.' Some people would resent being asked in as a last-minute replacement. I'm not proud and was happy that I was considered suitable enough to fit the bill.

As I had no medals worth wearing I presented myself unadorned at seven thirty the following evening. I had not been told who the other guests were to be and was pleased to find the Windsors present. I had met neither of them previously and in the course of the evening was able to observe their behaviour at close quarters. He struck me as a pathetic figure and I have often wondered if he regretted giving up a throne for the woman he loved. Both his and her life were bedevilled by their fury that she had not been accorded the right to be addressed as Her Royal Highness. To spend one's life bewailing something so incredibly unimportant showed an extraordinary lack of humour, particularly when he insisted that she should be accorded the honour within their own circle of friends. Conversely it can be argued that it was churlish of the Royal Family to withhold what was after all a matter of insignificance. In any case Her Royal Highness or rather the Duchess was not particularly interested in my existence and was content to remark to me how much she had detested the Bahamas where the Duke had been governor during the war, and how thankful they had been to get away from the place.

It was not until the time came for the party to break up that I had the opportunity to speak to Duff Cooper on my own. I told him what I roughly had in mind to write about for my paper. He begged me to go easy on de Gaulle and gave me the impression that the last thing he wanted was that I should offend the great man. I assured him that nothing could be further from my thoughts; that like him I only wanted to cement the entente cordiale. Just before leaving I asked him if by any chance he knew anything about a Comte de Chaumont.

'Yes, of course I do. Had an incredible record in the Resistance during the war. Was in charge of the entire operation in the Loire valley. Picked up a Croix de Guerre, a Legion d'Honneur and our own George Cross for his work, which takes some doing. Also a brilliant scholar. When I wrote my book on Talleyrand he was of considerable help to me. Why do you ask?'

'I would very much like to get in touch with him.'

'It may not be easy. Since the war he has become a virtual recluse and only sees a few of his friends. Used to have a château in the Loire valley. A beautiful place. I went to stay there when I was working on the book. He sold it up after the war and I believe it's been turned into some kind of hotel. He now lives in his house in the Avenue Hoche. I don't want to be inquisitive but why do you want to see him?'

It did not seem the time or the place to acquaint our ambassador with my reasons. I reckoned he had enough on his plate. So I said, 'It's about a mutual friend of ours who was killed in the war.'

'Did you know he lost his own sons? And his wife just before the war?'

'Yes I did.'

'Maybe that's what has made him shut himself away from everyone. Not that he was ever exactly a sociable kind of person. Do you know that he's a distinguished English scholar and that he was at Oxford in the twenties?'

'No, I didn't.'

'Came down with a first in English Literature. Anyway, give my first secretary a call in the morning, and meanwhile I'll see if I can arrange a meeting.'

After leaving the embassy that evening, I made a round of the night clubs and ended up in one in Montmartre where all the men were dressed as women and all the women dressed as men. But everyone seemed to be enjoying themselves, which made a change from London which six years after the end of the war was on the dull and drab side and filled with unsmiling faces. Probably this was due to the meagre rations on which the British still had to sustain themselves; they could be forgiven for believing that if they had won the war they had certainly lost the peace. The French may have lost the war, if only temporarily, but it was their firm intention to enjoy the peace to the full.

I returned to the Ritz about four in the morning, took a pill and was soon fast asleep. I was woken by my telephone ringing and looking at my watch was surprised to see that it was already midday.

It was the first secretary at the British embassy. 'His Excellency has asked me to inform you that he has made an appointment for you to call on the Comte de Chaumont at six o'clock this evening. He has asked me to warn you that the count is none too keen on the meeting and His Excellency is not hopeful that the count will be very forthcoming.'

I thanked the first secretary and made a note of the number of the count's house in the Avenue Hoche.

I spent the remainder of the day wasting it. I could not get down to any kind of work with the prospect of meeting the count within a matter of hours. But I did my duty and sent Lady Diana Cooper two dozen red roses, which I charged to the *Express*, together with a note thanking her for her hospitality the night before, saying that I would probably be in Paris for at least two weeks and asking her and her husband to telephone me at the Ritz and I would be pleased to dine them at their favourite restaurant.

At half-past five I made my way to the Avenue Hoche to locate the exact whereabouts of the house. It was not all that easy as when I finally discovered it, after making several enquiries, I found that the number on its front door had been obliterated and that the whole building was in need of a coat of paint. Having assured myself that there was no mistake, I went to a nearby café and drank a couple of large cognacs. At five minutes to six I went back to the house and pulled the bell.

The door was opened by an elderly lady completely dressed in black. Everything about her denoted widowhood. In France such women are a common sight as it seems that when the husband dies the widow goes into mourning and never comes out of it, at least not as far as her dress is concerned.

'I've come to see . . .'

She did not allow me to finish my sentence but turned her back on me. I sensed an enormous wave of hostility coming from her. At the same time I knew that she had been expecting me. Indeed the door had been opened so quickly after I had pulled the bell that she must have been just inside waiting for me. I shrugged my shoulders and followed her across the large hall. On all sides the furniture was draped in dust sheets. Although it was warm outside in the street, the interior of the house was distinctly on the cold side. I followed her up the wide staircase on to the landing where again all the furniture was covered. I noticed too that the walls bore imprints where pictures had once hung.

I followed her along the landing while she continued to ignore my presence. She stopped in front of the last door, knocked and, without waiting, opened it, indicating with a slight movement of her hand that I should go inside.

'Thank you,' I said.

She appeared not to notice that I had addressed her but turned on her heel and stalked away.

I do not think that I had ever tried to paint a mental picture of the Comte de Chaumont. But the man who rose from behind a large desk was certainly younger than I had expected, probably not more than fifty. As he walked across the room towards me I noticed that he limped badly.

He held out his hand. 'I'm Guy de Chaumont. My friend Duff Cooper tells me that you want to speak to me.' He indicated a leather-covered chair. 'Please be seated.'

I sat down and looked round the room. There must have been thousands of books neatly arranged in cases on all its four walls. Once again I noticed the spaces where pictures had been.

The count watched me closely but said nothing. I am not usually at a loss for words but on this occasion I did not know how to start the conversation. Maybe I had been put off by the hostility of the woman who had shown me to the library. I did not sense the same animosity in the count, although it was immediately clear to me that it was I who would have to make all the running.

'I understand from Duff Cooper that you helped him when he wrote his excellent biography of Talleyrand,' I said. All that produced was a slight inclination of the head in acknowledgement.

The silence in the room was unbearable. I gazed desperately round the walls of the room, searching for some inspiration from those thousands of books. When I looked back at the count he was still staring at me and once again I knew that he was not going to make any light-hearted conversation to put me at my ease.

'Did Duff Cooper tell you why I wanted to meet you?' I finally said, knowing I would have to come out with the reason for my visit if I was going to get anywhere at all.

'He said you wanted to speak to me about someone who was killed in the war whom we both knew.'

'That's not quite true,' I said. 'I mean I never actually knew the person in question, not when he was alive anyway.'

No sooner had I spoken than I realized it was pretty stupid to have claimed a mutual acquaintance with someone who was dead and whom I had never met. As if following my reasoning the count raised his eyebrows and, after continuing to watch me closely for what seemed to be a matter of minutes but which was probably not more than a few seconds, said: 'A statement which no doubt on reflection you would agree to be very strange, Mr Nelson.'

I think he must have sensed my embarrassment at what after all was proving to be the most difficult interview of my life, for he suddenly stood up and said, 'You must forgive my ill manners. Would you care for a drink? Or maybe some coffee? My house-keeper produces the best coffee in France.'

'A drink. A brandy if possible.'

He nodded and walked to a cupboard in the corner of the room. He came back with a decanter and a glass which he placed on the tripod table next to my chair.

'Help yourself. You know how much you require.' I appre-ciated the use of the word 'require'. It was as if he were telling me to go ahead and drink enough brandy to pluck up the Dutch courage I needed to come out with the true object of my visit.

I poured myself a brandy and took a mouthful. It was very smooth and I felt it warming me. 'A beautiful brandy. Is it from the château?'

He nodded.

I took another sip of the brandy still conscious that he was staring at me. I had been right in my supposition. If anyone was going to do the talking it was going to be me.

'Monsieur le Comte, I should tell you first that I am a jour-nalist. I work for a paper called the Daily *Express*. But I assure you that what I have come to see you about has nothing to do with my paper.' I could not help reflecting when I said this how many times during my investigations into the life and death of Antony Rattigan I had been at pains to disassociate myself from my paper.

I paused.

'I know. Your ambassador informed me. He did not wish there to be any misunderstanding between him and me on that account. I am glad to hear that you have not come to see me as a newspaperman. I never speak to them. Now perhaps you would be kind enough or brave enough to tell me the reason for your visit.' For the first time he seemed to relax and I had the impression that he was relieved that I had confirmed that I had not come to his house on official business as it were.

'I will be honest with you,' I said. 'That is, if you believe a newspaperman can be honest.'

'Continue please. Perhaps we can have an ethical discussion after you have revealed the purpose of your coming to my house.'

'I happened to stay in your château in May of this year. I was intrigued by something I found there. A plaque in the walled garden.'

The count leaned forward in his chair and said: 'Lieutenant Antony Fitzjames Rattigan, 1921 to 1942. He died for France. Remembering too his black cat whom he loved.'

To say the least, I was considerably surprised at the count's reaction.

'That memorial was put up by myself,' he said.

'What was Lieutenant Antony Fitzjames Rattigan like?' I asked.

'He was the bravest man, or rather boy, whom it has ever been my honour to know,' the count replied without hesitation.

Again I was disarmed by the count's reaction. I picked up my glass and took another sip.

'I was afraid that one day that plaque must bring someone like yourself to see me,' said the count. 'I am surprised that no one has come before. No doubt it needed someone with an aptitude to follow up a story. In what capacity have you come? You say not as a newspaperman.'

'Of that I can assure you, although it may be my journalist's nose for a story that has brought me here. I repeat what I have said to everyone since I read those words on that plaque, that anything told me will be in the strictest confidence. I've promised this to Antony's old schoolmaster, his grandfather, his sister, his fellow officers, to the people who trained him for his work as an agent and to Father Dominic.'

I could see that the count was surprised by the extent of my enquiries. 'You seem to have done a lot of research already,' he said. 'If you are not interested in the story for your paper, what is the purpose of your enquiries?'

'I can honestly say that I want to know the answers for my own satisfaction, for my own peace of mind. You see, I was also a soldier, but not a brave one. The exact opposite. I was a coward. Antony Rattigan would be exactly my age if he were alive today.'

'He would have been the same age as my elder son too,' said the count. 'As you have made so many enquiries I assume you already know that I lost both my boys in 1940.'

'At the German breakthrough at Sedan,' I said.

'You have been thorough.' He paused. 'What did you make of Father Dominic?'

'A remarkable priest,' I said.

'How much did he tell you?'

'He spoke of the bad feeling in the village of Les Saules. That there were those who wanted actively to oppose the Germans while others wanted to pretend that nothing had happened; that France had not been occupied. The latter clearly believed that there could be some sort of a compromise under the Germans. I learned from him of Antony's death on the morning of 30 May, of his being flung on to a dung heap in the farmyard of the Café de Boeuf by the bridge and how it was that you obtained permission from the Germans to bring him in and have him buried in the churchyard. I understand that Lieutenant Rattigan's body had been badly mutilated. Father Dominic described it as the work of a madman.'

'Let me ask you a question,' said the count. 'What do you know of Antony's childhood?'

'A mother and sister whom he loved. There is a beautiful house in the country called Malplaquet, which would eventually have been Antony's had he lived, where his grandfather Sir Henry Fitzjames Rattigan still lives. Antony's father was a colonel in a famous British regiment called the Dukes and was killed on the Normandy beaches.'

'Yes, you have done a great deal of research,' said the count. 'And what about his father?'

'He and Antony did not get on,' I said.

'Do you know why?'

'To begin with Antony was a bit of pacifist. He was sent to a public school called Wolfe College whose prime objective is to turn out officers for the British army. So you can imagine Antony's pacifism didn't go down well with his father. After all the Rattigan family had produced officers for hundreds of years.'

'What about the final split with his family. Do you know about that?'

'Yes. If you mean Antony's expulsion from Wolfe College. After that his father never spoke to him again. It was unforgive-able.'

'Indeed it was,' said the count. 'Not only did he never speak to him again but more or less prevented any communication between him and his mother and sister. He made the wretched boy feel so guilty that he did not even go back to Malplaquet to see his grandfather, who didn't care a damn about his being expelled from that ridiculous Wolfe College. After all, what was it for? For a mere triviality. For loving a boy of his own age, and that only from a distance. Oh, your public schools and their anti-quated masters almost turn me into an Anglophobe.'

'You seem to know a great deal about Antony,' I said.

'Naturally. He was with me for three weeks. For those three weeks I became his father in the place of the one who had rejected him.'

'Will you tell me about those three weeks?' I said. 'That is why I have made this visit. In coming here I have a feeling that I shall reach the end of my enquiries – shall come to the end of my journey.'

The count rose from his chair, went to the cupboard and returned carrying a glass which he proceeded to fill from the bottle on the tripod table next to my chair. 'You must give me your word that what I have to tell you must be between us only, unless I authorize you to pass the information on.'

'I give you my word,' I said. 'That is as much as I can do. I am not a religious man so I cannot swear it on the Bible.'

'Do you give it as an officer and a gentleman?'

'I was a bad officer and I am not a gentleman. I would rather give it, believe it or not, as a hack writer. For even a hack writer never discloses the source of his information. Not even the finest story in the world if he promises not to do so. Even in that hell called Fleet Street there is a code of honour.'

For the first time the count smiled. 'Frequent have been the days that I have wished I could have been killed with my two sons and Antony in the war. No doubt you have noticed that I walk with a limp. I was born with a club foot. If there has been any consolation it has been to know that your Lord Byron was similarly afflicted. That is the reason why I was rejected for military service. They would not so much as consider me. Now where shall I start? What a stupid question. I shall start at the beginning.'

It is thirty years since my first conversation with the Comte de Chaumont, and stupidly I did not make notes of what he said at the time. So what follows is only roughly what the count told me at my first meeting with him.

'I suppose the early morning of 10 May 1942 will be engraved on my mind for ever. It is as clear to me as I talk to you now as it was then. I was woken at first light by my housekeeper in a state of extreme agitation. I should explain that after the fall of France I had closed this house and gone to live permanently at the château. In fact this house has never been completely opened up again. You may have noticed the gaps on the walls where once the pictures hung. I had them sent in 1940 to vaults south of Bordeaux where they still are. On my death they will go to the nation. Anyway, to return to 10 May 1942, my housekeeper informed me that a young man wearing civilian clothes had come to the back door of the château asking to see me.

'As you may already have discovered, during the night there had been a plane flying very low, and my housekeeper, who was by no means stupid, was certain that this young man had been dropped from it. According to her he spoke impeccable French, but there was something about him that made her suspicious.

'Anyway, I dressed hurriedly and went downstairs. The young man, who of course was Antony, was sitting in the kitchen. He was in a state of shock, but when I told him I was the Comte de Chaumont he seemed visibly relieved. My housekeeper was still present and I realized that he was anxious about her. I assured him that there was nothing to worry about; that she had been in my late wife's service and was completely trustworthy. But she took the hint and left us in the kitchen. I made some coffee and when he took the cup I noticed that his hand was shaking. I got the impression that he was scared out of his wits. And he was. During all the three weeks that I knew Antony, I do not think he passed a minute absolutely free from fear. Just now I said to you that he was the bravest boy that I have ever had the honour to know. You see bravery is not performing feats of valour. Bravery is overcoming fear and still being able to act valiantly.'

'Did Antony disclose the fact that he was an agent?' I asked.

'Yes. Almost immediately. He didn't even trouble to check my credentials.'

'Did you have good credentials?'

'No,' said the count. 'Far from it.'

'I understand from my contacts who worked in the SOE that you were to be his contact in France; that the whole purpose of putting Antony into France was to liaise with you with a view to setting up a Resistance cell that would become operative when the Allies invaded France. At the same time if good opportunities for disruption, sabotage or even assassination presented themselves, he was to engage in them, bearing in mind that the building up of a hard corps of trained Resistance fighters was his prime objective.'

'That is correct. With my help he was to contact such men as were pro-Allies in that part of the Loire valley. Together we were to arrange for arms, explosives and so on to be dropped. Antony was to set about training a cadre of local Resistance fighters in their use.'

'So why do you say your credentials were not good?' I asked.

'F section of your SOE in London had been grossly misinformed as to the state of my mind. Quite simply I had only just begun to believe that resistance was necessary.' Seeing the look of surprise on my face the count continued. 'What had happened, as I subsequently discovered, was this. There was a very small Resistance cell at the time in Orléans besides a very active organization for aiding prisoners of war and airmen who had been shot down to escape into Spain. I had been contacted by the leader of the Resistance cell who was an old friend of mine. In a roundabout way he had suggested that I might join them.'

'Did you?'

'Not exactly. How would you say? I was still sitting on the

fence. I was still unsure of the future of Europe. I will come to that in a moment. Anyway, this friend of mine must have got a completely wrong impression and fed the information to London that I would make an excellent contact should they want to put an agent in to this part of the Loire valley. Does that make sense to you?'

'Yes, indeed. Without sound communications it is only too easy to misinterpret the situation.'

'I don't blame my friend,' said the count. The trouble rested in London, where there were two sections of the SOE. F section was run by the British and RF section, although under the command of the SOE, was de Gaulle's organization. In those early days there was considerable resentment felt by RF towards its British superiors, although as time passed this lessened. The direct result of this resentment, which, let us be honest, was in accordance with de Gaulle's attitude towards the British, was an appalling lack of liaison. Had F section, in other words, the British in London, made a more thorough investigation with RF into my background to determine my suitability for receiving an agent in the Loire valley, they might have come up with something considerably different from what they learned from my friend in the Resistance in Orléans.'

'What would they have learned?'

Without hesitation the count continued: 'They would have learned that I had been an active member of the French Fascist party known as La Cagoule since the mid thirties. Or have you discovered that already in the course of your investigations?'

'As a matter of fact I have,' I said. 'But I'm glad to have heard it from you personally.'

'To return to Antony on the morning of 10 May. Here I was with a boy on my hands who had been dropped blind during the night with instructions to contact a Comte de Chaumont who was apparently waiting to receive him with open arms.'

'Forgive me for interrupting,' I said. 'Here you are on the morning of 10 May 1942 with an unwanted agent on your hands. Why didn't you get in touch with your friend in Orléans and pass him on?'

'The answer to that is simple. Only a week previously my

friend had been arrested by the Gestapo and was being held in their headquarters in Orléans. There was no way I could get in touch with him.' The count paused. 'And let's be honest. I was too frightened even to admit that I knew him. Do you understand that? Do you know what fear can do to a man?'

'I would have acted in exactly the same way. I have never held it against St Peter for denying Christ. I believe St Peter was only human.'

'Thank you,' said the count.

'Did Antony say anything about the wireless operator who was dropped with him?'

'Yes, indeed. Apparently the wireless operator had jumped first. Antony was sure that he had jumped too soon. According to Antony there was a very high wind blowing at the time and he was frightened that his operator had been blown off target. It was this loss of contact with his operator which had put the wind up him. He felt completely isolated. I think that was his reason for being so relieved when he finally reached the château and got in touch with me.'

'Was there any subsequent news of the wireless operator?'

'Nothing. In the first week Antony was at the château he scoured the countryside looking for him. To begin with I was petrified Antony would be picked up, until I learned that he could move unseen about the countryside. It was uncanny.'

'I've heard a lot about that,' I said. 'It was something he learned at Malplaquet from his grandfather's gamekeeper.'

'In the end we were forced to the conclusion that the wretched man must have been dropped into the Loire or one of its tributaries. Later on, after the fighting that took place round here in 1944, a great number of unidentified bodies were recovered and buried in the war cemetery, but I understand the body of the wireless operator was never identified.'

'What happened next?'

'The cat. The cat happened next,' said the count and for the first time he smiled.

'You mean the black cat whom he loved?'

'That's right,' said the count. 'There we are, still sitting at the kitchen table, Antony shaking with shock and myself pretty scared too. After all, here I was with an unwanted agent on my hands and with no idea as to how to get rid of him. I couldn't exactly tell the boy to clear off. It would have been too cruel.' He paused. 'Anyway, I knew these agents had been trained to kill and, who knows, he might have knifed me then and there.'

'You are right,' I said. 'I have spoken to his instructors. They turned him into the perfect killer.'

'I was wondering what to do next, when the cat, the black cat, walked in through the back door. He took one look at Antony, leapt on to his lap and started to purr away and walk all over him. It was the most extraordinary sight. Up to that moment the cat had never come inside the château. Originally he had belonged to one of my gardeners. When he had been called up, the cat had gone wild. My housekeeper would put milk and food out for him but he would never come near her. He didn't seem to want to know the human race until Antony, a complete stranger, appeared on the scene.'

'What did he look like, this black cat?' I asked.

'Hideous. Very scruffy. He was a stray who had been rescued by the gardener. It appeared that he had no known mother and it was a miracle that he had survived. He hadn't even learned to wash himself properly. He really was an ugly cat. He had two enormous fangs protruding from either side of his mouth, and at his throat there was an off-white patch of fur. Otherwise he was completely black, paws and all. For eyes he had slits which never opened properly. As far as I ever discovered they were green with dark blue centres, but it was difficult to be sure. At one time I had considered having him shot but had decided against it in case his owner returned, although he never did. Like my own two boys he was killed in the fighting in 1940. It was bizarre to watch that cat, who all those months had run away when anyone tried to approach him, making such a fuss of a complete stranger. I remember well that I put out my own hand to stroke him and he hissed at me, his fur stood on end and he arched his back. I remember exactly, too, what Antony said: "I've always wanted a cat of my own, Monsieur le Comte. My father hated them and would never have one in the house. What is his name?" When I told him he didn't have one he said, "Then I shall call him the black cat, or just plain Blackie. Yes, I think Blackie will do very nicely." Whereupon Blackie curled up in his lap and proceeded to go to sleep.'

'What happened next?' I asked.

'The black cat, or rather Blackie, seemed to take the tension out of the atmosphere. Antony ceased to shake and some colour came back into his face which up to that moment had been absolutely white. For the first time since I had come into the kitchen I was able to think rationally. While Antony sat stroking Blackie I was able to decide on what immediate action was necessary. The first thing was to find somewhere to hide my uninvited guest. Antony was adamant that it must not be inside the château. First of all he pointed out that I would be compromised if he was found, while if he was in one of the outhouses or stables he could always say that I knew nothing about him. I then thought of the summer-house in the walled garden.'

'I saw it when I was at the château. It's next door to the plaque.'

'That's right. Antony thought it ideal when I told him that it had a door through the wall that led into the vineyard outside. If at any time the château was searched he said he could slip away unobserved. It wasn't until later, when I discovered how he could move unseen, that I came to believe him. The next problem was the fact that Marie, my housekeeper, had seen Antony and I was sure that she suspected that he was an agent. However, I trusted her completely. Indeed I trusted all the half-dozen employees who were still with me. They were the older ones. The younger ones had gone off to war and had not returned. They were still either in prisoner-of-war camps or had been transported as forced labour to Germany, although I had only just begun to suspect the latter. So, later that morning I did in fact call the staff together, told them as little as I could about Antony, and swore them to secrecy.'

'Not altogether successfully, I fear,' I said. 'When I was in Les Saules and started to make enquiries I was told there were rumours at the time of a stranger up at the château.'

'I know. But I would swear that the information never came from one of my people. In any case it was only a rumour, and you must remember that the whole village had heard that plane overhead during the night; or Antony may have slipped up in the first few days he was at the château when he went out to search for his wireless operator before he got to know the surrounding country thoroughly. Someone in the fields or vineyards may have caught a glimpse of him and mentioned it casually. I don't think any great significance would have been attached to it. There were a great number of strangers in the area at the time. It's probable that after Antony was killed, and the whole village knew about that, that the rumour grew that he had been at the château. We shall never know.

'Antony was very keen to move into the summer-house. I am quite sure he was concerned for me; was frightened that he might compromise me. I asked him if anything had been dropped with him. I meant anything in the way of explosives or weapons. He just shrugged his shoulders and I knew that there had been but he was unwilling or careful enough not to tell me. As soon as we had finished our coffee I led him out of the château and through the walled garden to the summer-house. The walled garden enchanted him. He told me that it was just like a part of his grandfather's estate. What particularly delighted him was that many of the trees, shrubs and flowers were exactly the same. He was also delighted with the summerhouse itself, and said that it was the perfect place for him to hide up until we could decide what we should do next.'

'I notice you say we,' I said.

'That's right. From when we first met, Antony had complete faith in me. I suppose this was partly due to the briefing he had received in London, however wrong it had been, and partly to relief at having come safely through a harrowing experience and made contact.'

'That is what he had been trained for,' I said.

'It is one thing to be trained, quite another to put one's training into operation,' said the count. 'Anyway we rigged up a wicker chair, one of those long ones for sunbathing which I had brought back from the South of France, for him to sleep on. It was immediately taken over by Blackie who had decided to attach himself permanently to Antony. Antony declined the loan of a blanket. He said if he had to get out in a hurry through the gate in the wall

he did not want to leave any signs that someone had been sleeping in the summer-house. He was from the very beginning, as he
was until the day he left, extremely solicitous about my welfare.
He did not want to compromise me with the Germans in any
way.'

'Were there many in the area at the time?'

'No. The main concentrations were nearer Orléans. The château had not even been requisitioned at the time. The Germans
were still trying to be friendly to people like myself who were
known to have had pro-Fascist sympathies. It wasn't until 1943
when they started to worry about invasion from the west that
an army headquarters moved in. Even then they behaved impec-
cably and did very little damage to the place. Certainly nothing
compared with the liberating troops who sacked the place. I
don't blame them. They were fighting in a strange country, a war
they hadn't been responsible for, and it was their way of getting
compensation for all the boredom and misery they had suffered.'

The count paused as if not knowing how to continue.

'That's a remarkably charitable attitude to take,' I said.

'I don't know,' said the count. 'I'm only trying to be fair. In any
case I have always thought the English the most civilized people
in the world. Even more so than the French.'

'Was that why you went to Oxford in the twenties?' I asked.

'Partly. It was also my father's idea. He was even more pro-
British than I am now. At the time the anti-war movement was
growing. It was inconceivable to him that a subsequent generation could mock all those millions who had sacrificed their lives.
It was his idea that I should write a thesis on the British poets and
writers of the 1914-18 war. As a matter of fact I think I enjoyed
collecting the first editions of their works more than the actual
writing.' He pointed to the shelves to his right. 'They're all there,
almost every one of them who was ever published. Many of
them were killed. One of the greatest disasters of the twentieth
century. In fact that war was far more disastrous than the one we
have just been through. It took away the cream, the people who
should have been the post-war leaders. We were left with a lot
of second-raters. But you don't want to hear about my obscure
writings, although it may be of interest to you that I am now

embarking on a study of the British poets and writers of the twenties and thirties. What a contrast they make. Floundering around like fish out of water, desperately looking for an ideology to embrace, some clinging to the extreme left, some to the extreme right. Both sides in search of a god with a message. I'm afraid I bored young Antony to tears while he was here talking about the First War poets and writers. But it was interesting to get his reactions, although I fear he was not a very well-read young man. He had been to the wrong school and left too early at that. But I got the impression that to him all wars were sad and useless. Which was strange considering he had decided to pursue one of the most dangerous wartime occupations, that of a secret agent and saboteur. But I keep digressing. To return to that memorable morning. After Antony had installed himself in the summer-house, together with the black cat, we had a long talk to decide what to do.'

'And what did you decide?'

'Very little. I was all for Antony sitting tight, a prospect which appealed very little to him. He told me that he had been dropped in France to do something to bolster the Resistance movement, not to sit on his bottom.'

'You didn't want trouble?' I suggested.

'That's about it. As I said, my first reaction had been to turn him out, to get rid of him at any cost. I suppose my better nature, if I have such a thing, rejected that idea. Frankly I didn't know what to do. There's a saying that when in doubt do nothing; that masterly inactivity will eventually solve all problems.' The count looked at his watch. 'And now if you will forgive me, Mr Nelson, I have an appointment with the director of the Bibliothèque Nationale.'

I must have looked surprised at this sudden dismissal for he added, 'No, no, don't worry. You shall hear the full story. Meanwhile I think it is best if you hear Antony's version of what happened during the three weeks after he came to the château.'

He went to the section where he had just indicated were kept the first editions of the poets and writers of the First World War and drew out a bound folder. He placed it on the table beside me. 'These are Antony's diaries which he kept while he was at the château in May of 1942. They're not the originals, of course, but photostats. I would never let the originals out of my hands.'

I turned back the covers of the folder and inside were fac-similes of exercise books used by French schoolchildren.

'Take them with you and read them,' said the count. 'I think you will know much more about Antony afterwards. They won't take long to read. Come back tomorrow if you wish. Say at ten. We can then pursue our conversation. No doubt you will want to ask me some more questions. The interval will give me time to consider how I should best answer them.'

He turned and rang the bell. A minute later the door was opened and I was conducted out of the house by the same hostile lady in black who had admitted me.

8

I can still remember vividly returning to the Ritz in Paris after my first interview with the count, going straight to my room without any thought of dinner, sitting by the window and opening the morocco-bound folder. What follows is necessarily edited, since much of the time Antony indulged in retrospection which involved a certain amount of repetition. The first entry is dated:

12 May 1942

It is two days since I was dropped in to France. It seems to me to have been one almighty cock-up. I am not at all optimistic about the outcome. The briefing at home must have been wrong. No sign of Henri, my wireless operator. God knows what has happened to him. I fear he is dead or lying injured. It is strictly against all rules to keep a diary but it might be useful later on, and someone might learn a lesson from it although, God knows, at the moment I have not much to tell. No, I must not feel sorry for myself although it's only honest to say that I'm scared out of my wits. I think it's the loss of Henri that frightens me more than anything else. I feel pretty isolated to say the least of it. Got these funny children's exercise books from the count. Have found a perfect hiding place for them where no one can find them so I can't compromise anybody. Maybe with luck I will come back after all this business is over and retrieve them. I must look on the bright side. I must not talk about luck. I was trained not to trust to it but to use my own initiative and assert my own willpower. It would be an additional help if I could pray to God for help. But the only help will be of my own making. The first time I felt really frightened was when I was driven to the airfield with Henri and Sally. She had warned me that weather conditions were not entirely favourable and the drop might have to be postponed. It was kind of her to come along. The funny thing is that all the time we were driving to the airfield I could not help wishing that she was coming with us. All through my training she has been a tower of strength. I am sure she has had doubts about me. I know some of the other instructors have and I heard a rumour that I have been too keen. I am sure they nearly returned me to my unit, or wherever they return a failure, especially when I nearly killed the instructor in unarmed combat. I still think it wasn't my fault. I do know I wasn't popular with the other chaps just because I was too keen. They felt I was trying to show them up. I couldn't help it. They could not know my feelings of failure. I just had to be the best at everything. I hope my father will find out one day. He might forgive me for what happened at Wolfe, though as far as I am concerned it is now beginning to seem to me to be of less and less importance. But it certainly did bugger up my life.

It was a beautiful night at the airfield with a nearly full moon. But the met chaps were worried about the wind which was blowing hard enough to make the drop dangerous and Sally said she wasn't going to waste us after all the bloody work she had put in on us. Henri was very morose. He had been dropped in northern France some months ago but his small organization had been compromised by some breach of security and he had been taken out by Lysander, which, he said, was more frightening than anything else he had experienced. I got the impression while we were holed up together in London, without being allowed out unescorted, just like a couple of kids, that he wasn't happy about going out again with me. Like me he has French blood so he can't fault me on account of my accent which he says is of number-one importance. It must be my youth. But I am twenty-one, if only just. Regret we did not have much of a party to celebrate it. I'll make up for it later when I have sorted out this shambles and got back home.

Waited around for hours, or at least what seemed hours, while met boys dithered about. At midnight they gave us the OK. Not with much confidence, I thought. Sally produced a bottle of brandy and we all had a good nip. She then gave me my death pill. I believe it's potassium cyanide. She said it was only to be taken in emergencies and not to exceed the dose. Wonder how many times she has made that joke? I didn't know what to do. Was about to salute her when she put her arms around me and kissed me. Only wish she had done it before. I never dared to approach her. Felt it would have have been out of order. Besides I have never been any good with girls. It has always been my misfortune to admire them from a distance. I just never had the confidence to make the running, except in the case of my darling Pearl. I thank God for that one night with her. Funny to think she is the only girl I have ever been to bed with.

Sally did not come with us to the Whitley bomber waiting for us already warmed up. Was still thinking of her and that last kiss as I climbed aboard. In a funny kind of way it made me less frightened. I tried to concentrate on the routine that lay ahead of me. Only one container to be dropped with us. This must be concealed together with our own parachutes, and we must make the château at first light before the local population starts work in the fields and vineyards. I kept visualizing the map of the area and felt that I had got it right.

Although it was warm when we left England we flew high to avoid flak and I was soon shivering. One of the dispatchers put blankets round me and gave me coffee. Could not talk on account of the noise of the engine. Soon after three I knew we must be near the dropping area as we started to descend and the red light went on. The trap in the floor was lifted. An appropriate word, trap. We had made jokes about it in training. Now I really did feel the noose round my neck and that I was going to my death. Had never felt it during training, but now I had a strong disinclination to jump. Looking through the hole in the floor the countryside below was clear, but I was unable to pick out any of the landmarks

I had memorized from the maps and aerial photographs. Henri looked tense and so did the two dispatchers. He was to go first, then me, and last of all the container, so that we could both pinpoint it when it hit the ground. I saw the dispatcher knock Henri hard on the shoulder and he was gone. I was looking through the hole in the floor when to my horror all I could see below was water. I looked at my dispatcher who shook his head. The plane banked and we started to circle. I was petrified. It was obvious that the pilot had come in on a wrong heading. My immediate inclination was to make for home. The dispatcher held up his hand indicating for me to wait and went forward. After what seemed an hour he came back and shouted at me to wait. All the time we had been climbing. Through the hole in the floor I could see the moonlit landscape receding. I noticed the red light had gone out. After we had retraced course for five minutes or more the pilot banked and we started to descend again. All the time I was looking through that bloody hole in the floor. I was terrified and frozen into the bargain. We came in low over the river, at about 600 feet. Suddenly I recognized the village of Les Saules, its church at one end of the street and the château to its east. The red light came on. I felt a thump on the shoulder. Then I jumped. No problems. No broken limbs and I saw the container hit the ground two hundred yards to my right. Everything silent except a few dogs barking probably in Les Saules. Surprised by the silence. Suppose I had feared a welcoming party from the German army. Wherever Henri had been dropped I was in the right place. The château was clearly visible in the moonlight about two miles to the south and I could hear a river behind me. Carried out the routine. Hid my parachute in culvert which was conveniently nearby and moved off to locate canister. No problems. Removed its parachute and concealed it in vines. Took its parachute and concealed with mine in culvert. Spent about half an hour searching the land towards the Loire. No sign of Henri so made my way slowly in direction of château. Worried terribly about Henri. Reached château at four-fifteen as dawn was beginning to break. Lay up in hollow in front of château. Just the faintest hope that Henri might turn up but only the faintest. Felt more and more certain that he had jumped into the Loire. It might have been me had it not been decided that he should go first. Thought made me more frightened.

Waited till five. No sign of life at château or in the vineyard which stretched for miles on all sides. At least there would be no shortage of wine in France as there is at home. Approached château directly from its north side and made my way into court-yard at back. Was only armed with a Smith and Wesson .38 and knife. Did not wish to scare potential friends by carrying sten. Looked through windows into kitchen but could see no move-ment. Waited until shortly before six when a woman came down to make coffee. Felt very thirsty. Still terrified. Knocked on heavy door. Kept hand on Smith and Wesson inside coat pocket. Middle-aged woman opened door and without waiting for her to speak said I must see Comte de Chaumont on urgent business. Got the impression that she was as scared as I was. She admitted me to the kitchen and without a word went off to wake the count.

I recognized the count immediately from the photographs that had been shown to me and from his pronounced limp. I did not beat about the bush but told him straight away who I was, all the time keeping my hand on my Smith and Wesson in my pocket. I don't think the count was frightened like me or the woman who opened the door to me, but I felt that he was not at ease with me; that he had not expected my arrival. Could it be that my briefing at home on him and his background had been wrong? We drank coffee and I gave him a rough outline of what my orders were. I think had he told me to leave I would have killed him together with his housekeeper. That was the woman who opened the door to me as I later discovered. They were the only two people who knew of my presence in the area. But even if he seemed confused he was not frightened.

The sudden arrival of a scruffy black cat relieved the atmos-phere. The cat came in through the back door which was still open and leapt on my lap and started to purr. I think this aston-ished the count more than my own arrival. He told me it was a stray that had belonged to one of his men who had been called up. I have always wanted a cat. I didn't expect though that my first one would be a scruffy black stray.

Still got the impression that I was unwanted. Finally count

suggested that I should hole up in the walled garden in some kind of a summer-house. Knew about this garden from aerial photographs. Ideal situation with a gate in wall through which I can slip out in an emergency.

13 *May*

Count has no news of Henri. Spent all day in summerhouse hoping that he might turn up. Count brought me out food at midday. Asked him if there had been any Germans in the area looking for me. Reassured when he said as far as he knew, none. Slightly more confidence in him. Still scared and feeling hopelessly cut off. Black cat, whom I have christened Blackie, has taken up residence with me in summer-house and seems to have fallen for me in a big way. At least it's good to have one friend in this mess. He seemed very hungry and ate half of what the count brought out to me, including vegetables. He's very skinny. Ribs stick out. Scratches all the time. Presumably he's got fleas. Hope they don't transfer themselves to me. Know nothing about cats as Father would not have one about the place. Thought for the first time of my family and hope they are all well – even Father. At times over the last three years I have hated him for what he has done to me, especially taking my mother and my sister away from me. I suppose I cannot blame him. I was never cut out to be a soldier in the Rattigan tradition, but at least I have proved to myself and I hope to him that I am not the cowardly degenerate (as he called me) that he imagined. But after all the efforts I have made it is ridiculous to end up in the position of not knowing what to do next.

Of all the problems it is the loss of Henri that concerns me most.

The count visited me in the summer-house shortly before dark, bringing more food. Blackie wolfed most of it and curled up on my 'bed'. He refused to move over when I lay down and tried to sleep – without much success. When I did finally doze off he woke me by snoring. Count says that it still does not appear that my presence is suspected by the Germans. Bit perturbed when he said that he had informed his staff of my being at the château but he assured me that they were completely trustworthy. I only hope so.

14 May

At first light I left the summer-house very carefully. Made my way back to where I was dropped and checked contents of container. Everything in good order, sten, ammunition, plastic explosive, detonators, bren-gun and so on. Carried it and concealed it together with parachutes in culvert. Scouted north as far as the banks of the Loire and spent some time searching for hiding places in case I have to leave château in hurry. Saw trout in one of the small tributaries. Also mallard, but best of all a kingfisher. Found small island covered with willows. Waded out to it and decided it would be eminently suitable. All the time I kept look out for sign of Henri. More and more depressed that there is no trace of him. Fear he must have drowned. Further north could see the spire of the cathedral in Orléans. Wondered whether I should make for there and try to make contact with Resistance. What a lovely part of the world this is. I have always liked water, and this Loire valley is tremendously beautiful. Will definitely come back here when this is all over.

Cut across vineyards in the direction of Les Saules. Reached a bridge by café and derelict farm which I recognized as the Pont de Boeuf. Decided that this was as far as I could safely go. Signs of life on road leading to village. Spire of church looked beautiful in early-morning sun.

Here saw my first Germans. Was lying up about fifty yards from bridge scanning village with my glasses when heard sound of car approaching. Open Mercedes with Nazi flag fluttering at bonnet came fast out of village escorted by two outriders. Driver in front and some high-ranking officer in the back looking straight ahead. Through glasses could distinguish insignia of SS on his lapels but not time to identify his rank. Car crossed bridge and instead of taking right turn in direction of château kept going north on the main road in the direction of Orléans. Thought occupant of car would have made a good target for the bren, but going too fast for an individual shot.

By half-past seven too much activity on all sides for my liking. Was undecided whether to return to the château by road or across country. Both have their advantages and disadvantages. Had been told that there would be refugees in the area so that my presence would not arouse any particular interest. Although my identification card is in order as far as is humanly possible, and I carry all the correct papers, there is always the chance that these might have been altered. Theoretically it would be safer and more natural to use the road. If I am found slinking along the vines I would be at once suspect. Finally decided that as long as possible I would keep to the country. I know that this is my strength thanks to my days at Malplaquet.

God, how careful one has to be every second! One cannot relax. Was thinking about the German officer in the open Mercedes as I was approaching the château from the direction of the village through the vines. Turned the corner at the end of a row and walked straight into an old man. He was carrying a basket of eels and coming from the direction of the Loire. Only hope he did not notice my look of surprise. I wished him good morning but he did not even look at me, just plodded on. Can only hope he thinks I am one of those refugees. It was an unforgiveable mistake on my part. It was one-hundred-per-cent blunder and shook me up considerably.

Blackie went crazy when I got back to the summerhouse. He was lying on my bed with his eyes closed as I came in and immediately leapt all over me making strange cries. He does sometimes purr, usually when he is lying on my lap. At other times he squeaks. I suppose it is his method of communication. Near Malplaquet Grandfather had some friends who bred Siamese. Very beautiful, but how they did talk. Blackie isn't up to their standard, but he does his best. Looking at his pointed ears I wonder if he may, way back, have had some aristocratic ancestors. Noticed that he keeps scratching his ears. Looked inside and found them full of a black damp mess. Got a piece of cotton wool from my first aid kit, wound a piece on the end of a twig and did my best to clean them out. Did this carefully as I do not want to damage his hearing. Removed an awful lot of evil-smelling muck. He did not like it one bit and cried, but made no effort to scratch me. After I had finished he made a great fuss of me.

Count's housekeeper came out at midday bringing the food. Her name is Marie and she has been with the count twenty years. Does not say much but seems friendly enough. Clearly worships the ground he walks on. Asked me what life is like in England. Could not believe me when I told her the size of civilian rations. She says it is all right in the country but terrible in the towns. Says too that the peasants round Les Saules are all millionaires from the black market and that at weekends the countryside is swarming with people from the cities in search of food.

Marie does not think much of Blackie and calls him a dirty beast. She suggests that he must have some English ancestors. She was amused when I told her that we talk together in English. I suspect that she thinks I am out of my mind. So do I when I wonder what possessed me to come here in the first place.

Slept for an hour in the afternoon. About four it was very hot. The most perfect May day. Wandered round the walled garden identifying the trees, shrubs and flowers. It is like spring at Malplaquet. Thoughts of Malplaquet made me feel very low. But couldn't help laughing when I thought of the dressing-down Pullen would have given me for my carelessness in blundering into the old man in the vineyards this morning.

Wonder if I have not made a dreadful mistake in cutting myself off from Malplaquet and Grandfather for the last five years. Why did I? I suppose it was partly guilt. I was dreadfully ashamed at being chucked out of Wolfe at the time. Now I couldn't care less. If Father had not reacted so violently things might have been very different. But he forbade Mother and Henrietta to see me. I love Mother and I know she loves me. But she loves him too. God, what an awful position to put her in. After I left Wolfe and worked on the paper at Rochester things were never quite the same between me and Henrietta although I shall always be grateful to her for coming to see me there. At least she brought me news of the family and of Malplaquet. I don't blame Father for what happened. His code of conduct is his own and he believes what he does to be right. It's an awful thing to say but I have never loved him as I love Grandfather, Mother and Henrietta. But if I had gone back to Malplaquet and seen Grandfather that would have only caused more trouble, and Grandfather and Father would have started fighting one another. It was probably better that I faded out of the picture, at least for a while. But perhaps five years was too long. I should certainly have gone and seen Grandfather at Malplaquet before embarking on this lark.

Count came to see me in the evening, bringing a bottle of white wine. I am no expert but he told me it was the vin ordinaire off the estate. It tasted far better than that to me. He is a most cultured man. Was most amused by my briefing on his background and although he put me right on a few points, I suspect he was quite impressed how much was correct. The only snag is that I still feel he does not really want me here and is wondering how he can decently get rid of me! He knows a great number of high-up people in England, and all the clever ones up at Oxford. He gives the impression of having devoted himself to a life of scholarship now that he has lost not only his wife but also his two sons. Every time he mentions them there is a look of grief on his face. He says he hopes that this war will not prove as disastrous as the last. According to him all the future leaders on both sides were killed off in the 1914-18 war leaving only the dross who have brought us to this war. I argued that all the leaders before the 1914-18 war had not been killed off but still the war took place. He seemed very amused by this argument but did not agree with me.

After the count had left I used my own comb to try and get rid of some of the bugs from Blackie's fur. Not very hygienic, but highly successful. He is literally infested. They are the same fleas that used to torment my dogs. Little devils to kill, so I dropped them into the dregs of my wine glass. Counted roughly up to fifty of them. No wonder he has been scratching himself. But he loved every moment of it and when I had finished kept pushing his black nose against me, asking for more. Who says that cats are not affectionate? I would even go so far as to say that Blackie shows uncatlike symptoms of utter slavishness.

The count has left me some books, mostly light paperbacks. I mean light in content. I tried to read an Agatha Christie, but found it boring. I suppose the truth of the matter is that I am worrying about Henri. I feel very cut off and frightened. It occurred to me to say a prayer, but I decided, as I have never said one since I was about fifteen, there is not much use in starting now. I don't think God will help me out of this. The only person who is going to help is myself. I will wait a few more days in case Henri turns up or I find him. Then I will do something on my own, even if the count is not willing to help me. I don't think he will because when I talked of a local Resistance he more or less told me that it didn't exist; that the peasants are more interested in making money on the black market than in killing Germans. He pointed out that we in England have not suffered a war that has ravaged our countryside and cities, and that it is too early for Frenchmen to think about rising against the occupation forces. This seemed to me to be a bit defeatist. I am more and more sure that my briefings on him were cock-eyed. But I still like him. He is very friendly and treats me like a son. In any case he is all that I have at the moment.

15 *May*

Slept for four hours last night. Woke before dawn and removed Blackie, who had slept on my tummy, much to his annoyance. He made even more noise when I left to make a further search for Henri. I really believe that he would have followed me through the door in the wall if I had let him.

Spent at least three hours going over the ground near the Loire but with no success. Was very careful how I moved after yesterday's experience but there were very few people about and no one saw me. At seven I made my way to the Pont de Boeuf and hid up in the vines fifty yards from the bridge where I had hidden yesterday. At seven twenty heard the noise of a car approaching and the same cavalcade came out of Les Saules. The Mercedes, the driver, the officer and the two outriders. Nothing like the Germans for punctuality and routine. I was half expecting them so had my glasses ready and focused.

I identified him as a general in the SS. I could not help wondering what he was doing at that time of the morning. I have seen no other troops in the area. Once again the car crossed the bridge and raced off down the road in the direction of Orléans. Again it occurred to me what a wonderful target he would make. Obviously there is no Resistance in this part of the world or he would be taking more precautions. The thought depressed me. I felt completely isolated. Me against the whole German army. Spent a very restless day pacing up and down the walled garden. Watched a pair of wrens feeding their young. Amazing the amount of food such small birds can carry in their beaks. The ratio of weight of food to the weight of their bodies must be out of all proportion. I wonder how they manage to get off the ground. Was visited by a robin who was very friendly. Blackie did not take the slightest bit of notice of him. What did he live on when he was a stray? Out of the dustbins from the château, I suppose. He does not show the slightest interest in hunting. He doesn't even chase the butter-flies. He is utterly lazy. What the army would call 'idle'. The only time he seems to show any sense of excitement is when there's grub about. He gobbles it up as if it's his last meal on earth and then starts pestering me for more, making his strange uncatlike miaows. I notice too that he loves to be in contact with me. When he is not sitting on me he likes to be near me and have at least one paw in contact with some part of my body. Once again I cleaned out his ears and they seem better. He let me do it under protest, but made no effort to claw me. I am glad someone has confidence in me. I wish I had more in myself.

While Blackie went to sleep on my lap in the evening I thought about Tom Makepeace and wondered how he was getting on. I don't know why he suddenly came into my mind. He certainly never loved me. I can see now that he treated me very badly. But it was my fault for not realizing that he was not in the slightest bit interested in me. I realize now, even at my age, that you can never make people love you. They either do or they don't. I suppose I am a bit annoyed with him for making me frightened of women for so long, although I may be wrong about this. The trouble is that I can never really make up my mind about anything. I am just ignorant.

Somehow the conversation got round to education when the count was with me this evening and we were drinking his beau-tiful wine. I more or less told him about Tom. He told me not to worry; that only the British would have such a stupid system of education; that in France they managed things in a much more civilized way. He went on to point out that the French attitude to sex was altogether more civilized than ours and that it was not something dirty, not to be mentioned, but something splendid to be enjoyed. He said that the English upper class came nearest to the French ideal because it had escaped the excess of puritanism which had overcome and weighed down the middle class right up to the present day. He didn't think the working class had been affected in the same way and said it had a lot in common with the upper class. I pointed out that I was middle class, but he would not hear of it. He said that with my military ancestry I was definitely upper class. I was rather pleased about this. We talked a lot about Malplaquet and what I would do when it was mine. I realize that we have a lot in common. Strange considering he is about the same age as my father. He feels the same about the château as I do about Malplaquet.

The only fly in the ointment is that he doesn't want to talk about my future. I told him that I cannot sit here for ever in this summer-house. Again he repeated that nothing is accomplished by hurrying. I asked him if there had been any news of Henri in the village. He said no, and that if there was he would have been the first to tell me.

16 May

Was at the banks of the Loire very early this morning, well before dawn. Once again Blackie kicked up a fearful row when I left but I am getting cunning. I had kept a piece of meat from last night's supper and I put this on the floor. While he was gobbling it up I slipped out through the door. The only thing he loves more than me is food.

I did a very stupid thing. It had occurred to me that Henri may have dropped on the north bank. If he did he would have made his way over here to the south coming by one of the bridges and trusting to his papers to get him through. The fact that he has not turned up must mean that he is injured or dead over on the north side. I decided to swim across.

The current runs very quickly, particularly after the spring rains. I chose a crossing where there were two islands in the centre of the river. Stripped right off and put my shoes, trousers, shirt and beret into my ground-sheet which I secured to my shoulders. The water was much colder than I had expected. To cut a long story short I only just made it. Can't say what a relief it was to reach the opposite bank. Was completely exhausted. I couldn't possibly have attempted this unless the moon had still been full and the weather clear and fine. I spent an hour on the north side going over the ground near to the bank, but there was no sign of Henri. I don't think I shall trouble to do this again. If Henri is dead, there is not much point in getting myself drowned. But I hate the idea of him lying out in the open badly injured. Coming back across the river was even worse than going over. It took me far longer than I expected. I was feeling pretty exhausted even when I went into the water and I did not make the south bank until I had been swept two miles downstream. Of course it was now broad daylight and there were plenty of peasants in the fields and vineyards. Put on my clothes in the reeds and only hope I didn't look like a half-drowned rat. Made my way back along the bank which took me another hour. The banks of the Loire here are not banks in the sense they are at home. The Loire is wide and has numerous inlets and tributaries. In the summer it subsides considerably leaving large areas of pebbles or sand. Did not reach the summer-house until after eleven. The count must have been on the lookout for me for no sooner had I slumped down on my bed than he arrived in quite a state. I told him what I had done and he told me more or less that I was a bloody fool; that none of the locals would so much as think of trying to swim the Loire here because of the currents. I pointed out to him that they had no reason to.

When he had gone I decided that tomorrow I would make one more search for Henri and that's that. But is it? I shall then have to decide what to do.

Soon after I had come back Marie brought me out some bread and coffee. Told me that coffee was very short in France. I don't think this was a hint but suggested that soup if she had any would do just as well in future. Anyway it is far better for me. Wondered whether I should hand over some of my emergency rations. Suggested it but she assured me that there was plenty of food at the château and reiterated that it was only in the towns that people were beginning to feel the pinch. She seemed very friendly and wanted to know who I was. Of course, I could not tell her anything, and I think she understood. I felt embarrassed when she told me that I was a brave young man. She more or less intimated that I was wasting my time putting my life in danger for a load of ignorant peasants. I got the impression that she considers that because she works for Monsieur le Comte, as she always calls him, she is a cut above the rest. The count told me that she had been his wife's personal maid, was the bastard child of one of his grandfather's house servants and that her airs and graces made her highly unpopular in Les Saules.

Gave Blackie another combing. Yesterday's seems to have made little impression on the little monsters that torment him and he is as lousy as ever. The only place he won't let me comb is the tangled hair on his belly. When I try, however gently, he cries out loud. He doesn't make any attempt to scratch me, but it is such a howl of utter anguish that I have to give up. So I suppose his tummy is the citadel where the fleas retreat to. Perhaps I should give him a bath. I am worried about his right eye. I made a very weak solution of iodine and wiped away the mucus that comes out of it, hoping that cats are not allergic to iodine. He didn't like this very much and glowered at me. But then he always glowers as he never opens his eyes fully at any time, although I am pretty sure now that they are green. I am fascinated by the two fangs that protrude from either side of his mouth. They should make him look fierce, but they don't. Just different from other cats I have seen. I tried to examine his teeth which he let me do without protest. Discovered that they were thick with tartar. I managed to scrape some off with a hard piece of wood. He didn't like this much, especially when I cut into his gum and made it bleed. I never thought to find myself, a highly trained agent, acting as a cat dentist in the middle of France. After the bleeding had stopped Blackie made a great fuss of me. What a strange little cat he is! Whatever pain I had caused him, nothing was going to put him off his food. I gave him a few scraps of bread softened with milk and they disappeared down his throat in a matter of seconds. He is the noisiest eater I have ever heard. Talk about bad manners!

They say when you are about to die all your past life flashes in front of you. It certainly didn't this morning when I thought I was going to drown while swimming the Loire. All I thought about then was how to survive and overcome the current. It's when you've nothing to do but sit and wait that you think about the past. All day I paced round and round the garden. I tried to occupy my mind by identifying all the birds and butterflies, having already gone through the flowers and shrubs. Blackie followed me all the time. When I stopped, he stopped. He would have made the most perfect ready-trained gun dog. It would be fun to produce him at one of Malplaquet's grand shoots and say: 'Oh, yes. It's my new gun cat, don't you know?'

Unfortunately my mind wasn't altogether on my identification programme. I thought a lot about my Rochester days and had to admit to myself that I had been a ghastly failure. What made me join the wretched paper in the first place? I hated the work. I hated asking strangers questions. I hated the local court work, listening to the petty crimes and watching the local bench behave as if they were judges of the High Court. I particularly hated the funerals, intruding into people's private grief, and asking questions about the deceased. One was never allowed to use the word dead. People 'passed over'. They were even allowed to 'drift peacefully away'. They never died. Death is such an absolute, such a final word.

I suppose I went to Rochester because there was nothing else I could do. At least I got the job on my own. At least I proved I could do something on my own, however badly. But they were the most miserable two years of my life. I thought too often of Tom. On the other hand I did have fun with Janet at weekends. It was fun showing her the countryside. What amazes me is that someone like her should be so ignorant about it. Looking back, what a disaster that I didn't fancy her in the way I did Pearl. But then Pearl would never have spent a day with me in the country. She just wanted to go to bed with me as she did with every other young man who took her fancy. I can see now that I was just another challenge. Still, I must not be nasty about her because when I finally did sleep with her, it was a fantastic experience. I wish I had more experience with women, but I am clearly what they call a late starter. If I come out of this alive I must make up for lost time. The silly thing is that if I had not been so terrified of Pearl while I was at Rochester, I could have slept with her then and there. Just as well I didn't. I would have been just another scalp, and I would have been utterly shattered when she chucked me to one side and went on to conquer fresh fields.

If there's one thing this war has done it has toughened me. I suppose there is nothing wrong with the ideals of youth, but they are horribly painful. When one is young one believes in purity, even in the ultimate goodness of people, but after what I have seen I am beginning to have serious doubts.

I was glad when the evening came and the count arrived as usual with a bottle of wine. He says he looks forward to our little chats as he calls them. I certainly do. I don't think I could survive without them. I told him what I had been thinking about in the afternoon, and he says if he had his life all over again the one period he could do without is adolescence. He says that the brain is not sufficiently tempered by experience to deal with the emotions that are at their keenest at that period. He thinks it is one of nature's failures. He points out that a great many adolescents commit suicide. This he says is a waste of human life, and incidentally another reason for not believing in God. He thinks that if there is a God, he has a perverted sense of humour. I agree. I remember the padre at Wolfe trying to explain suffering and evil in the world, taking the line that without suffering there would be no good. What a load of rubbish. Pleasure and happiness would be no less enjoyable or right just because evil was abolished. The count says that religion is nurtured on ignorance. The witch doctors exploited the tribesmen. They even wore outlandish clothes to make themselves different. He points out that the vestments of the dignitaries of the Church today are nothing more than an extension of their decor. We discussed Christianity at length and he says that while he believes there was a Christ in the historical sense there is no reason to associate him with a god. He says that the great weakness of Christianity is that it is too obsessed with blood and sacrifice just like so many other religions. Worst of all it is fundamentally a passive religion. He points out that if Christ had come down from the cross that would have been a positive action; that dying for the sins of the world is completely negative; that the whole of Christianity has got too bogged down in death, and heaven and hell after death.

17 May

My worst day so far. Went out this morning as usual to look for Henri. Nothing. This is the last day I shall look. Utter dejection all day. No, that's not quite true. On the way back to the château I came across a bank covered with *fraises des bois*. Funnily enough I smelt them before I actually saw them. I filled my beret with them and brought them back here to the summer-house. Blackie afforded the only light relief of the day when he tried to get at them. What an extraordinary animal! Is there nothing he won't eat? I wonder what he would say to a really hot curry?

In the evening the count came over and I offered him some strawberries. He put them in the wine. Says they really need a touch of sugar but some people prefer them in wine. They certainly were delicious. He tried desperately to cheer me up. I'm afraid I did not do much to help him.

18 *May*

This beautiful walled garden is turning into a prison. This morning I woke long before dawn and went down to the culvert and checked the contents of the container. The bren and the sten are in perfect order but to make certain I cleaned and lightly oiled them. Rest of the day mooned about the garden trying to decide what to do. Have definitely written Henri off. Of course I came to no decision. Tried to read but find that I get to the bottom of the page only to discover that I cannot remember a word I have read.

Blackie followed me about all day. I think he must have sensed my mood because, although he stayed close to me, he kept very quiet. In the early evening I tried to play with him using a length of string with a blackbird's tail feather attached to one end. I trailed this along the grass. He looked at me as if I had gone out of my mind. What kind of a childhood – or should I say kitten-hood – can this cat have had? But he does look a little bit fatter and his ribs are not sticking out so much. For the first time too he has started to clean himself. Can it be that he was so matted and dirty before that he didn't trouble to? Now that he is being looked after it is almost as if he has decided to turn himself out a bit more smartly. Anthropomorphic thinking, I fear.

19 *May*

Another completely wasted day. Did not even trouble to go outside the garden. Utter depression. Try to think of Sally and what she would do. She would certainly tell me not to mope but to think positively and stop drifting. It's easy for her to talk. She's safe in England. How on earth did I allow myself to be talked into this crazy mission? I know Sally had doubts about me. She should have followed her instinct and taken me off the course. Anything would have been better than this. This is just turning into another of my failures.

20 *May*

Went out at dawn for the exercise more than anything else. If any brilliant idea does come into my head I might just as well be fit. Went to the Pont de Boeuf and at seven twenty precisely the usual cavalcade came by. The German general never seems to look to right or left. Only straight ahead. Wonder what he is thinking about. After he had gone by I waited until eight and then walked into the village of Les Saules. I just had to do something. Beautiful as the walled garden is I am fed up to the teeth with it. This wasn't just foolhardiness on my part. I wanted to find out whether people would take any notice of me. I might as well not have existed. Most of the men were going to work, many of them on bicycles. I did not encounter a single car. I suppose there is no petrol available. I walked past the lane at the bottom of the street which leads to the church. On the corner is a grocer's shop and there was a queue of women outside it. Just like England. The same at the baker's halfway up the street. The garage was deserted, I suppose because of the petrol shortage. At the top of the street is another café-cum-restaurant called the Café des Fleurs. There were in fact flowers in pots outside the café but as there seemed to be no one inside I decided not to risk going in. I retraced my steps and returned to the château by the road. No one took the slightest notice of me.

On reflection this was a bloody stupid thing to do. I don't mean going into the village, but returning by the road. Someone may well have noticed me walking into the château. With any luck they might think I'm on the scrounge or looking for casual work. But it was unfair on the count. It was extremely stupid and thoughtless of me. After all he has done for me it was wrong of me to put him under suspicion, however slight.

21 *May*

The count didn't pay his usual visit last night. Marie came over with some food about six and said that he had gone into Orléans on business. She thinks it may be something to do with billeting of troops at the château. She calls them *'sales Boches'* just like one reads in the war books. It's all I need. A regiment of Germans at the château. She tells me not to worry. 'Monsieur le Comte' apparently thinks the world of me and would give me ample warning of the arrival of any filthy Germans. While she was talking to me I was feeding Blackie with scraps off my plate. She was most shocked and said I should not waste food on such a scruffy animal. I pointed out that he is one of God's animals, not of course adding that I did not believe in God. It did not impress her at all. In typical Gallic fashion she asserted that animals were made for man and not vice versa. I realize that her whole life is devoted to getting hold of food for the delight of Monsieur le Comte. She says that they will be killing a pig in the next day or two and that she will produce me a dish of pork such as I have never tasted before. There is no false modesty about her. She went on to say that before the war there was a chef at the château. She clearly detested him. Apparently he wasn't fit to cook at the local Café de Boeuf, which I gather has a very poor reputation. I asked her about the Café des Fleurs. She says it is good, although naturally not up to her standard. She went on to say that most of the villagers are, if not pro-German, certainly not against them; that they spend all their time thinking about their stomachs, many of which are too large anyway. I get the impression that she is not a lover of the human race, Monsieur le Comte excepted. I asked her about the count's wife. She clearly did not want to discuss her except to say that she was most beautiful and most gracious. Gracious was the word she used. When I asked her about the count's two sons I thought for a moment she was going to burst into tears. All she would say was that before this dreadful war the château had been a place of sunshine and laughter. Now it was like a tomb. She felt she was already underground. She expected that after the war was over the count would go and live in Paris now that there was no more love and life at the château.

After she had gone I wished that she had not come to the

summer-house. She made me think of Malplaquet. But I do feel sorry for the count.

22 May

Early this morning I went to the Loire and picked some more strawberries. While I was near the river I put up some mallard and sure enough in the reeds I found the nest with a clutch of six eggs. I took one as a present for Blackie. When I got back and cracked it open I found it had a chick inside which I had suspected by its weight. Blackie didn't care a bit but gobbled it up. I suppose to him it was like poussin is to humans. He followed it with a handful of wild strawberries. What an extraordinary meal for a cat.

23 May

The count is back from Orléans where he spent the night. Says that Marie has got it all wrong about the Germans being billeted at the château. Apparently it is her permanent phobia. I asked him if he had any contacts in Orléans who might be able to help me, but he was most unforthcoming. He swears that he is not in touch with the Resistance, which according to him is non-existent anyway in this area. I point out to him that that is the reason why I was dropped, and he says that my superiors in England must be out of their minds. He keeps harping on the fact that the time is not yet ripe. I argue that when the time is ripe we must be ready with some kind of organization; that it must be built now so as to be in place when the time comes for the landings in France. But he argues that the landings are at least two years away; that the situation of the Allies is critical; that they haven't even won a single battle so far and are struggling to hold on to Egypt and the whole of the Middle East and that the battles must be won there first before they can even begin to think of Europe. I tell him he is a defeatist, and point out that the whole secret of strategy is to be one step ahead. The reason why Hitler never invaded Britain after the fall of France was that he had never expected to get to the Channel ports so quickly. When he got there he hadn't a plan. I was really quite angry with him but I am glad he did not mind. When I even went as far as apologizing he seemed surprised and said that the point about a civilized conversation is that one can say what one likes without coming to blows.

24 May

Last night Blackie was sleeping with his face against mine – one of his less pleasant habits as he dribbles and snores – when I came to a decision. I looked at my watch and saw that it was two o'clock. I felt as if an enormous weight had been lifted off my shoulders. What I had to do would require a bit of planning. It was so obvious that I should have thought of it before. I was so relieved that I turned over on my side and was soon asleep. The last thing I can remember is Blackie resting a paw on the back of my neck.

When I woke at first light Blackie's paw was still on my neck. I turned over and looked at him and he squinted back at me. I have started to talk with him so I wished him good morning. I must be daft. Anyone seeing me with this cat would have me carted off to the nearest asylum. I literally said to him, 'Good morning, Blackie.'

Then I said, 'Blackie, I'm going to kill that SS general.'

I will go over the ground tomorrow. I must not hurry. A few days won't make much difference one way or the other.

Spent all day thinking of different angles and the pure logistics of the problem, not least my getaway route. Have no intention of making this a Custer's last stand. If I plan it properly there is no reason why I shouldn't do the job and live to tell the tale. Couldn't help thinking of the last time I killed Germans. I have tried to wipe the Arras disaster from my mind. It was another of my failures. I think at that time I was still so miserable with my life and failures that I wanted to prove to myself and my father that I could be brave. But that wasn't bravery. It was sheer stupidity. But I was frightened, scared out of my wits. I suppose it was only the discipline that had been instilled into me by the army that kept me there at all. But I couldn't stand the mortaring. This time there won't be any mortaring.

I suppose they would never have taken me on for a job of this sort if they had known that at heart I am a coward. Is everyone else as cowardly as I am? Are the other agents in France at his moment living in perpetual fear, as I do?

Funnily enough this evening when the count came over the conversation got around to bravery. He says there is no such thing as bravery in the sense that people in general think of it. People who are decorated are no more brave that those who receive no decorations. The brave person is the person who is terrified but who overcomes fear. A person who does his job in battle is just as brave as the person who performs what are known as outstanding feats. It's purely a question of degree. He particularly mentioned bomber crews. He rates their bravery as highly as that of the greatest heroes. He does not believe in cowardice either. The so-called cowards are people who cannot overcome their fear. They should not be despised for that. They simply do not rank among the brave.

The subject of bravery naturally led us on to the subject of death. The count is not afraid to die, but like me is afraid of pain. I told him that I would never be taken alive by the Germans willingly; that I would take the death pill which Sally had given me at the airfield. He agreed with me that this would not be the action of a coward when I pointed out to him that I did not think I could stand torture, and that I would reveal all I know about my organization in England. I jokingly added that it would be to his advantage as I would not be able to give away the fact that he had hidden me at the château.

A rather high-falutin conversation, but I think I got the gist of what he was trying to say. At Arras I rated among the so-called cowards because I could not overcome those mortars. God willing, this time there will be no mortars.

Before the count left I asked him if he knew anything about a general in the SS who came through Les Saules in the morning. Of course, I had not told him of my early morning recces in the surrounding countryside. He seemed surprised at my question, but told me that the general commanded a SS Panzer division resting north of Orléans. Apparently this general is the lover of a French widow who lives in a large château south of Les Saules. Her husband who was in the cloth business in Lyons left her a fortune. According to the count they were both upstarts and he never received them. After he had gone I wondered if I should have asked him. After all it didn't make any difference to me who the general was. I wish I could keep my big mouth shut. One of the things most dinned into me on the course is the less people know about anything the safer it is for all concerned. When I kill the general the mere fact that I asked about him must put the count in danger.

25 *May*

At bridge early. Cavalcade on time.

Thought a lot today about Grandfather, Father, Mother and Henrietta. Also about Pullen and the great days we had together at Malplaquet. Without his teaching I would never be able to carry out this job. Wonder if Sally would approve. I hope so. I want her approval more than anyone else's. It will be fun to see her reaction when I tell her what I have done.

26 *May*

After watching general go by at seven twenty this morning, decided where I will set up my bren. There's a mound to the west of the road opposite the bridge. To the right is the broken-down farm and the Café de Boeuf. I have noticed that the car slows down as it takes the bridge. Not more than thirty miles an hour. I shall be at dead right angles to it as it crosses the bridge so can rake it. I'll take the general first, then the driver, and finally the outriders. They'll probably be clear of the bridge by then but they'll be in my sights for at least another hundred yards, so there should not be the slightest chance of their getting away. Back at the summer-house I drew a map of the area. I cannot fault it.

Blackie was a bit restless today but I noticed one good thing. Up to now all his defecations have been runny as he suffers from permanent diarrhoea. For the first time he produced a firm stool in the grass. He seemed very pleased with himself and walked round it several times as if to say, 'See what I've accomplished.' I suppose it's the rubbish he's been living on up to now. I noticed too that for the first time he made some effort to cover it. Up to now he has never troubled. I suppose he was never trained by a mother. Why then should he suddenly start to do it now? Very mysterious. Funny how a silly thing like that pleased me in a childish kind of way.

27 *May*

Watched general go by this morning. Am sure I have chosen the right location. The getaway is good. Plenty of cover in the vineyards north to the Loire where I will turn east and lay up in the hide in the willows on the island in the river until everything quietens down. Count came over in the evening. He seemed a bit worried. Asked me if I had any plans. When I questioned him as to what made him ask he said the mere fact that I had not moaned about being stuck in the walled garden had made him wonder. I'm afraid that stupid question as to who the SS general is has made him suspicious. Played with Blackie. For the first time he began to chase the blackbird's feather tied to the piece of string. Once he got the idea he would not stop. He was just like a baby wanting more. Every time I stopped playing with him he started to howl. Absolutely pathetic. Naturally he won every time. At last he was exhausted and lay down in the centre of my bed and fell fast asleep. When I decided to get some sleep in too, he refused to move over. Every time I pushed him away he protested and rolled back close beside me. If only he didn't snore so!

28 *May*

I was up two hours before dawn. I went to the culvert and undid the container. Took out the bren, magazines, the sten, ammunition and four grenades. I still had my Smith and Wesson and killing knife hidden in the vineyard outside the walled garden.

Hated carrying them back to the summer-house although it was unlikely that anyone would be about at that ungodly hour. But I presume there is a local policeman, although I have never seen him. I must have looked a decidedly shady character slinking through the vineyards with a bulky parcel halfway through the night. The count did not come to the summer-house today. I was rather glad as I kept going over the plan in my mind and was somewhat distracted. I think too that Marie found me rather uncommunicative and went off in a bit of a huff. After she had gone I brought the bren and the sten into the summer-house and checked them thoroughly. Blackie sniffed around them. I understand now why people say that cats are curious. He is fascinated by anything new. He is very much an animal of routine. I decided, for instance, to go to bed early, but it was too early for him and he wanted to play, so he kept walking all over me until, for the first time, I shouted at him. He got the message and slumped down against my side. Then gradually he began to move up the bed until his face was against mine. When he had made me thoroughly uncomfortable he let out a big sigh and went to sleep; snoring, of course.

29 *May* 10 p.m.

I am scared about what I have to do tomorrow morning. But I have worked it out to the best of my ability and it will not fail. This is what Sally would call positive thinking for you! My main worry is Blackie. Without him I don't think I could have survived my three weeks' hiding here. I shall always be as grateful to him as I am to the count and to Marie. But they can look after themselves. Blackie cannot. He senses that something is wrong and literally wants to be in contact with me all the time. I pick him up and he clings to me and gently places his paws against my face. But he will not purr. He is quiet the whole time and this worries me. I tell him everything will be all right but he just looks at me, through those slits of eyes, in the most reproachful fashion. Marie brought me fish for my midday meal. Blackie wouldn't so much as look at it. He just came to me, rubbing himself against my legs. It was ghastly. The count has just been to see me and we have drunk our last bottle of wine together, for the present that is. I have not told him of my plans. I'm afraid he will find out soon enough after tomorrow morning. We had one of our usual philosophical discussions and put the world to rights. I can't help thinking if we had more people like him ruling the world it would be a far better place. Before I left him I casually mentioned how much I love Blackie and asked him to take care of him if at any time I should have to go away. He asked me if I had any immediate plans and of course I lied and said no. He said that he had never seen such a relationship as had developed between me and Blackie. He found it beautiful. He used the word *beautiful*.

30 *May* 3 a.m.

I am writing this by candlelight and then I shall put it with the rest of the diary in the wall behind the loose bricks. I wonder how it will read when I return and pick it up. I have just taken Blackie in my arms and said to him: 'Thank you, Blackie. You are my first cat, and I shall never find a better one. Goodbye, for the present, Blackie. I love you so much.' He hasn't even purred back at me. He just nuzzled his nose against my face. I have put him on the bed and he has begun to miaow. I can't stand it.

I am leaving now. I must be in position well before dawn.

9

At ten o'clock I rang the bell of the count's house in the Avenue Hoche. It was immediately opened by the same lady in black who had admitted me the previous day.

'Good morning, Marie,' I said.

For the first time she looked me full in the face, but did not say a word.

As I walked into the library the count came to meet me and shook my hand. I inclined my head towards the door behind me. 'Is that the same Marie who was your housekeeper at the château during the war, the same as the one in the diaries?'

'The same.'

'How come she is in widow's weeds?'

'She went into mourning on 30 May 1942, the day that Antony was killed, and has stayed in mourning ever since.' He indicated a chair, and I seated myself. 'Did the diaries enlighten you?' he asked.

'Yes, considerably.'

'What else do you want to know?'

'First of all, how did the diaries come into your possession?'

'Sheer luck. When I was having the plaque put up by a local mason he found them hidden behind a loose stone in the wall where he was erecting it.'

'I don't really know where to start. Can you pick up the story from the time that Antony left the summer-house at three in the morning to set up the ambush?'

'Yes, I can. My source of information is one-hundred-per-cent reliable. To understand why I had better remind you of how I stood politically in the spring of 1942. I have never made any secret of my political affiliations in the years before the war. I was violently anti-Communist and I think I told you I was a member of La Cagoule. I also think I said yesterday that when Antony was at the château I was, as it were, sitting on the fence. I did not know what to think. I certainly wasn't pro-German. If I had been called up like my sons I suppose I would automatically have gone and fought like them for France. But on the other hand I wasn't violently against the Germans. I was far more frightened of the Russians than them.' He smiled. 'Indeed in view of what has happened since the war it is arguable that they were the greater enemy. In spite of that nothing that they have done can begin to excuse Hitler and his cronies. Anyway, as a result of my pre-war record I was well thought of by the Germans. Indeed I was on friendly terms with the area commander who had his headquarters in Orléans. He was one of the old army types, a regular soldier with an old-fashioned code of honour. After the war when the full horror of the Hitler regime came out he shot himself, leaving a note saying that although he had not known the full extent of the atrocities, he had known enough and should have had the courage to attempt to bring down Hitler earlier. It was from him that I learned what happened.

'Antony must have been in position while it was still dark as we know from his diary that he left the summerhouse at 3 a.m. He obviously had to leave so early as he had to get his sten and bren to the mound by the bridge under cover of darkness. At seven twenty precisely the Mercedes with its two outriders, driver and the general in the back came out of Les Saules. As it slowed to cross the bridge, which you may have noticed has quite a hump, Antony opened up with his bren. He was a brilliant marksman. He killed the general, the driver and the two outriders. It was all over in less than ten seconds according to my friend the colonel.

'Then something that Antony hadn't bargained for happened. He did not know that a hundred yards behind the Mercedes was a lorry carrying twenty of the most highly trained German soldiers, the equivalent of your commandos. The colonel suspected that if Antony did see it following the Mercedes he decided to ignore it. It was a covered lorry and there was no reason for him to suppose that it was carrying troops. Within a matter of minutes they had deployed and surrounded the mound where Antony was hidden.'

'So it was over quickly?' I said.

'Not a bit of it. You see the German soldiers had been ordered to bring Antony in alive.'

'But that means someone . . .'

The count held up his hand. 'We'll come to that in a minute. In fact the battle, because that was what it was, lasted twenty minutes. The German discipline was superb. There were no ifs and buts about their orders. They had been ordered to bring him in alive and bring him in alive they would. Gradually they inched closer and closer. Antony was alone and couldn't keep an enemy at bay on all fronts. But in the first stage of the battle he killed two of them. They were about to move in for the final assault when Antony did an extraordinary thing. By now he must have exhausted the ammunition for the bren. Suddenly he stood up and rushed down the slope in the direction of the farm firing his sten. He didn't kill any more soldiers but wounded at least three. Again the discipline of the Germans was superb. They could easily have gone berserk and shot him to pieces then and there. But quite calmly their officer, a young lieutenant, shot Antony in the legs, and he fell, twenty-five yards short of the farm. Then, showing incredible bravery, the German officer inched forward to where he lay, suspecting at any moment to be met by a grenade. But everything remained quiet. When he finally reached Antony, Antony was dead.

'I thought you said he had been shot in the legs.'

'That's right. He had. Soon after the battle a German doctor arrived to tend the German wounded. The officer and his men were appalled when they discovered that they had failed to take Antony alive. To begin with the officer suspected one of his men had disobeyed orders and had shot Antony. But when they examined his body there were no other wounds – only two shots in the legs which certainly could not have killed him. The doctor gave them the answer. Antony had taken his death pill. Further examination revealed death by potassium cyanide.' He paused. 'Yes, I know what you're going to ask. How did the Germans know that Antony had set up an ambush at the Pont de Boeuf, and if they knew why didn't they alter the general's route?'

I nodded.

'To take the second question first,' said the count. 'The Germans didn't alter the route because they wanted to capture Antony. They knew he was an agent. They wanted him alive to extract every item of information from him. He was to be handed over to the Gestapo in Orléans. You know what that would have meant.'

'You mean to say that they were prepared to sacrifice a general, a driver and two outriders for the sake of one agent? But that was murder.'

'You could argue that it was incredible bravery on the part of the outriders and the driver to risk the ambush. They knew one was possible, but they didn't know where. It could be anywhere between the château where the general spent the night with his mistress and his divisional headquarters north of Orléans. For what it was worth all three German soldiers received posthumous Iron Crosses.'

'And the general?'

'Oh the general, he was all right.'

'I don't understand.'

'A general commanding an SS division could not be put at risk. No, he wasn't a coward. He would willingly have made that last journey and taken his chance along with his men, but his superiors refused to allow it.'

'Who was riding in the back of the Mercedes then?' I asked.

'A volunteer. A German corporal dressed as a general. He also received a posthumous Iron Cross.'

'They were all brave men,' I said.

'Now we come to the first question,' said the count. He paused, stood up and came back with a bottle of brandy and two glasses. He filled both of them and handed me one. 'Yes, now we come to the first question. How did the Germans know that Antony had set up an ambush?'

'I heard in the village talk of betrayal.'

'Exactly,' said the count.

'But who? Why? So someone did know that he was hiding at the château. But even then how could they have known that Antony was going to try to kill the general. Who on earth was it?'

'Me,' said the count. 'I betrayed Antony Fitzjames Rattigan.' There is no word to describe what I felt. He was still looking at me hard. 'It was me. I betrayed Antony,' he said again.

I stood up, walked to the window and looked down on to the Avenue Hoche. I was tongue-tied. I remembered what our ambassador, Duff Cooper, had said to me about the count's war record only two days ago. 'Picked up a Legion d'Honneur, a Croix de Guerre and our own George Cross for his work in the Loire valley in 1944 and 1945.' I could not turn and face the count. As I stood staring down at the street below, I heard him say, 'I will not attempt to make excuses. I will give you my reasons. I will try to explain to you my state of mind in that spring of 1942. As you know I was not pro-German. Had I been I would have handed Antony over the first day he came to the château. Quite simply, I was frightened of reprisals. Only in October of 1941 forty-eight citizens of Nantes had been shot in revenge for the assassination of one German colonel. The number of hostages who would be taken from Les Saules and the surrounding villages for the assassination of a general commanding an SS division would have been far greater and insupportable. And Nantes wasn't the only place. Reports of other hostages being shot were beginning to filter through. Does this mean anything to you?'

I was still staring out of the window. I nodded. I was hating every minute of this confession. I could not bear to turn round and look the count in the face.

'So I was presented with a moral problem. One British agent or possibly a hundred Frenchmen, many of whom would leave their wives and children behind them. What would you have done?' The count wasn't pleading with me. He was asking a straight question.

I turned and faced him. He was looking calmly at me. 'What would you have done, Mr Nelson?' he repeated.

'I would have to think about it,' I said.

'I would like your answer when you have thought about it,' he said. 'But no doubt you have some more questions?'

The first shock of the count's disclosure was over. 'If you felt you had to inform the Germans, why didn't you do so earlier. They could have picked him up at the château any time.' I paused. I didn't like to say it but I had to. 'Was it because if they picked him up alive you were frightened he might incriminate you? Was that it?'

The count was not at all offended. 'You had to ask that question. The answer is no. I was not afraid to die although I admit the thought of torture frightened me. But neither of those problems presented themselves, neither death nor torture. Antony told me that he would never be taken alive. I knew he was telling the truth. You will recollect there is a reference to killing himself in the diary. Antony was too highly trained to have made a mess of it. Of course I should have betrayed him earlier. I would have saved the lives of those brave German soldiers. Nothing was accomplished by their deaths. Nothing. It may seem strange to you to hear me talking about German soldiers, particularly in an SS division, like this.'

I shook my head. 'How did you actually betray him?'

'The only way I knew. Very early on 30 May I simply picked up the telephone and called police headquarters in Orléans and, without identifying myself, informed them that a British agent would be waiting somewhere between the château where the general slept and his headquarters in Orléans with the intention of assassinating him.'

'Why did you leave it so late? Why, if you were not frightened to incriminate yourself, did you leave it so late?'

'Because I did not put two and two together until the early hours of 30 May. Then suddenly I saw the connection between Antony questioning me closely about the SS general and his black cat.'

'What had Blackie to do with it?'

'Everything. When Antony said, and these were his actual words, "Take care of Blackie. I love him. I want you to promise to take care of him if at any time I have to go away." It was obvious wasn't it? He loved that cat and would never have asked me to do that if he wasn't leaving. There was one other thing. I had dropped in at the Café de Boeuf a few days previously about some money they owed me for wine, and one of the Boudin family happened to mention that he had noticed a young man near the bridge on two occasions. He had fair hair and his description fitted Antony's. It wasn't very difficult to come to the obvious conclusion. Soon after three o'clock on the morning of the 30th I went to the summer-house. Antony had gone as you will know from his diary. Only Blackie was there, crouching on his bed. I then went back to the château and called the police. You know the rest.'

'Not quite,' I said. 'Why was his body thrown on to the dung heap? Why was it shot to pieces?'

'After the doctor had pronounced Antony dead of poisoning, the German soldiers went berserk. Even their officer took part. They literally pumped hundreds of bullets into his corpse. A kind of useless and symbolic revenge. It was the SS officer who gave orders that the body was not to be removed. As you know I was able to get the order rescinded with the help of my colonel friend in Orléans. The SS general was furious but even he was unwilling to go so far as to have Antony's body, or rather what was left of it, dug up and thrown back on the dung heap after Father Dominic had brought it into the churchyard and buried it.'

I picked up my glass and drained it in one. 'Have you ever told anyone else about this?' I asked.

'Father Dominic. It is hardly the sort of secret one can carry alone all one's life. I suppose not a day has gone by since May 1942 when I have not thought about it. Father Dominic thinks I went to him in the role of a penitent. I didn't. But I had to talk with someone and I knew that my secret was safe with him.'

I remembered Father Dominic's actual words: 'This is a very strange affair. May I plead with you to leave the young man in peace?'

'What did Father Dominic say?' I asked.

'He evaded the issue. He said that if he were ever confronted with such a moral problem, he would pray to God for guidance.' He picked up his glass and sipped his brandy. 'Is that all, Mr Nelson? When you have had time to consider the problem, perhaps you would be kind enough to let me know what you would have done under the circumstances. But please don't cite the For-sterian choice of betraying country before friend. It sounds good, but it doesn't make sense. I had to choose between betraying my friend and murdering a hundred of my countrymen.'

'I have one more question,' I said. 'What happened to Blackie? Did you take care of him?'

'No. I didn't have to. I was in the kitchen at seven-twenty on the morning of 30 May when I heard the sounds of firing from the direction of Les Saules. I knew, of course, that it was Antony; that he was doing what I had known he was going to do. Marie joined me shortly after seven-thirty and we both sat listening to the sound of firing from the village. I never said anything to her, but I knew she was thinking of Antony and praying for him. At seven-forty the firing ceased. I made my way to the summer-house. I knew that Antony would never come back, but I forced myself to hope that he would.

'Blackie was lying stretched out on Antony's bed. I went to stroke him, expecting him to hiss and claw at me.'

'And did he?'

'Blackie was dead. He was still warm. He had only been dead a matter of minutes. Marie and I buried him in the garden that morning. He lies in the earth under the plaque between the wis-teria and the climbing rose.'

EPILOGUE

That is the story of the life and death of Lieutenant Antony Fitz-james Rattigan.

I do not think any explanation is needed as to why I could not write it sooner. I had given my word not to harm anyone and I am pleased to say that I kept it.

I am glad I kept copious notes and records of conversations that took place in 1951. They are as vivid to me now as they were then. Over the years I have thought often about the people involved, especially about Antony and the Comte de Chaumont.

For the record here is what happened to those who were most involved in Antony's life, short as it was.

Philip Hanbury, Antony's housemaster at Wolfe College, died in 1960 after ten years of happy retirement at Bluebell Cottage, Etchingham, in Sussex. He left his collection of boys' books to Wolfe College, who promptly put them up for auction where they fetched exceedingly good prices.

Father Tom Makepeace found the martyrdom he sought in the civil war in the Congo in 1959. He was hacked to death along with several other missionaries by the Freedom Fighters. Possibly without him Antony might still be alive today and living at Malplaquet. But that can only be conjecture.

General Sir Henry Fitzjames Rattigan died at Malplaquet in 1955 at the age of eighty-seven. I attended his funeral and watched his coffin being carried from the great hall of the house. It was of plain deal, with no ornamental handles.

Father Dominic died at his house next to the church in Les Saules in the spring of 1971, of a sudden heart attack. I like to think that he died with the taste of *écrevisses Nantua* on his lips.

Antony's mother died in 1952, only a year after I had first come upon that plaque at the château in the Loire valley. According to her daughter, Henrietta, she never recovered from the loss of her husband in Normandy, and her boy in the village of Les Saules.

I made extensive enquiries as to what happened to Pearl, the only girl Antony went to bed with in his twenty-one years of life. I never found out. I do not suppose that anything I have written will harm her or even cause her offence. I have a very soft spot for Pearl.

The Comte de Chaumont outlived them all. From 1951 onwards we kept up a desultory correspondence which gradually faded away until we ended up exchanging cards at New Year. The list of letters behind his name grew longer and longer over the years as his distinguished academic career went from strength to strength. He became the expert on English poetry of the twentieth century, and was much disliked by the left-wing poets of the thirties for whom he had nothing but contempt. I have often wondered if he ever really came to terms with his solution of the moral problem that confronted him in 1942. I am grateful that I have never been placed in his position.

During the course of our exchange of letters, and subsequently of cards, the count always communicated with me through my bankers, Messrs Coutts and Co., 440 Strand, London, simply because in the nature of my work I have never been able to put down permanent roots.

What finally enables me to write the story of Antony's life is a package which was forwarded to me by Messrs Coutts in the spring of 1979. It contained the original exercise books in which Antony had written his diary during the last three weeks of his life. With them was a letter which read:

Dear Michael Nelson,

When you receive this letter, which I have asked my bankers to send to you through yours, you will know that I am dead. That is not meant to sound dramatic, but I detest euphemisms for the word *dead*.

I would like you to know that over all the years since Antony died I have never in my mind resolved the moral problem involved without misgivings, although scarcely a day has passed without my thoughts turning to it. Incidentally, I notice that over the years you have not come up with the answer. If you have, you have not communicated it to me.

I know you have a photostat of the diary, but I feel you might care for the original. I do not think I have to tell you how grateful I am that you have not published the story during my lifetime. I well remember your words when we first met in 1951, when you said that you could not give your word as an officer and a gentleman because you were neither, but that you would give me your word as a hack writer. 'Even in that hell called Fleet Street there is a code of honour,' you said.

Frankly I was dubious at the time. I apologize for doubting you.

Antony has throughout my life remained the bravest boy that it has ever been my privilege to know.

Thank you again for your kindness.

Guy de Chaumont

After I received this letter I made the journey to Les Saules which I described in the Prologue to this book. I returned convinced that I could now write the full story without fear of harming anyone.

As I said, I shut myself up with the telephone off the hook, and worked hard. By the end of June, the story was on paper. As soon as it was finished I parcelled it up and sent it by registered post to Antony's sister, Henrietta, who was still living at the dower house at Malplaquet.

Two days later she telephoned me. I should say that I had not been in touch with her since 1951. I had discovered too much, and I could not face the prospect of lying to her about her brother's death, the brother whom she loved so much.

'I have read the story,' she said. 'Would you like to come down here to Malplaquet this evening? Say between five and six?'

'Yes, of course. But you haven't said anything about the story. Has it upset you in any way?'

'I'm so sorry. No, it hasn't upset me one little bit. I just feel sorry for the Comte de Chaumont.'

I set out to drive to Malplaquet that same evening, taking with me Antony's original diary. I was about to lock my front door when I remembered something. I went back into my flat and took out Antony's cap badge from the black box where I had kept all the notes I had made about him thirty years ago. It was very tarnished. I wondered what had happened to the rest of Pearl's trophies.

It was a glorious evening as I drove up through the park to Malplaquet. I felt a certain melancholy. As I passed Malplaquet and turned on to the road that led to the dower house I noticed that visitors were coming out of the main door. It was now National Trust property and had been well provided for in the will of the old general.

Henrietta was waiting for me at the dower house. We shook hands and I noticed at once how striking she was. I suppose she could not have been more than sixty. She asked me to come into the house. The drawing room was very cool and filled with roses. I noticed a bottle of champagne wrapped in a white napkin sitting in a bucket of ice.

We were like two strangers, which in fact is what we were. 'I'm sorry that I did not get in touch with you before,' I said.

'I understand.'

'I did see you at your grandfather's funeral, but I kept well in the background.'

I opened my briefcase which I had brought with me into the house, took out the diary and handed it to her. 'I think you should have it,' I said. I felt in my pocket and took out the badge. 'And this too.'

She took the cap badge, looked at it and read aloud, '*Semper fidelis*. Always faithful.' She smiled at me for the first time.

'I could not help laughing at the way Pearl seduced you,' she said.

I do not often blush, but I felt myself going red in the face.

'No, no,' she said. 'It's nothing to be ashamed of. Just very funny.'

'I'm glad the story has some comic relief.'

'I think Antony's life calls for a toast,' she said. 'Will you bring the champagne? I'll take the glasses.' Seeing the look of surprise on my face she explained, 'I think we should drink Antony's health in the place he loved, don't you?'

I carried the bucket out to the car and placed it on the floor in the back. Henrietta got into the front seat beside me and I drove back to Malplaquet. In front of the house I stopped the car. I picked up the champagne and placed it on the balustrade that separated the house from the park.

'You open it,' she said.

I eased the cork. The wine had been shaken in the car and foamed out, but I managed to fill the two glasses. We sat on the balustrade looking towards the house. The evening sun was just above the limes, turning Malplaquet slightly pink and making the tall windows shine.

'To Antony,' she said.

'Antony,' I said.

We raised our glasses.

'And to Blackie,' I said.

'The black cat whom he loved,' she said.